DENY
TOMORROW

A NOVEL

ANN HEATHMAN

ASH
Publishing

Cover, interior book design, and eBook design
by Blue Harvest Creative
www.blueharvestcreative.com

DENY TOMORROW

Published by
ASH Publishing

ISBN-13: 978-0-692-30959-9
ISBN-10: 0-692-30959-4

Visit the author at:

Website: *www.annheathmanauthor.com*

Facebook: *www.facebook.com/annette.heathman*

Twitter: *@AnnHeathman*

For Casey and Haley who have enriched my life
beyond what I could have ever imagined.

CHAPTER

1

"F ire in the hole! *Fire in the hole!*" came the echo.

Zach Acevedo covered his head as debris rained down on him. The cave held a treasure trove of ammunition and had blown like the Fourth of July.

"Damn! How much shit they have in there?" Tony Soto, the team's second in command asked, spitting and sputtering dirt. "This is bound to get someone's attention."

"Roger that," Zach said to Tony and the three other men who were dusting themselves off. "Gentlemen, let's get the hell out of here before any Taliban show up."

Zach and his team of Special Ops were making their way to Nabolis, a village in the northern province of Kervistan. Their mission was to find and assassinate a Taliban warlord, Ali Hamdra Fasi. With him out of the way, that part of the country would be a prime insertion point for U.S. troops. But this mission, like the all the others they had undertaken, was yet another operation that wouldn't make the nightly news.

The route to Nabolis was mountainous and the group had to pick its way over one rocky crag after the other. They'd 'gone in light' compared to the usual equipment they carried, but the trek was still physically demanding.

"Hold up, guys," Zach said about an hour into the trek. "Take five while I check our location."

He retrieved a GPS from his backpack and was checking their coordinates when a rocket-propelled grenade came sailing at them, detonating twenty feet away. The explosion knocked the group off its feet as a wall of dirt blew back on them.

Zach staggered to his feet and checked to see if any men were down. No one down, but everyone had been roughed up. Shaken and somewhat disoriented, he willed himself to scan the horizon for the source of the attack. High on a ridge above he caught sight of a white pick-up truck and another RPG sailing toward them.

"Incoming!" he yelled, and everyone dove behind a boulder as a second missile flew by. The Taliban had an ample supply of missiles, but thank God, they were not very precise. This RPG had missed its mark as well, landing several feet off to the right.

"Everyone all right?" Zach asked, dabbing at some blood on his forehead as he rolled to his feet.

"Fuck, that was a close call," Juan, the group's demolition expert, replied. "Where the hell did these guys come from?"

Zach unshouldered his weapon. "Tony, you take the right flank. I'll take the left. Juan, you and the rest of the guys cover us. We're going after these fuckers."

Snaking their way up through the hills to an area just above the pick-up, Zach and Tony could see there were only two Taliban fighters.

"On three," Zach signaled to Tony. Taking careful aim, they fired and dropped both occupants just as they were about to launch a third RPG. They threaded their way down to the truck... weapons still locked and loaded. A quick body check confirmed both shots had been fatal.

"Nice shooting," Zach said as they started going through the truck. "No radio equipment to radio our position, but we've got to get rid of this truck and these bodies." He signaled the kill to the rest of the men who quickly joined them. "Let's push this into that ravine over there, down into that underbrush."

"I'd like to know what dumb-ass general decided we should blow up ammo dumps on our way to Nabolis," Tony said as they rolled the truck over the edge. "We might as well have taken out a fucking front page ad announcing our arrival."

"Yeah, well, we can't worry about that now," Zach said. "We've got a job to do, and right now, we need to keep moving."

He checked their coordinates one more time. "We hike to the next ridge due north about two hours away. When we get on the other side, we'll stop for the night. That puts us about three clicks outside of Nabolis. Everybody, keep your eyes open. We're moving right into a Taliban stronghold. Things could get worse before they get better."

"Yeah, most people move away from the enemy, but not us," Tony quipped. "I ought to have my head examined for being in this line of work."

A faint smile crossed Zach's lips. Tony was right. This was dangerous work, but that was exactly why the government generously financed his operation. He and his team did what most men wouldn't do... move right into the mouth of the enemy and hide in plain sight.

"Well, you can reflect on your true calling in life later," Zach replied. "Right now we've got to get the hell out of here. Let's move out."

THEY CAME over the ridge to the place they would stop for the night. Kervistan was a bleak, barren country with very little vegetation. They would have to make do with a small alcove amidst some large boulders as their campsite.

The wind howled, and the temperature was dropping, but it wasn't safe to build a campfire. Staying warm would be a major struggle, and dinner would once again be a cold MRE... meals ready to eat.

"Listen up," Zach said as the men gathered around. "Chow down and then, try to get some sleep. Tomorrow morning we go into Nabolis and find Fasi." He turned to Juan and asked him to take the first watch. "There could be Taliban all over the place. Keep an eye out. Tucker will relieve you in two hours."

"Roger that," Juan said. "I've been here less than a week, and I hate this fucking country."

Everyone let out a groan of agreement. Kervistan wasn't one of the more environmentally friendly assignments they'd had.

"Okay. Okay," Zach said. "We'll be out of here in a few days, so everybody just suck it up."

With that, he moved to the back of the encampment and spread out his gear. He opened a MRE and stared at it a moment before putting it down. He was starving but not hungry for yet another cold pre-packaged meal.

As he looked around at the group and their surroundings, this all seemed so odd and so far away from his real life. Here were five Hispanic men in Kervistani garb, sporting long, scruffy beards and wearing turbans on their heads. Their naturally dark complexions and brown eyes allowed them to pass as someone indigenous to the area. They also had a basic command of the local language which would make it easy for them to blend into the background when they entered the village in the morning. At least that's what he counted on. Otherwise their plan to get close enough to assassinate Fasi would fail miserably and probably get them killed.

He tried to get comfortable on the cold, lumpy ground, but he ached all over from being blown off his feet earlier in the day. He reached up and scratched the long, thick beard covering his normally clean-shaven face. He took his turban off and ran his fingers through his hair… hair that hadn't seen a bottle of shampoo in more than a week. Retrieving a stocking cap he had tucked inside his tunic, he pulled it down over his ears, relishing the warmth it provided against the cold Kervistan night.

He was far from home. The Caribbean island of Costa Luna was his legal address. He and some of his men lived there in his private, gated compound amidst a sea of luxury. He had maids and servants, a private plane and expensive cars. His life there was the complete opposite of the miserable condition he found himself in now.

However, being here in this bleak environment begged the question of just what was his real life. Was it the life of a modern day gun for hire, off on one dangerous assignment after another, or was it the life of a wealthy bachelor living in luxury back in Costa Luna? Truth be known, he loved both lives. He loved the thrill and adventure he got from being a special agent on assignment, but he also loved the finer things wealth brought him. There certainly was a dualism to his life that even he didn't understand. Making your living in Black Op's came with a price. There was a deep emptiness he tried not to think about.

IN THE morning, everyone rose slowly from their hard, earthen bed, breakfasted on a spaghetti and cheese MRE, and then, began to assemble their gear. This country was a throwback to the Stone Age, but not so the equipment they'd brought with them. At their disposal, they had a state of the art communication system, explosives, and a mini-arsenal of weapons each man had hidden under his baggy tunic. What they couldn't conceal, they would bury at the campsite.

"Here's the plan," Zach said as they huddled for one last strategy session. "We'll pair up and enter the city separately from different directions. We don't have any intel on this, so we'll finalize things once we get some eyes on Fasi's compound. Then, we'll make the kill and head for the hills. Once there, we'll call in a helo and get the hell out of here. As usual, we're all alone in this, guys. If we get in trouble, no one's coming to help us so let's not screw this up. And keep the chatter to a minimum with the locals. We only know enough Farsi to get by so don't press your luck. Any questions?"

There were no questions. They were all keenly aware that the assassination had to be a sterile operation. There couldn't be any 'made in the USA' fingerprints associated with this, otherwise the fragile coalition that currently supported the U.S. war effort would dissolve and leave the U.S. to go it alone. As had been true many times in the past, a lot was riding on the ability of Zach and his men to complete their mission.

Putting their hands together in a circle, they whispered a collective *Hoo rah* and then, moved out.

CHAPTER

2

F uck this story! I say we turn the hell around and go home."

"Chill out," Arianna Garret said to fellow journalist, Kevin Baxter. "We worked hard to get this assignment, so take a deep breath and relax."

They had come to Kervistan to do an exposé on the plight of Muslim women. First, all of their equipment and luggage had been lost on the flight over, forcing them to hole up in a cheap hotel in Pakistan for three days until their belongings were recovered. Now, less than four hours into their journey to Nabolis, they were stranded by the side of the road as their Kervistan guide attempted to repair the sorry excuse of a vehicle they'd rented that morning.

The noonday sun was brutal, and Arianna was finding it stifling beneath the burqa she'd been forced to wear. The scratchy cloth irritated her face, and sweat ran profusely down her back. It was such a humiliation, but their guide, Tarique, had told her she would never be allowed into the country unless she covered herself as all Kervistan women did.

"If I'd just brought some tools," Tarique said, "I could fix this car."

"Great," Kevin snapped. "I don't suppose you might have thought of that before we left Pakistan this morning. You know it's not like we can call Triple A or anything."

"Triple A?" Tarique asked. "What is a Triple A?"

"Nothing. Just keep working on the car," Kevin mumbled.

Arianna threw the veil back off her face and felt instantly refreshed and alive. Being under that veil made her feel queasy and claustrophobic. The only good thing about wearing the traditional garb was she would be able to write a firsthand account of what it was like to be imprisoned in such a restrictive garment.

"Need any help?" a voice asked in Farsi.

Arianna spun around and came face to face with a Kervistani man who had walked up to the vehicle. He was amazingly handsome and had coal, black eyes that seemed to look right through her. She knew he couldn't, but it felt like he could see her naked form right through the burqa she wore. Despite the extreme heat, a shiver rippled through her body. *What a waste!* There could be nothing worse than having a man from this country lay his hands on you. Even so, despite the scruffy beard and primitive dress, this guy was stunningly gorgeous.

"What's wrong with the car?" a second Kervistan man asked in Farsi and began to look under the hood.

"Tell him we'll pay him a lot of money if he can fix this car," Arianna said to Tarique as she came around to the front of the vehicle.

Tarique took Arianna by the elbow and spun her around, flipping her veil back over her face as the two Kervistan men stared in disbelief.

"Please, madam," he said in a hushed tone as he abruptly escorted her to the back of the car. "You must keep your face covered, and you must not speak English."

Arianna began to do a slow boil that had nothing to do with the heat. She hated this subservient role. She had been stubbornly independent all of her life, and it irritated her to take orders from a man like this.

ZACH HAD heard it as plain as could be. The woman spoke English, and by the way she so boldly came forward, it was clear she was no Kervistan woman. Also, she wore her veil up. A woman could be stoned for showing her face in public in this country. But what a face she had. Beneath that veil was a beautiful girl with sparkling, azure, blue eyes that danced with devilment and a complexion nicely tanned from many days in the sun. It was a face that certainly had not been hidden behind any veil for very long.

He glanced into the back of the SUV and could see several cameras and other photographic equipment. If he had to make a guess, he would say these were American journalists here on an assignment. Only the guide seemed to be from this region. Thinking it was a Kervistan couple they'd come upon, the idea was to get a ride into town with them which would be a perfect cover. Now, Zach wasn't sure what he and Tony had walked into.

"Let's see what we have here," Tony said in Farsi as he tinkered with something under the hood. "Give it a try."

Tarique slid behind the wheel. No luck. The only sound was the clink of metal against metal. Tony looked under the hood again and made a couple more adjustments. "Okay, try it again," he said.

This time the engine sputtered to life.

"Thank you. Thank you," Tarique said in his native language. "Let us pay you for your help."

"No, we don't want any money," Zach responded in the native language, "but we would take a ride into Nabolis with you."

"Oh, yes. Please, get in," Tarique said, bowing in respect.

"Are you men from Nabolis?" Tarique asked, as the Land Rover rumbled down the unpaved road.

Tony shook his head. "No, we are from Bekistan."

"We are not from here, either. We have come to meet with Ali Hamdra Fasi. This man," Tarique said, pointing to Kevin, "is doing a report for a Western news group, and he wishes to feature Fasi in the film."

So, it was as Zach suspected. He'd hitched a ride with the wrong companions. Even more worrisome was that these journalists had chosen a very bad time to come to Kervistan.

ARIANNA RODE in silence, sandwiched between Kevin and the handsome looking stranger. She dared a sideward glance at the gorgeous hitchhiker, knowing he could not see her face. As if he sensed her stare, he turned in her direction and looked directly at her, his obsidian eyes searing her to the seat. She felt herself blush from head to toe. It was the first, and no doubt would be the last, time she would be thankful to be wearing this face-hiding burqa. Suddenly, the Rover hit a bump and bottomed out, jostling her into the passenger's lap. The stranger's strong hands caught her and helped her to right herself. His touch was electric. She felt tingly all over. *God, this guy was so hot, but why, Lord, did he have to be from this male dominated country?*

As they entered the center of the village, the vintage SUV chugged to a stop, and Zach and Tony exited. Before leaving, Zach paused and said to Tarique in Farsi, "Tell your friend Kevin this is not a safe place for him to be right now. The three of you should leave the country immediately." With one last look back at Arianna, he and Tony made their way into the marketplace.

"What did he say?" Arianna asked after they left.

"He said to leave this place… that it is not safe to be here, but I do not know why."

"So what's new?" Arianna asked. "This entire region of the world has been a troubled spot for years, but the problem is, this is where we find the Muslim women for our exposé. It's not like we can shoot this story on the French Riviera."

"Well, speaking for myself," Kevin chimed in, "I must admit this is not the journey I envisioned it to be. I'm feeling more and more uneasy all the time. I say we find Fasi and a couple of Muslim women, get their stories fast, and get the hell out of here."

"Okay, but just think. When this documentary airs, it's going to catapult our careers into the national spotlight. Every major news organization in the country is going to want to hire us," Arianna said.

"Oh, and aren't you just the little optimist?" Kevin shot back. "For all the hassle we're going through, I hope you're right."

"So where do we start?" Arianna asked Tarique.

"First, we find some lodging. Then, we try to get an appointment with Fasi. Please wait in the car while I make some inquiries."

Arianna pulled out a small mini cam she kept hidden under her burqa and began filming the marketplace. The first thing she noticed was the large number of stray dogs that wandered freely around the village. Most of them were skin and bones. Next, she spotted an ox that was currently taking a dump next to a produce stand.

"Eww! Gross," she said to Kevin. "Look at that ox. Now, that's a scene you won't see in the States."

"For sure," Kevin said. "Thank, God!"

There were several produce stands, but from Arianna's vantage point, all the vegetables seemed limp and over ripe. Nothing looked fresh. Nothing even looked familiar. Other vendors were selling household items such as rugs, vases, pots and pans... it looked like the American version of a rummage sale. Hanging from poles at another stand were some skinned goats with flies buzzing all around them. They were as unappetizing as oxen feces next to the produce stand.

"This will make some good B-roll for our documentary. Notice how few women are in the market place and those that are there, are completely covered, of course, and accompanied by a man. How could you live like this day after day?" Arianna asked.

"I guess you just would," Kevin replied. "You'd have no choice, plus you wouldn't know any better if this is all you've ever known. I think their contact with the outside world is non-existent, so this is normal for them."

Arianna zeroed in on the two Kervistanis that had helped them. She couldn't take her eyes off the one who'd made her heart race on the ride here. Even in his grubby, unkempt condition, there had been an animal magnetism, drawing her to him. *For Pete's sakes. Get a grip and try to remember this is about Muslim women, not Muslim men.* Just the same, she made sure she took numerous pictures of him to show the girls back home.

"You need to be careful with that camera," Kevin said. "We don't exactly have permission to film here, especially you, as a Kervistan woman. I know these windows are tinted, but you're still taking a big risk."

"Oh, you worry too much," Arianna said. "If you want to get the story, you have to take chances, and I intend to do what I have to do to get this amazing story."

Kevin rolled his eyes. "Arianna, your impulsiveness is going to get you into trouble one of these days. Mark my words, sweetie. Mark my words."

CHAPTER
3

Tarique returned with a man who led them to a mud and timber hut on the far side of the village. This was to be their home during their stay. The primitive dwelling had a kitchen with a wood burning cook stove while a large, tattered rug covered the floor of a sitting area. An additional side room would serve as Arianna's bedroom…a thin mattress on the floor, her bed. Kevin and Tarique would sleep on the floor in the main room. In either case, a good night's sleep wasn't in anyone's future.

"Hey, guys, just let me enjoy a moment of freedom before we head out again, please" Arianna said as she wrestled out of the burqa. "It's so unfair that the men can come and go as they please while the women are stuck wearing this thing. Personally, I think this is just another way to control women in the name of religion."

"Way to take one for the team," Kevin replied, giving her a quick hug. "Anyway, you have no choice. You either wear the damn thing, or you don't get the story. Sorry, sweetie. I feel your pain, but it's the only way."

Arianna felt refreshed as she lounged in her khaki shorts and t-shirt, but she knew she was just postponing the inevitable. She downed a quick bottle of water and then, looking at the burqa with disgust, exhaled deeply and said, "Okay, let's do this before I change my mind." Stepping back into the 'walking detention center', she headed out the door.

THE THREE strolled back to the market place. Tarique and Kevin led, and as was the custom, Arianna trailed behind.

"We have a Western journalist interested in our culture," Tarique said to one man after another, looking for someone who might agree to an interview. "He'd like to interview a woman in the village. Do you know any women who would agree? My friend is willing to offer some compensation?"

Most men looked at him as if he was crazy. Finally, one man asked, "How much?"

"Three hundred rubles," Tarique answered.

The man looked around suspiciously. "And we could do this without anyone knowing?"

"Yes. Yes. Very secret," Tarique answered. "No one in the village would know."

"I agree then," the man said. "I believe my sister would give an interview."

Tarique pointed to Arianna. "We brought another Kervistani woman so your sister would not feel uncomfortable talking to a man. This is good, right?"

"Very good. We will do it. Three hundred rubles. You meet me here tonight at five-thirty, and I will take you to my house to meet my sister."

"I will give you half the money now and half when we meet." Tarique counted out one hundred-fifty rubles from his pouch and handed them to him.

"We also need to find a way to get an audience with Ali Hamdra Fasi," Tarique continued. "Do you have connections to get an appointment with him?"

The man scratched his beard and thought for a moment. "I think so, but this may be a little harder to arrange. You will be paying money for this, too?" the man asked with a gleam in his eye.

"How much do you want?" Tarique inquired, beginning to tire of this guy gouging them for money.

"I think maybe five hundred rubles would be enough."

"Five hundred rubles! Ah, well. A moment, please," Tarique said, pulling Kevin aside to translate what had transpired so far.

"What the hell! That's outrageous. Do you trust this guy?" Kevin asked.

"I do not know, but we must start somewhere," Tarique answered. "Fasi is the only one who could give you a clearance to film openly in the village. If you want to film everywhere, you must have Fasi's permission."

"Okay. Pay the guy," Kevin said reluctantly. "I think he's fleecing us, but we're stuck. We need this appointment."

"Okay, we agree," Tarique said, turning back to the villager.

"Fasi is a media whore," the man said. "If you feature him in your film, you will surely get his permission to go wherever you want."

"Where does Fasi live? Can you take us there?" Kevin asked and Tarique interpreted.

The man hesitated and looked expectantly at Tarique. "Well, maybe, yes for another small fee, I think I can do that," he said with a sheepish grin.

Kevin turned and whispered to Arianna. "Jesus Christ! I see these people understand capitalism quite well. This guy's a fuck-ing entrepreneur."

Tarique paid the man fifty more rubles, and they were off to Fasi's dwelling on the far side of the village, sitting off by itself. His house was much larger than the small stone huts most people inhab-ited, and Arianna thought that by Kervistani standards, this must be considered a mansion. A tall, stone wall surrounded the unadorned two-story dwelling. In the front courtyard, several young boys were in the midst of a soccer game. Any girls that lived there were seques-tered inside.

Kevin took out a small, digital camera and began shooting the warlord's compound. He made sure he got shots of the children, the guards, and some local villagers who were milling around. This kind of footage would really add to the authenticity of their documentary.

"They say Fasi is with his men in the hills," Tarique informed them. "He will return tonight, so we will see if we can get an audience tomorrow."

"That seems so long," Kevin groaned. "Why can't we just start filming? We've still got several hours of daylight. I'd love to film the marketplace and get some quick interviews."

"Oh, that would not be wise. These are a suspicious people, especially of Westerners. If we were to begin filming everywhere in the village, we would be rounded up and put through a terrible interrogation. You know we have to get Fasi's permission. Even filming with your small camera is a risk. So please. Put your camera away. Let us return to our headquarters to eat and rest. Then, we will meet the sister at five-thirty."

The three turned to leave and collided with some villagers who began making a big fuss. Infidel was the one word Kevin clearly understood as an angry man bumped hard into him. A sharp look from Tarique told Kevin not to retaliate as he pulled him away.

"Heathens!" Kevin yelled after them despite Tarique's admonishment.

"Shh! Please, it is okay," Tarique said. "We do not want to anger these people. Anyway, they do not understand what you are saying. Let us go."

As the three of them rushed back to their rented lodging, they came upon a group of women, dressed in traditional garb, wailing and moaning. For some reason, a man with a switch was beating them. The women were huddled on the ground in a big burqa ball with their backs to the man. Though the stings had to be quite painful, the women made no attempt to defend themselves. It was as if they were resigned to their fate.

"Quick, Kevin," Arianna whispered. "Get a shot of this."

Arianna watched in horror as the man continued to strike the defenseless women as other men looked on, approving the beating. This was exactly the kind of abuse she hoped to document. She wished she could pull the mini cam out from under her burqa and film the whole thing herself, but that was not possible.

"Hurry, Kevin," Arianna said again, but as she looked in his direction, she saw he was fumbling through his camera bag, a bewildered look plastered on his face.

"I can't," he said, patting his clothes and digging through the bag.

"What do you mean, you can't?" Arianna asked.

"The camera. It's gone! I can't find the fucking camera."

"What? You were just taking pictures with it back at Fasi's compound. How could you lose it so fast?"

"I was sure I put it in my bag, but now it's not there. The camera and all my film are missing. God! You don't think they have pickpockets here do you? That scuffle... I mean, you might expect that in a large city, but not in a primitive place like this. These people don't even have pockets for Christ's sake!"

"Well, we may as well forget it," Arianna said. "That camera, wherever it is, is long gone. Luckily we've got other cameras back in the car, but we have to be much more careful from now on. Let's get the hell out of here before anything else happens."

ZACH AND his men had been checking out Fasi's compound when Kevin and the phony Kervistani female had shown up. It wasn't too bad until Kevin took his camera out and started taking pictures of everything and everybody in sight, including Zach and his men. That was a big problem. There was no way those photos could leave this country. So, he had signaled the men to relieve Kevin of the camera. In one of the oldest tricks in the books, one man created a diversion while the other picked him clean. Kevin never knew what hit him.

But something nagged at Zach about these two. In less than twenty-four hours, Fasi would be dead and all hell would break loose in this area. Fasi's men would immediately take Kevin captive as well as his female companion as soon as it was discovered she wasn't really a Kervistani woman.

But how to warn them to leave? He'd already told them once, but it appeared they had no intention of leaving. He needed to figure out some other way to warn them of the danger they were in, but he didn't know how to do that without blowing his cover.

When the CIA was formed under President Truman, no one envisioned a renegade group such as Zach's. This covert arm of the agency secretly worked to subvert foreign powers and overthrow enemy governments. Officially they didn't exist, and Zach had to make sure it stayed that way. But at what point do you risk blowing the mission, never mind blowing your cover for all time, to save two people. After all, these were journalists. Did anyone think for one second they wouldn't write about Zach and his men at the first opportunity they had? And once outed, his career would be over, and he'd likely be the target of some assassin himself.

The plan was supposed to be a quick in and out of the country, but the presence of the two journalists was an unexpected complication he hadn't counted on. … a complication that weighed heavily on his mind. One he may have to respond to sooner or later.

CHAPTER
4

W e're late," Kevin said as they hurried to their rented house. "I'd like to get my hands on the son-of-a-bitch that stole my camera. I'd beat the bloody hell out of him." He grabbed another camera from the equipment case and checked to see if it was fully charged. "Do we have anything to eat around here? I'm starving."

Arianna rummaged through her bag and found some bread and cheese. She broke off a hunk of cheese and laid it next to the bread on the table. "Dinner is served."

"Boy, this is barely edible," Kevin said, peeling off one moldy end of the cheese. "Don't we have anything else to eat?"

"Maybe some peanut butter," Arianna replied, digging deeper in the bag. "It's going to be slim pickings until we get out of here."

"Well, this will have to do, then" Kevin said as he made a sandwich. "I just hope this guy shows. He was all about the money, but maybe he decided to take our down payment and run."

"I believe he will be there," Tarique said. "I trust him."

Kevin gobbled down the food and washed it down with warm bottled water. "Ah, that hit the spot," he said and punctuated his satisfaction with a belch.

"You are such a pig!" Arianna looked at him and shook her head. "Just get your camera and let's go. And try not to lose it this time, okay?"

Kevin shot her a dirty look. "Very funny. Cut me some slack, okay? It's been a very long day, and it's not over yet."

"Okay. Sorry. You're right. Hang in there. We'll get through this together."

THE GROUP breathed a sigh of relieve when the local contact was at the meeting place. He led them to the other side of town to a hut that looked similar to the one they had rented. Made of stone and devoid of any modern amenities, it was the home of the villager's sister.

"This is Turilla. She has agreed to talk to you," the man said as he led them into the house.

The young woman had a gaunt look and sallow skin that had not seen the light of day in quite a while. Her teeth were rotted or missing and a nasty looking rash partially covered her body. In this country, no man other than a woman's husband could touch her. Most of the doctors were men, so Turilla, like most women, was forced to go without needed medical and dental treatment.

"My sister is a widow, so she now lives with me. Without my help, she would be begging on the street," the man said.

Arianna removed her burqa and smiled at the girl who seemed shocked to see an American woman under the veil. "Turilla, my name is Arianna. I am a journalist," she said as Tarique interpreted. "We are here to do a story about Muslim women and life under the Taliban rule. You do not have to fear us. We will make sure anything you tell us is kept a secret in your country. We will never use your name, so I'm hoping you will answer some questions for me."

Turilla waited for the translation and then, looked at her brother who nodded his approval.

As Kevin filmed, Arianna began asking the woman questions. She wanted to know everything about her life—education, marriage, children… her dreams for the future.

"Do you think you have been treated unfairly because you are a woman?" Arianna asked in the middle of the interview.

"Yes," she answered through Tarique. "Always, as well as every woman I know. We have no freedoms. No life. Under the Taliban rule, it is as if we don't exist."

Tears began to form in Turilla's eyes as she poured her story out. It was as Arianna suspected. The life of a Muslim woman in Kervistan was very dismal. They hated their lives but felt trapped with no way out.

"It is very oppressive under the Taliban regime. Girls used to be able to go to school, but now, not even that is available to us. We have nothing. Nothing!" Her tears of despair were beginning to turn to anger.

"Maybe this would be a good place to end," Tarique said, feeling Turilla's growing anxiety. "I believe you have enough information, Miss Arianna. We should stop now, yes?"

Arianna agreed. She could see it was painful for the woman to discuss this any longer. "Do you know of any other women who would agree to share their story?" Arianna asked.

"There is another woman I know… Fadia. She lives far outside the village. My brother knows her and can take you there, but you must never let any of the men of the village know that we have spoken with you. Please, do you promise?"

"I promise, Turilla," Arianna said, giving her a hug. She pulled out a handful of rubles and gave them to her. "Please, take this money. I just hope you find happiness somehow."

"Thank you," Turilla said. "You are a good person and very lucky to be born in the USA. Please be safe in my country. There are those who are treacherous. Be careful."

"I will," Arianna assured her. She slipped back into the burqa, and the group started back to the village.

"I fear we may have stayed too long," Tarique said. "It is against local custom for a woman to be out so late, even in the company of her husband. Let us hurry." However, as they came around the corner, their worst fears were realized. A group of men were gathered at the street corner.

Arianna's pulse quickened. A sense of foreboding came over her. It was late. She was a woman, and she knew she was in trouble. They tried crossing on the far side of the street, but the men spotted them. As soon as they saw Arianna, they began to question Tarique about why the woman was out so late. He tried to offer an explanation, but no one seemed interested in what he had to say. One man took out a switch and began beating on Arianna.

"Hey," Kevin said as he tried to fend the guy off. "Stop! Leave the woman alone."

This only made matters worse as they then began to question who Kevin was. Arianna fell to the ground and curled up in a tight ball. The man kept striking her with some kind of strap. She bit back the pain—defenseless against the attack.

Just when she thought she couldn't take it anymore, a man came up and pushed her attacker away. Then, he reached down and lifted her from the ground. As she looked into his face, she instantly recognized the handsome man who had hitched a ride to town with them. No one could forget those eyes. He shoved her into Tarique's arms and said something in Farsi. Tarique took off running, pulling Arianna along with him. Kevin followed quickly behind.

Arianna stopped and looked back. All the men were yelling and scuffling with each other. She couldn't understand a word they were saying, but she was worried for her rescuer's safety.

Kevin took hold of her arm and jerked her along. "Come on, Arianna. We've gotta get out of here." Everyone took off again and didn't stop until they were safely inside their house.

"Are you all right?" Kevin asked trying to catch his breath.

"I think so," Arianna panted, as she examined a welt on her arm. "Boy, it's even worse than I had imagined over here. These guys are evil."

"Except for two that is," Kevin said. "That's twice now our two Kervistan friends have come to our rescue... once to fix our car and now this. Guess not all of these people are bad."

"Well, two out of two million hardly counts," Arianna said. "This incident makes me all the more determined to bring this story to the attention of the world. Someone has to speak out for all the defenseless women that endure this treatment on a daily basis."

"We got a good start tonight with the interview. And I hate to say it, but your beating will make for an interesting story too," Kevin said. "Too bad I didn't get any of this on film."

Arianna had to agree although it was a tough way to get a story.

"Here, let me put some cool water on those welts," he said to Arianna. "I'm afraid we're fresh out of ice, honey." He dabbed the three large welts on Arianna's neck and arms with a wet cloth. "You know, we don't have to do this documentary. We can pull out whenever you say."

"I appreciate your concern, Kevin. I couldn't ask for a better partner. But I need to gut this out. This story is too important for me to wimp out, but right now, I'm exhausted. Let's turn in and call it a day."

As she settled into her bed, a mix of emotions washed over her. The day had been full of highs and lows, but for the most part, it had been a good day. She had a fabulous interview and some great footage to go with it. Just a bit more material like that, and they'd have all the makings of a powerful documentary.

Another image flashed through her head too as sleep closed in. It was the vision of the Kervistan man who'd come to her rescue tonight. She was very grateful for his intervention, and the thought of him lifting her out of harm's way made her feel warm all over. There was something very intriguing about that guy. Thinking about him was a silly waste of time, but he definitely added some spice to what had been an otherwise rough day.

"FUCK!" ZACH said to Tony, as the Kervistani men moved on. "That was too close for comfort."

"Yeah, but I think they bought our story," Tony said.

"It's a good thing, or we would have been in a lot of trouble."

Zach had convinced the men that the Kervistan woman was his cousin and that she and her husband were visiting from the province of Maza Sharif. He told them the couple had lost their way home and that's why they were out late. Have mercy he urged them. Fortunately, though skeptical, they finally dropped the matter.

Zach's concern about the fate of these two Americans had just deepened. By this time tomorrow night, they would be in more danger than they could handle, but no one would be here to help.

"So what do we do about them?" Tony asked.

Zach shrugged his shoulders. He still did not know, but they should have rendezvoused with the rest of the team twenty minutes ago. "Let's get going. The men are going to think something's happened to us and come looking," he said.

Zach and Tony rushed to meet the rest of the team at a remote location, far outside the city. "You've seen Fasi's compound. What do you think?" Zach asked the group.

"We've got the compound layout from Massi, our undercover connection in Pakistan," Juan said. He drew a rough outline of the dwelling in the dirt. "Carlos and I will take out the two guards at the front gate, so you can enter here." He pointed to the location on the diagram.

"You're sure you can trust Massi to have the gate open?" Zach asked.

"He better have it open. He cost us enough."

"If the gate's not open, this op will be severely compromised."

"Don't worry, Zach. He'll be there," Juan reassured him.

Looking around the team Zach said, "Okay, then, we strike tomorrow night at zero dark thirty. Fasi will be back in his compound by then. In the meantime, everybody lay low for one more day."

With that, they put their hands together and whispered a soft *hoo rah* then, disappeared into the night.

CHAPTER

5

Arianna woke stiff and sore after a fitful night's sleep. With no modern plumbing, her morning toilette consisted of a bowl of tepid water and a rough towel. Next, she brushed her teeth using bottled water from her knapsack and finished by running a brush through her hair while asking herself why. As soon as she put the lovely burqa on, no one would see her hair anyway.

In the sitting room, she found Kevin and Tarique eating a breakfast of some kind of gruel accompanied by a piece of flatbread. "What?" she quipped. "No fresh-squeezed orange juice or Western omelet?"

"Western omelet?" Tarique looked confused. "What is a Western omelet?"

"Never mind. It's a joke," Arianna said. "This food will do. I'm starving."

"Okay, today we meet Fasi," Kevin said scraping the last remnants of cereal from his bowel. "And also we go for the interview with the woman Turilla told us about, Fadia. I have the directions to her house written down somewhere."

"I also have a time set up with a group of men who have agreed to be interviewed on women's issues," Tarique said, and then paused.

"That's great!" Noticing Tarique's puzzled look however, Kevin asked, "Is there something more?"

"I think so. Arianna will not be allowed to go with us. No women are allowed."

"That figures," Arianna grumbled. "After all, what else would you expect in this male-dominated society?"

"I won't go if you don't want me to." Kevin came over beside Arianna.

"Don't be silly. Of course, you have to go. We need lots of material for our exposé. Now, if everyone is ready, let's go get this interview with Fadia. Then, we'll meet with Fasi."

FADIA LIVED in an area far outside Nabolis, so they packed up their camera equipment and piled into the Land Rover. The road to her house was more like a rutted cow path than a real road. The Rover bounced along causing Arianna to feel carsick by the time she arrived.

A young girl greeted them at the door. Though only three years older than Arianna, she looked many years her senior. Life here was hard and aged a woman fast. Her story, as interpreted by Tarique, was much like Turilla's.

"I have a cousin who was killed by her own father, my uncle," Fadia began, "all because she dared to choose her own husband. It is called an 'honor killing'. It was said she had dishonored her father by choosing her own husband, something no girl would dare to do."

"Is this a very common thing?" Arianna asked.

"I'm afraid so," Fadia explained. "The only way for my uncle to save face, he believed, was to kill his daughter. And worse yet, the man has never been arrested nor do I believe he ever will be. All the authorities are men, so you see, there is little hope for justice."

"This is terrible!" Arianna was fuming inside. "Is there no one to speak for these women?"

"No, there is no one. You will tell our story?" the girl pleaded, grabbing Arianna's hands.

"Yes," Arianna assured her. "We will tell the world. In the meantime, you must be brave and be safe."

Thanking Fadia, they loaded their gear into the Land Rover and began the bumpy trip back to town. They'd captured another powerful, yet sad testimonial.

When they arrived in the city, they went immediately to their appointment with Fasi. He had agreed to give them five minutes of his time. Before the guards led them into his headquarters, they thoroughly searched both Kevin and Tarique for any weapons.

"Your Excellency," Tarique began, "I have brought you my good friend, Kevin Baxter, from a Western newsgroup. He wishes to do a story about all the great improvements you have brought to this province. He only needs your permission to move about the village and take photos and talk to the villagers. I have also asked my sister here," he lied, "to accompany him so there would be a woman present if we speak with any women. It would only be proper."

"Hmph!" Fasi grunted. "And what will your story say?"

"It will tell about all the prosperity you have brought to your village. You will be known as a great leader in Kervistan. It will greatly enhance your image in your country and in the world."

"I see," Fasi said, suddenly pleased. "I will agree to this, but you will have only two days to get all your stories and photos, and you must not take any photos of my army or their weapons. If you abide by these rules, I will tell my people to allow you to go freely in our village. Do you agree?"

Tarique interpreted for Kevin who nodded his approval.

"My friend agrees," Tarique replied. "Thank you, your Eminence. We will follow all of your rules. And before we go, may we take a picture with you?"

"Yes," Fasi smiled and posed for the camera. As the one man had said, he loved the media attention.

Having shot several photos, and also gotten some video, they took their leave and got into the Rover for the ride back to the house.

"Well, that was easier than I thought," Arianna said. "Two days is a not much time, but we can do it. Actually, I don't think I could stand to be here much longer than that anyway."

"Okay," Kevin said, "I better get moving. The clock is ticking. I'm going to interview that group of men Tarique spoke about. I shouldn't be long. Will you be alright staying by yourself, Arianna?"

"Sure. Just get us more good footage, and when you return, I'll have a nice hot meal ready for you, honey."

"Right," Kevin said, laughing. "We both know that's not happening."

LATER THAT night, Zach and all his men were in place outside Fasi's compound. "Okay, gentlemen. Time to get your sneak on."

Juan and Carolos set up their sniper rifles, silencers attached, a hundred yards away from the front gate of the compound. Firing off two shots, both guards at the front gate dropped to the ground. As soon as the guards were down, Zach, Tony and the other two mercenaries dashed across the open hundred yards and stopped at the gate. With a slight creak, the gate swung open and Massi, the Pakistani plant, ran quickly away... his job done.

Tony entered first, followed by Zach and the rest of the team. The compound layout was exactly as they had studied. The team moved stealthily in the darkness to the building where Fasi slept.

At the front of his building were three guards. Two stood at the door while the other sat twenty feet away and appeared to be sleeping. Zach snuck close to the sleeping man and waited for his snipers to take out the two at the door. The two fell dead to the ground. Zach stepped up behind the third guard who had awakened with the sound of falling bodies. He snapped his neck, then dropped him to the ground.

The two snipers waited and watched outside for any other guards who might happen along, while Zach and the team hurried into the home of Fasi. They found him sleeping in the upper bedroom with two women. Without hesitation, Zach put one shot in his head. Fasi was dead. Thankfully the women sleeping beside him never stirred. Zach had no heart for taking them out too. The mission was accomplished, so wasting no time on target, the group left as they came, clandestine warriors of the night.

"Well done, men," Zach said as they met up a short distance from the compound. Now, take off for the hills. I have one more thing to do before I meet you at the rendezvous point."

Everyone stared at him in surprise, not moving.

"I have to go get the American journalist, the girl. This place is going to be a war zone in the next twenty-four hours, and she'll never make it out of here. I just can't leave her. You guys go on."

"We're not leaving you," Juan said. "We'll all go."

It was Zach's turn to stare. He knew they were loyal and wouldn't budge without him, but he couldn't let them stay.

"No, there's too many of us. It will attract too much attention. You guys take off. I shouldn't be more than twenty minutes behind you. Now, go. That's an order."

"Roger that," they said reluctantly, and headed for the rendezvous point... everyone except Tony.

"I'm going with you and don't try to stop me."

Zach looked at Tony and knew there was no talking him out of staying. "Okay, let's move then. We don't have much time."

They darted in and out of the shadows of the sleeping village and quickly reached Arianna's hut.

"What about the guy... Kevin?" Tony whispered.

"There's no way to take him. We'd risk too much if we tried. He's a man so at least he stands a fighting chance of coming through this especially once the Americans arrive. We just take the girl."

"Roger that," Tony answered.

They silently stepped through the glassless, bedroom window where Arianna slept. As the moonlight shone in the room, for the first time, Zach saw the girl without her burqa on. Her shimmering blond hair lay tumbled around her shoulders. He couldn't help but notice the bikini panties and t-shirt that revealed her long legs and nicely rounded breasts.

God, she looked enticing. But there was no time to enjoy the view since they had to get out of there. He pulled a hypodermic needle out from under his tunic. He signaled Tony to cover her mouth should she rouse while he was sedating her. He plunged the needle into her hip.

She began to rise even as Tony held her down. He put a scarf over her face so she couldn't see or scream. She struggled for an instant, but the powerful sedative took only seconds to work. She slumped into a deep coma. As soon as she was out, Zach grabbed the khaki shorts that lay near by and pulled them on. He threw her over his shoulder, climbed out the window, and took off for the rendezvous point.

"Do you want me to carry her for awhile?" Tony asked about a mile into their trek.

"No, I got it," Zach said. This reminded him of boot camp in special ops training. Part of the training was carrying a heavy log around for hours to build up endurance. If he could manage that, he could certainly handle a woman weighing a little more than a hundred pounds. Plus, she was his burden to bear. A half an hour into the hills, they caught up with the men. At this point, he was happy to hand Arianna over to them.

"If she starts to wake, sedate her again. We need to make sure she doesn't come to while we're around. She must never know what happened to her. Since according to our government, we don't exist, we cannot have any witnesses to say otherwise."

He got on his two-way radio and made a call to the USS Hornet stationed in the Indian Ocean. They would send a helicopter to take them to Turkey where they would get a private plane home. The government would never acknowledge their existence, but they would get them out of there. He called in their coordinates and waited for the chopper.

One of the men gave a low whistle, looking down at Arianna lying unconscious on the ground. "I can't believe this is what was beneath that burqa. Very nice!"

Zach nodded as he bent down to check her pulse. The girl was beautiful. Under different circumstances he might have enjoyed getting to know her, but that was impossible now. He planned to take her to the Isle of Costa Luna, the resort island where he lived. She would wake up and find her way back home, their paths never to cross again.

CHAPTER
6

O oow!" Arianna tried to raise her head off the pillow only to fall back in pain. She had the worst headache of her life. She lay there hoping the veil of fog that consumed her would soon lift. Images floated in front of her in slow motion. Everything was a blur.

Rising up again, she blinked rapidly to adjust her eyes to the surroundings. By the looks of the room, the only thing she was pretty sure of was she was no longer in Kervistan. The bed had sheets and a comforter. The room was carpeted and air-conditioned, and drapes adorned the windows. Also, she could see a bathroom with real plumbing just past the foot of the bed. She fell back on the pillow once again, her mind scrambling to make sense of things. She was absolutely sure when she'd gone to bed, it had been in Nabolis, Kervistan.

She dozed for a few more minutes and then, woke with a start. Struggling to a sitting position, she slipped back the covers and saw she was still wearing the same t-shirt and panties she remembered going to bed in, and her khaki shorts lay on a chair beside the bed. These were the only things that seemed even remotely familiar.

Thinking her bladder would burst if she sat there one more minute; she rose gingerly, wobbled and grabbed the nightstand to steady herself. It was then she noticed some money on the stand. Reaching over, she fingered through twenty, one hundred dollar bills. Two thousand dollars! *Whew! What was going on?*

She made a visit to the bathroom and as she pulled her panties up, she noticed a large bruise on her hip and wondered how she'd gotten it. Taking a closer look in the mirror, she detected a couple of needle pricks. Of course! She'd been tranquilized with something. That's why she had no recollection of how she'd gotten here. But who and why?

Moving back into the bedroom she threw open the drapes and was stunned to see the ocean in the distance. With sand, surf, and rows of palm trees, she realized she was in a tropical location—somewhere, but where?

She slumped back onto the bed and sat there a moment with her head in her hands, massaging her temples, hoping to assuage her screaming headache. Exhaling deeply, she stood and slowly pulled her shorts on. Shaky or no, she had to go and search for answers.

It was about ten o'clock in the morning as she came down into the lobby of what resembled a small, turn-of-the-century hotel. The only people she saw were a desk clerk and a young woman painting a mural on the far side of the room.

"Umh, excuse me," she said to a young man behind the desk. "I was wondering if you were on duty last night." Actually she wasn't sure when she would have checked in. Wasn't even really sure what day it was. She could have been here for days as far as she knew.

"No, Madam. I'm afraid I came on early this morning. May I help you with something?"

"Uh, my room. Room 323. Well, I know this is an odd question, but what name is that registered under?"

The clerk frowned and arched an eye brow.

"No. No. It's not what you think. You see I admit I was a little, well, shall we say, 'under the weather' when my, uh... uncle dropped me off, but really I'm here on vacation, partying, you know and.... and I just wanted to know, uh, which uncle I needed to thank for taking care of me." *God! Such a lame excuse.* It was all she could muster at the moment.

The clerk had a skeptical look on his face, and replied, "Yes, Madam. Well, let me see then. Hmm! That's curious. There is no name on the registration. You said room 323, right? It looks like someone evidently came in and paid in cash for three night's lodging. I wonder why the night clerk didn't post a name. This is highly irregular. I can call our manager. It's his day off, but he might know what the situation is."

"No, that's okay. Thank you anyway," Arianna said. "I'll speak with him later."

"Yes, Miss. Is there anything else I can help you with?"

"Aspirin. Would you happen to have some aspirin and maybe a soda?"

"Certainly. Please have a seat over there, and I'll bring it right out. I think there may even be a pastry left from the breakfast bar if you're hungry."

Arianna sat down on a sofa and rested her head in her hands. This was so crazy, she didn't even know where to begin to start putting her life back together, and right now, her head hurt so much she could hardly think. Whatever she had been tranquilized with was extremely powerful.

"Are you all right?" someone asked. The girl who'd been painting the mural spoke to her from across the room. "Is everything okay? You look a little pale."

"Yes, thank you," Arianna said, trying to put her best face on. The clerk returned and handed her two Tylenol and a can of Coke.

"Hang-over?" the girl asked.

"No, I wish," Arianna replied. "At least that would be easy to explain. Mmm, say. Can I ask you a question? One that you might think is stupid, but…" Her voice trailed off.

"I'm sure it's not stupid. What's your question?" the girl asked.

"No, that's all right," Arianna said, changing her mind. She popped two Tylenol into her mouth and washed them down with a swig of Coke.

"Hey, are you in trouble?" the girl said, laying down her paint brush and coming over to where Arianna sat. "I don't mean to pry, but you don't look too good."

Arianna was sure that was true. Her hair was matted and tangled. She had no make-up on. Her eyes had dark circles under them, and here she sat, shoeless and wearing dirty crumpled khaki shorts. No, she didn't look too good at all.

"My name is Lisa Calder," the girl continued. "I'm the interior designer for this place."

"Uh… Arianna. Arianna Garrett," she whispered, then cleared her throat. "Ahem. My name is Arianna Garrett." She looked at Lisa for a moment and then, said, "I don't know where I am."

"Excuse me."

"I don't know where I am," Arianna repeated, watching Lisa's reaction.

Lisa frowned. "This is the Cass Hotel. Does that ring a bell?"

Arianna shook her head. "No. I mean I don't even know what city I'm in."

"You don't know wha… what city you're in?" Lisa said, trying to conceal the surprise in her voice. "You're kidding, right?"

Arianna shook her head.

"You're not kidding, are you?" Lisa said, calmly. "Well, uh, you're on the Caribbean island of Costa Luna."

Arianna was stunned. How had she come half way around the world and not been aware of it?

"How… how is it you don't know where you are?" Lisa stuttered, surprised at Arianna's revelation.

"You wouldn't believe me even if I told you."

Lisa leaned forward. "You might be surprised. I have three sisters, so I've heard some pretty crazy stories."

"Well, I'm sure you haven't heard this, but I'll try. You see, I'm a journalist who until yesterday, well at least I think it was yesterday since I don't know what day it is either."

Lisa's mouth fell open. "Wow! This is wild. It's Wednesday, Arianna."

"Wednesday? Oh, my God. I've lost almost two days," Arianna said, shaking her head. She cleared her throat and began to pour out her story. "Lisa, as I said, I'm a journalist who was on assignment in Nabolis, Kervistan. Two nights ago I went to bed in that city, but about an hour ago I woke up here in this hotel, and I have no idea how I got here. I know all this sounds crazy, but it's true. I haven't been drinking or doing drugs. This is honestly what happened to me."

Lisa stared at her a moment. "Kervistan as in Eastern Europe next to Pakistan? I mean, you're not pulling my leg, are you?" Lisa asked.

"No. I can prove all of this except for the part about how I got here because I have no idea how I got here. I did find a bruise on my hip where I believe someone might have sedated me, but I have no idea who or why anyone would want to do that."

"Whew! This sounds like something out of a spy novel. What about calling the police?" Lisa asked.

"I thought about that, but really what can they do? I don't think they exactly have jurisdiction in Kervistan. It's not like they can send someone to investigate and since I have absolutely no clue what happened, they would have no leads to work on. But more than that, I'm afraid they'll think I'm some kind of nut case, or worse."

"Worse?"

Arianna hesitated a moment, unsure if she should say any more or not. She really didn't know this girl. Of course, she didn't know anyone on this island, but right now she needed a friend. Lisa looked trustworthy, so she forged ahead.

"Lisa, whoever abducted me left two thousand dollars in hundred dollar bills. To me that has hooker written all over it. If the police ever found that out, they'd dismiss me as a drugged up prostitute."

Lisa nodded her head. "You know, I think you're right. So what do you do now?"

"I'm not sure. I don't have any idea where to even begin to sort this out. My partner is back in Kervistan. Maybe he knows what happened if I can reach him. I really don't know where to start."

They both sat there, silent for a moment. Arianna finished her soda and stood. "Lisa, if you'll excuse me, I better get going. You've been very kind to listen to me."

"Sure," Lisa said, standing and giving her a hug. "If I can do anything to help you, well, please let me know."

Arianna returned the much needed hug. "Thank you. I'll keep your offer in mind."

BACK IN her room, Arianna stood motionless for a moment. She wasn't sure of anything except that right now she wanted a long, hot bath. She filled the tub and stepped in. Sinking into the hot steamy water, she couldn't remember when anything had felt so good in such a long time. Grabbing the hotel shampoo and soap, she lathered up from head to toe and sank below the water to rinse off. Coming back up, she laid her head on the back of the tub and closed her eyes. She just wanted to soak and think for a moment. Her headache had subsided and for the first time since she'd woken that morning, she felt half way normal.

Also, for a brief moment, she almost forgot her troubles. Whatever happened, she was still alive, and she hadn't been raped or maimed. All she needed to do was to pick up a phone and get a flight home. Her abductor had even left her money to pay for a ticket. She could go home and life would go on as usual. Except it wouldn't. You didn't just walk away from an experience like this and go on without finding some answers.

She pulled the plug on the tub, stepped out, and wrapped up in a towel. Feeling refreshed, she walked to the bedside and stared at the phone. She thought she should call someone, but who? Picking up the phone, she dialed her mom in Milwaukee.

"Mom," she said, when Kathryn Garrett answered. "This is Arianna." She didn't know why she felt the need to identify herself. She was an only child, so no one else would be calling her mother, mom.

"Oh, thank God, it's you. Honey, where are you?"

"Well, Mom, it's kind of complicated, but I'm on the Isle of Costa Luna in the Caribbean."

"Where? Costa Luna? You mean you're not in Kervistan? Oh, that is such good news."

"What do you mean?" She couldn't figure out why this would be good news. She doubted her mom even knew where Costa Luna was.

"Haven't you heard? War has broken out in Kervistan."

"What?"

"Some warlord, Ala Hamra Fadi, or something like that was assassinated and the Northern rebels are blaming the South and are ready to attack them. The U.S. and the British are backing them, so we're sending troops to the area. I'm not sure what is going on, but I'm so happy to hear that you got out of that place. I can't tell you what a relief it is to know you're safe."

"Yeah, me too," Arianna replied, stunned with the news. Fasi assassinated! She wondered if her situation could possibly be related, but how? She didn't know any assassins or of any anticipated assassination plans, but things were getting weirder by the minute.

"Well, anyway, Mom. I just wanted you to know I'm fine. I'll call you again later. I love you."

"Yes, I love you, too. You take care now."

"I will, Mom. Bye."

She didn't see any sense in worrying her mother by telling her what had really happened to her especially in light of what she'd just learned about the current upheaval in Kervistan. She'd give her all the details later when she had some answers.

She reached for the remote and snapped on the TV. The story was on every news channel. Fasi had been assassinated and the minister of defense for Kervistan was claiming the U.S. was responsible. The U.S. State Department on the other hand was vehemently denying any connection to the assassination. Fasi's rebels in the North had moved troops to the South and had attacked a small outpost. In the meantime, the U.S. had positioned two aircraft carriers in the Indian Ocean, ready to launch air strikes.

Kevin. Oh, no! He was right in the middle of that. *Please, God! Let him be okay.*

She picked the phone up and tried to remember the number to Starline Productions, the small independent film company she and Kevin worked for. She had the number in her purse, which of course along with every other piece of information about her, was long gone. She had to talk to her boss, Harold Major. Maybe he'd heard something. After getting the number from the operator, she dialed Starline and waited for Harry to pick up.

"Arianna! Where the hell are you? Are you still in Kervistan?"

"Harry, you're not going to believe this, but I'm in the Caribbean resort of Costa Luna, but I don't know how I got here, and I don't know what's happened to Kevin. I was hoping you had heard from him."

"What the hell? You're where, and what do you mean you don't know how you got there? My God, all hell's broken loose over there. If Kevin's still there, then he's in serious danger."

She did her best to explain, but it didn't make sense even to her.

"Look, kid. I'm not sure what's going on, but I do know I put everything I had into this assignment. Now, I find one of you is missing, one of you is on some damn island in the Caribbean, and all my camera equipment and start-up money are down the fucking drain. I'm practically bankrupt. None of that equipment was insured, you know?"

"Oh, Harry. I'm so sorry. I know we let you down. I just don't know what to say."

"Don't say anything. I guess it's just the hazards of the business. I'll try to do what I can to see if I can find Kevin, but I don't know where to begin... with no money and no contacts, it seems hopeless. What a frickin' mess, but I gotta go. Let me know if you hear anything. Glad you're ok, kid," Harold said and hung up.

Could things get any bleaker, Arianna thought as she hung up? Here she was in a strange place with nothing... no identification, no shoes, and barely any clothes. And now, it appeared she had no job to return to. She looked over at the cash on the nightstand. With no other options available to her, she was consoled by the thought that at least she had the means to get a flight home.

She picked up the phone and dialed the airline for tickets but hit a snag immediately when the agent asked for a credit card. "Uh, it was stolen. My purse and all its contents have been stolen. I'll be paying cash," she said. *Stolen. Lost. Two thousand miles away. Whatever. They were gone.*

"Everything?" the agent asked. "You know the new security regulations require you to have two pieces of ID for all international flights. You'll never be allowed to board a plane without some form of picture ID and your passport. You need to postpone your travel plans until you can replace your identification."

Of course, the agent was right, Arianna thought as she hung up the phone, but didn't they have some kind of system for emergencies such as hers? It seemed not. She felt helpless and out of options.

She sat there, staring at the floor, not sure what she would do next. Then, it suddenly dawned on her that maybe she wasn't supposed to go home yet. If she ever hoped to find out what had happened to her, the answers were here on this island. If she went home, she'd never know how she got here, and it would bug her for the rest of her life. The not knowing would consume her. After all, she was an investigative journalist who had experience in finding information. She ought to be able to solve the mystery of how she got here.

Yes, that's it! She could. She just needed a plan and some help. She threw on the only three items of clothing she owned and started to reach for the cash, but paused. Running into the bathroom, she tore open two of the sealed water glasses and brought the plastic baggies back to the nightstand. Using the hotel pen, she slid the top and bottom hundred-dollar bill into one bag and the hotel room key into the other.

Fingerprints! Unless they'd been obliterated from her touching them earlier, she thought she might just get lucky and have her abductor's fingerprints. At least it was a start. She scooped up the rest of the money and headed downstairs. She would not be defeated. She would find out what had happened to her if it was the last thing she did.

CHAPTER

7

E xcuse me," Arianna said to Lisa as she crossed the lobby.
"Oh, hi Arianna," Lisa replied, turning and smiling. "You're looking much better than the last time I saw you."

"Same clothes, of course," Arianna said with a sheepish grin,
"but I did get a shower and so I feel a lot better. Say, I was wondering.
You wouldn't happen to know where I could rent a room here on the
island, would you? Something really cheap."

"Costa Luna is a popular vacation retreat, so finding something
reasonable might be difficult. I went through this myself about six
months ago." Lisa paused, and then added, "You know, I have an extra
room I could rent to you if you're interested."

"You do? That would be wonderful, but are you sure? I mean you
hardly know me, and I do have this crazy drama going on. Also, my
funds are limited. I'm not sure how much I could pay."

"Understood, so how about this? Let's give it a two-week trial...
a hundred dollars a week, and if it's a bad fit, we shake hands and go
our separate ways. How's that sound?"

"Sounds great," Arianna said, offering her hand. "It's a deal."

"Well, then, let's go get you settled in." Lisa started packing up
her equipment.

"What about your painting?" Arianna asked.

"Oh, it can wait. I'm the designer, the painter, and the clean-up person. A real one-woman show," Lisa chuckled. "The one perk I have is that I can set my own hours, and right now, I say it's quitting time."

Arianna smiled. "Well, okay, then. After you."

Lisa led the way outside to her vintage, yellow Volkswagen convertible. "Hop in. I'll give you a tour of the island on the way home."

As they cruised down Oceanside Drive, Arianna laid her head back on the seat, relishing the warmth of the sun on her face. Pent up anxiety flew away with the wind that blew through her hair, and she began to relax for the first time since she'd awakened that morning.

"What a beautiful beach," she sighed, looking out at the crystal blue water. "And look at all these cute little shops and restaurants. Such a big contrast to where I came from. The country of Kervistan is quite bleak and has little modernization. Waking up here makes me feel like I'm in some kind of time warp."

"Lots of tourists come here to vacation and scuba divers love to explore the reef and sunken Spanish galleon off the coast," Lisa said, as she stopped to let some beach goers cross the street. "Also, we have several yachts that anchor out and bring their guests ashore for dining and gambling. By nine o'clock tonight, this entire strip will be jumping with people hitting the local nightclubs. That's about all there is on the island—tourism. There are some cattle ranches and banana plantations on the far side of the island, but those residents stay pretty much to themselves."

"How did you happen to move here?" Arianna asked, as they continued on down the ocean highway.

Lisa grimaced. "It's a long story. Not a pretty one, either. I arrived about six months ago with my boyfriend. He was a drummer with one of the local bands. Well, to make a *long* story short, we were only here about a week when he ditched me and headed back to the States."

Arianna winced. "Oww! What a bastard! I'm sorry to hear that."

"No, it was for the best, really. But I'd given up my job back in Chicago, so I had nothing to go home to. Didn't have any money to get home on anyway. Maybe that's why I can relate to your dilemma."

Arianna nodded. It seemed they had at least one thing in common.

"Anyway, in order to survive," Lisa continued, "I started working as a cocktail waitress at night while I tried to get my design business going during the day. It's been a struggle, but I think I'm making it."

"I'm sorry about your boyfriend but impressed with how you landed on your feet. It makes me think if you can make it, I could too. I at least need to find a way to support myself while I try to find some answers about how I got here."

"Sure. I'll help you all I can," Lisa assured her. "And as far as the boyfriend goes, well, it was the best thing that could have happened really, so don't feel sorry for me. Say, are you hungry?"

"I'm starving. I have no idea when I last ate. I do remember what I ate, however, and it wasn't the greatest. I could really go for a nice, juicy hamburger."

"Done," Lisa said, breaking to swerve into a McDonald's. "Here, I'll buy this time. You can buy when you get on your feet. And speaking of feet, I see we're going to need to get you some shoes."

Arianna looked down at her bare feet. "Thank God, I'm in a tropical climate. I have no shoes and no clothes. I'm wearing the only things I own."

"I think we can fix you up. The dress is very casual here so you won't need anything too expensive."

Arianna bit into a Big Mac, grabbed a handful of fries, stuffed them into her mouth, and washed it all down with a big swig of Coke. "I can't remember when anything tasted so good. By the way, do you know where I might find a job of some kind?"

"Well, the club where I work is always looking for help. Maybe I can get you on there. It's not glamorous, but tips are outstanding."

"I'll do whatever I have to do to get by. I waitressed my way through college, so I guess I can do it again. I have to find a way to finance my stay while I solve this mystery."

"We'll figure out something," Lisa said as she pulled into the carport of a tiny, stucco cottage, a block from the ocean. "Here's where I call home these days. Come on. Let's go get you settled in."

The house was small but cozy, and Lisa's designer touches could be seen everywhere. The kitchen, dining area, and living room all opened up together to make one big room and had been decorated in an island motif. A royal blue sofa was nestled beside a blue and white striped, chair and matching ottoman in the living room. A white, painted parsons table sat in the dining area with a fresh bouquet of spring flowers in the center. The kitchen had a small butcher-block center island and a built-in wine rack overhead. The entire house was light and airy and had an inviting feel about it.

"Your place is lovely," Arianna said as she looked around. "Did you decorate it?"

"I agreed to decorate this house in exchange for a reduction on the rent. So far I think the owner got the better end of the deal. Here, you can have the second bedroom," she said, leading Arianna down the hall. "By the way, I'm meeting some friends at the beach this afternoon. I have an extra bathing suit if you'd like to join us."

"That sounds wonderful. I'd love to."

"Great!" Lisa replied, opening the door to Arianna's bedroom. "It's pretty bare bones, but the bed is very comfortable. Why don't you change while I pack the cooler? How does a cold beer sound?"

"Perfect. I can sure use something to help me relax. It's been a rough day. And, hey Lisa, thank you again for helping me out. This means a lot to me."

Lisa smiled and handed her a bathing suit. "Not a problem. I've been where you're at, well, at least sort of. Helping you out is the least I can do. Now, go get ready. I think this suit will fit you."

Arianna put the plastic baggies with the money and room key in the top dresser drawer. She was banking on these two items to provide some answers to the identity of her mysterious abductor. It was a long shot though. Even if there were finger prints on the money, there was no guarantee they were in a data bank somewhere, but it was all she had for now.

At the beach, she wasted no time downing three quick beers in an attempt to numb her senses. It had worked. Drinking to excess wasn't usually her thing, but today the alcohol greatly eased her anxiety about what had happened to her in the last twenty-four hours. Listening to the waves rush back and forth on the shore, she felt relaxed and free. But she wasn't free. Though no burqa bound her, she was imprisoned in a veil of mystery. Until she found out how she had gotten to this island, and who had brought her here and why, she would never be free. That's why she was determined that no matter how many obstacles she faced, she would never give up until she solved this mystery.

CHAPTER
8

Now, less than fifteen hours since he'd left Kervistan, Zach stood in the shiny marble bathroom of his multi-million dollar, seaside estate on the resort island of Costa Luna. He studied his naked image in the mirror and thought he looked like a Cro-Magnon man. His jet-black hair hung in dirty strands and a big, bushy beard hid the entire lower part of his face. At least three inches would have to come off before he could even begin to shave. He took a long draw on a cold Heineken, then picked up a pair of scissors and began cutting away big tufts of beard. Trimmed to a manageable length, he shaved the last remnants of the Kervistan disguise off his face.

Draining the rest of his beer, he stepped into the shower and let the hot water pour down on him. Grabbing a bar of soap, he lathered from head to toe, and then shampooed his wild mop of hair, rinsing it until it squeaked. He stood immobilized for a moment, savoring the smell of lime verbena shampoo. It was funny that the things you missed the most could be as basic as a little soap and water and the smell of "clean".

Retrieving another beer from an ice bucket on the counter, he stepped back into the shower and sat down on the built-in bench. As the water streamed over his chest and legs, he sat back and closed his eyes. The last twenty-four hours had been hell.

The event was all over the news—the assassination. It had accomplished just what it was supposed to, and he should have been pleased, but Fasi's death brought him no joy. He disliked killing, but with Fasi's passing, the U.S. could move in and bring about a regime change. Everyone won including the people of Kervistan. He rationalized the completion of this assignment as performing a public service for many, though his good deeds would never be publicly acknowledged.

Then, there was the girl he had saved from certain rape and torture, probably even death at the hands of the Kervistani's. She was supposed to be just someone he was getting out of harm's way, but once he got a good look at exactly who was under that burqa, everything had changed. She was amazingly beautiful, and it occurred to him that she must possess extraordinary courage to brave those conditions to get a story... the kind of woman he'd love to meet, but seldom did. Not that there weren't plenty of women in his life. Through the years, there had been lots of women, and all quite eager to be the one he finally settled down with. But at thirty-one and single, it was obvious it was going to take a special type of woman to capture his heart.

He'd tried to keep his distance from the girl during the fifteen-hour flight home, but he found himself going over to monitor her vital signs more times than were actually warranted. If he went over there one more time, he knew the men would start to razz him, so he had turned the duties over to Tony. Thus, it was Tony who sedated her one last time when she began to rouse just as they were landing. She was going to have a huge, fucking headache when she woke up, but it was the only way. She could not be allowed to come to and recognize them. It was a matter of national security as well as a matter of his own personal safety. His life would be in grave danger if his identity ever got out.

When they arrived home, the men loaded their gear into a Hummer limo waiting to take them to his gated compound on the far side of the island. He stayed behind to see to the girl personally. After putting her in his black Escalade, he drove to a small hotel in an older section of the city. There, he met Hector Alvarez, a friend of his who was the manager of the hotel. He paid him for three night's lodging and an additional large sum of cash as hush money. Then, he carried the girl up the back stairs into a room. Once in the room, he laid her on the bed and removed her shorts. He felt like a voyeur as he stared down at her luscious body. Something stirred in him, but at that point, it didn't take much. It had been more than a month since he'd been with a woman.

He thought again about how, in a different time and place, he would have been eager to get to know this girl, but that was not possible now. It was doubtful she could ever recognize him once he was clean-shaven and dressed in civilian clothes, but he could never take the chance. So he put twenty, one hundred dollar bills on the nightstand, pulled the comforter and sheet up over her, and then, despite all he was feeling, he left. He knew he'd saved her life, though there would never be any acknowledgement of that either.

Now, as he sat in the shower, loneliness permeated his thoughts. He'd be hooking up soon with Lydia, a girl he'd been dating at the time he'd left for the Kervistan mission. He wondered why he hadn't thought of her the whole time he was gone and was only mildly interested in seeing her now.

He knew why. Because of the kind of work he did, how could he ever hope to have a meaningful, long term relationship? Lydia had no idea where he'd been for a month never mind what he'd done. And he sure as hell hadn't written or called during that time… would lie about everything now that he was home. Yet, as he sat alone, quietly getting drunk in his shower, a yearning for something more rained down on him. He rose and snapped off the shower and smacked the wall. *God, this was a damn lonely business!*

CHAPTER
9

"M y feet are killing me." Arianna slipped off her shoes and began massaging her toes. It was 3:00 AM, and she'd just finished a six-hour shift at *Poseidon's Adventure,* a trendy disco on the beach where both she and Lisa waitressed. "At least I made some good tips tonight. That makes my feet hurt a little less."

"Me, too," Lisa said, counting her money. "Had some really big tippers in my section."

Arianna had been on the island for about three weeks, and Lisa had given her a place to stay and helped her to get a job. She had been right by Arianna's side as she scoured the island, looking for answers to her mysterious arrival on Costa Luna... a search that so far had hit all dead ends.

She'd interviewed all the staff of the Cass Hotel who had been on duty the night she arrived. There was no name on the hotel registration. No video surveillance existed. A key had been coded for the room, but no employee remembered or fessed up to coding the key. After being put off for nearly two weeks, the hotel manager finally agreed to meet with Arianna. In the vein of "the customer is always right" accompanied by "fake sympathy for her plight", he pledged to look into the matter and get back with her, but it all rang hollow. Arianna could tell he was only patronizing her and was sure he had no intention of following up on anything.

She'd also made the rounds at the airport trying to check inbound flight records. Jet Blue was the only airline that flew into Costa Luna's small international airport. Five flights had arrived that day.... all from the States. But she'd been in Kervistan, not the States. Common sense said there was no way to get a comatose passenger off a commercial flight without someone noticing anyway.

This left the possibility of arriving on a private plane. By using her beauty and charm, she circumvented official airport policy and convinced an air traffic controller to allow her access to the flight logs for that date. They revealed no private planes had filed a flight plan for the day she arrived. It didn't mean no private plane had landed. It just meant someone might have been paid off not to report the plane's arrival, making it a completely untraceable event unless a witness came forward to say otherwise. There were only three traffic controllers and none recalled any private plane landing that day. End of story.

Finally, Arianna considered the remote chance she could have been brought here by boat. Yachts frequented the island all the time, their guests coming ashore for dining and gambling. She had no idea how to follow up on this option. Those yachts were not registered and were long gone anyway. Besides, boats are slow. She would have been at sea too long to have arrived when she did. Arrival by boat was out.

Adding to her frustration, no one had heard from Kevin. Her former boss, Harold Major, had heard nothing, nor had Kevin contacted his parents. They were worried sick and had turned to the State Department for help. U.S. forces had invaded Kervistan and the nightly news had shown fierce fighting with the Taliban. The situation was too hot to get any reliable information out of there. In her private moments, Arianna was very worried about Kevin. If he were alive, she thought he would have contacted someone by now. The fact that no one had heard from him was a worrisome sign.

"I should just give up and go back home," she told Lisa, as they pulled into the carport after work. "I don't think I'll ever find out what happened to me."

"Oh, no, Arianna," Lisa pleaded. "Don't do that. How about the key and money with the fingerprints? Isn't it time to see if they can help solve this mystery?"

"I guess you're right," Arianna said without much enthusiasm. "I'm out of options, so I think it's time to run those prints. That will probably turn out to be a dead end, too."

"Come on now, Arianna. Think positive. I think you're going to get a lucky break with those prints."

"Sorry. I'm just tired. You're right. I need to stay positive." Pouring herself a glass of wine, she sat down and put her feet up. "I need to figure how to go about getting those prints checked. I don't think you just walk into a police station and ask them to run a set of fingerprints. I wish I knew a private detective or someone who could run them without starting a major investigation."

"Hey, wait a minute," Lisa chimed in. "I might know someone. There's this guy, Paul Vega, who's some kind of a detective here in Costa Luna. He comes into the club all the time and keeps trying to get me to go out with him. He's a nice enough guy, but not my type so I've been avoiding him. I could cozy up to him and see if he'll help you."

"Maybe, but you'd have to be careful about how you approach him. We don't want to give him too many details until we're sure we can trust him."

"Right, so the next time I see him, I'll ask him if he'll meet with you. I won't give him any details. I'll just tell him you have a private legal matter you want to discuss. What do you think? Want to give it a try?"

Arianna thought a moment, unsure. She was eager to see if the prints revealed a name but at the same time, afraid they would reveal nothing and that would be the end of the line...mystery never solved.

"Ahh!" She blew out a ragged sigh of resignation. "I guess it's time to play my last card. Nothing else has worked, so see what you can line up. Let's do this."

IT WASN'T long after their conversation that Lisa was able to arrange a meeting with the detective. He agreed to meet for coffee at a small diner on Oceanside Drive.

"I still can't believe you insisted on dragging me along," Lisa said, as she sat waiting with Arianna. "I don't want to give this guy the impression I'm interested in him."

"I know. I know, but I need you for moral support."

Paul Vega strolled into the diner and slid in beside Lisa. "Good morning, ladies. Arianna, I'm Paul. Lisa said you had a legal matter you wanted to discuss with me. How can I help?"

"Well, it's complicated," Arianna began, then paused as the waitress brought Paul a cup of coffee and refilled hers. "You see I have kind of a situation which I don't really want the police involved in. At least not yet."

Paul held up his hand. "Okay, hold on a minute. Be careful what you tell me. I'm duty bound to report any illegal activity."

"Oh, no," Arianna said, shifting in her seat. "It's nothing illegal, at least not on my part, but my situation is a little unusual." She looked at Lisa for a sign she should continue.

"Paul," Lisa said, jumping in, "Arianna needs your help regarding something that happened to her about a month ago. Ari, just tell him. It's not anything bad, you know."

"Okay," she said clearing her throat. "About a month ago I was a journalist on assignment in Kervistan."

"Wow! Like the real Kervistan in the Middle East?" Paul asked.

Arianna nodded. "Anyway a month ago, I went to bed in Kervistan, and when I woke up the next day, I found myself in the Cass Hotel here on the island, and I have no idea how I got here."

"What? Say that again. You had no idea how you got here?" Paul asked, an astonished look plastered on his face.

"None," Arianna said, shaking her head. "Someone in Kervistan drugged me then brought me here and dropped me off in the hotel. I don't know who, and I don't know why. That's where you come in. I need your help to find out who brought me here. If I can find out who, then maybe I can learn why. Right now it's all a big mystery."

"Uh, I don't mean to get personal, but uh, well, had you been raped or anything?"

"Yes, I understand and no, I hadn't been raped or harmed in any way."

"Oh, glad to hear that. And now, excuse me for being a little dense, but don't you think waiting a month to call the police is a little long?"

"Probably, but I never figured they could do much to help me. No one at the hotel where I woke up saw anything. No one at the airport saw anything. I can't find a single witness who had any information about this situation, and of course, there's no way to question anyone in Kervistan. There's really nothing to go on."

"Hmm, very interesting," Paul said, sitting back in the booth, sipping his coffee as he mulled the situation over. "You're probably right about the police. We have a good group of men at the station, but the biggest thing they've handled this year was a drunken brawl on the beach. I don't think they're equipped to investigate an international incident. So what do you need me for then?"

Arianna hesitated. *Can I trust this guy? He seems like an honest, decent person, but how can I be sure?* She looked at Lisa who nodded her approval, so she continued.

"Well, you see, Paul, I believe I might have my abductor's finger prints."

"Well, now. That would change everything, assuming the guy is in a data base somewhere, otherwise you don't have jackshit."

"That's true so I need someone to run the prints and see if anything shows up. If there's a match, then I promise I'll let the police take the whole case and run with it. Until I have something definitive, I'd rather keep the police out of it. Are you willing to help me?"

"Okay," Paul said slowly. "Seems harmless enough. I think I can run these without getting my department involved. I have some connections in the States who will help me. Do you have the prints with you?"

Arianna pulled out the two baggies that contained the money and the room key and laid them on the table.

Paul's mouth dropped open. "Money? This guy gave you money?"

Arianna could hear the skepticism in his voice. "Yes. He left money on the nightstand. Twenty one-hundred dollar bills. I think he thought I would take the money and go home. I obviously didn't. This is the top and bottom bill. I'm hoping there's a thumb print on the top bill and maybe one of the other four digits on the bottom. And this is the hotel room key. Maybe there is a print on that, too."

"Ahem," the detective said, clearing his throat. "Are you sure there isn't something you're not telling me about this money and this entire situation?"

Arianna let out a small groan. "Your reaction is just what I expected and another reason I haven't called the police before now. You think maybe I was just turning tricks and got dumped in some hotel and that now, I want to find the john that jilted me or something fishy like that. Maybe I've made a mistake coming to you." Arianna started to gather her things to leave.

"No. No. Wait!" Paul put his hand on her arm to stop her. "I'm sorry, but I had to ask. Please. Have a seat." Looking her straight in the eye, he continued, "Arianna, listen. I'm willing to help you with this, but do you promise you've told me everything? My career could be on the line if you get me involved in some shady deal."

Arianna met his gaze. "Paul, I swear. I know it sounds crazy, but what I told you is the absolute truth."

"Okay, then. Give me your evidence, and I'll see what I can do."

Arianna hesitated once again. *I want the truth, so why am I afraid to let go of the money and key?*

"Go ahead, Ari," Lisa urged. "Let Paul take them. It's your last chance to find this guy. You've got to trust him."

Arianna exhaled deeply, and then, handed the baggies over. "Please take good care of this evidence. I'm really banking on these to solve my case."

Paul patted her hand. "I'll guard them with my life. You know, of course, that just because we ID this guy, doesn't mean he's not or ever was on this island. He could be anywhere in the world. Then, what will you do?"

It's something that hadn't occurred to her until now. *How naïve to have assumed my abductor was on this island, just sitting there waiting to be discovered?*

"I don't know. I guess I'll cross that bridge when I get to it. Right now I'd be happy to just get a name."

"Well, then sit tight, sweetheart, and I'll see what I can do." He grabbed the check and got up to leave. Winking at Lisa, he said, "Take care. I'm looking forward to seeing you around the club."

"Sure," Lisa said weakly, a half-smile on her face. "See you around the club."

After he was out of sight, Lisa turned to Arianna and slugged her on the arm. "Did you see him wink at me? I knew it was a mistake for you to drag me along. Now, I'll never get rid of this guy."

"I hope not," Arianna replied. "Not until he gets me the information I need anyway. So until then, keep smiling. He's our new best friend."

"Great," Lisa murmured. "Just great."

CHAPTER

10

"Veritas wants to meet," Zach said staring at the message on the computer screen. Veritas was the code name for his contact in the CIA. The only time the two of them met was to discuss a new assignment.

"Damn!" Tony moaned. "We just got home. I'm not ready to go back to work yet. Hope they don't send us back to Kervistan."

Zach silently agreed. Kervistan was one of their worst assignments to date. With any luck at all, maybe they'd send them to Central America. Fighting drug cartels in a warm climate was much more to his liking. He knew what he preferred, but he also knew he'd go wherever they sent him if the mission was in American's best interest and the price was right.

On the agreed upon day, he and Tony watched the helicopter land on a deserted beach on the leeward side of the island. Stepping out of the chopper, Veritas walked briskly toward them.

"Gentlemen, let's walk and talk, shall we?" It was more a demand than a question. "First of all, I'd like to tell you the president sends his thanks to you and your men for the excellent job you did for us in Kervistan."

Zach nodded his acknowledgement but was sure the president had no idea who he and his men were. The president's advisors had probably informed him one of their operatives had completed the mission in Kervistan and that would be the extent of his knowledge. Still, it felt good to get at least a modicum of recognition from so high up.

"So, what's next?" Zach asked.

"Actually, I didn't come to give you an assignment," he said.

Zach stopped. A look of surprise crossed his face. Something was up. Veritas wouldn't come all this way just to chit chat.

"I've come to tell you someone's been running your fingerprints."

"What do you mean?" Zach asked.

"Well, I was hoping you might tell me what that's all about. We know her name. We just don't know why she's running your prints."

"Her? Some woman is running my prints? Is she with a law enforcement agency?"

"No. As near as we know she's just an ordinary citizen. We thought maybe she might be one of your ex's or something. Maybe a jilted lover?" he asked, knowing Zach's reputation as a wealthy, playboy bachelor.

It was true. Most people, if they knew anything about him at all, thought he was simply a wealthy, bachelor who held fabulous parties at his seaside estate here on the island. That was fine with him. It provided a good cover. As far as jilted lovers? Probably not too many of those. Most of his ex-girlfriends were probably still in love with him and anxious to get back in his good graces.

"So, who is this woman who tried to run my prints?" Zach asked.

"Her name is Arianna Garrett, and she actually lives here on the island? Do you know her?"

Zach shook his head. "Not that I'm aware of."

"Well, the prints came through a local policeman, Paul Vega. He had a contact at the Bureau who agreed to run them for him. Our agent thought it was just a routine check, but when your prints came up marked classified, alarms suddenly went off. One of our agents questioned the guy and found out the name of the person who had submitted the evidence."

"So, how'd this girl happen to have my prints?"

"Well, I understand they were lifted off a hotel room key and a couple hundred dollar bills, so maybe you could tell me. Have you had any romantic trysts in a hotel lately?" the agent asked, amused at the thought.

Zach did a double take. He instantly knew where the prints had come from…the girl from Kervistan. He'd always assumed she was long gone, which he now knew was a careless assumption on his part. Thinking to lift the prints off the key and the money was quite clever, though not clever enough to lead her to him. He knew his fingerprints were classified.

In fact, practically all of his identity had been scrubbed. The only thing a background check would reveal is that he was born thirty-one years ago to wealthy parents in Puerto Rico. His father, Rafael Acevedo was Puerto Rican, and his mother, Muriel was American. Existing school records would show that he had dropped out of high school at sixteen but nothing beyond that.

A background check would not show he had dropped out of school because he was bored with the lack of academic challenge, nor that he had immediately gotten his GED so he could enroll in the local community college. He tested out of freshman comp, math, and chemistry, and at eighteen, he transferred to Texas A & M in the States where he graduated cum laude three years later. Following his graduation, he joined the Navy and became a Navy SEAL. After spending five years as a SEAL he was recruited as an undercover agent in the CIA.

Working as a Black Op, he had amassed a considerable fortune by charging substantial fees for the services of himself and his team. He had invested his money wisely, compounding his wealth. All this information scrubbed. No other personal information existed, and his current reputation as a supposed high school drop-out, wealthy, playboy bachelor living here on the island, was fine with him.

"I don't think I even want to know what your connection to this girl is," Veritas lamented.

Zach had never mentioned the girl in his Kervistan report. No need to discuss it now.

"So is there something else?" Zach asked. "You didn't come all this way just to tell me this, did you?"

The agent shook his head. "There's potentially another problem. Possibly serious. The hit on your fingerprints has piqued the interest of someone else."

Zach arched an eyebrow and looked at him. "And who might that be?"

"That's just it. We don't know for sure. We've always known we have a mole in the agency, but we don't know who. Whoever it is has also been showing a strong interest in your fingerprints. Evidently, they'd like to know who you are too."

"Meaning...."

"If I had to make a guess," Veritas continued, "I'd say he'll try to find out who this girl is and see what she knows. He probably feels she can lead him to you. If so, then she'll be a very important piece of property to him. I wouldn't want to be her though. Since this mole is one of the bad guys, once he gets the information he needs from her, she'll become expendable to him."

"She can't ID me," Zach said. "She has absolutely no idea who I am."

"You're sure?"

Zach just stared at him. He didn't like being questioned about what he said.

"Then, I guess there are no worries as far as you're concerned. It could get really ugly if you're wrong."

"She can't ID me," he repeated, irritation just under the surface.

"Well, you and I know that, but our mole doesn't. I think he's going to come after her. Might be a chance to catch him. I'll let you handle this locally. Let me know if you need any Agency resources."

Zach nodded slightly. "Yes, sir. I'll handle it."

"Very good, then. Please keep me posted." He approached the helicopter to leave. "You'll be hearing from me soon with a new assignment."

"Something in a warm climate would be nice, sir," Tony interjected.

The agent chuckled as he buckled himself in. "Can't guarantee anything, but I'll see what I can do, boys."

They watched until the chopper was but a fluttering black speck in the distance. Then, Zach turned to Tony. "I want our own people to snoop around and see what they can find out about this girl. I'm not worried about her identifying me, but I am concerned about the mole in the CIA." He hopped over the side of the car and slid into the seat of his Porsche 911 Carrera convertible. "In a way, it's ironic that I hauled her ass out of Kervistan to save her, only to plunk her right back into danger."

"Yeah," Tony said, hopping in beside him, "but who knew she'd try to play private eye. She was supposed to wake up and catch the next flight home. Instead, she's put herself right in the middle of something that's probably going to get her whacked."

Zach slammed the car in gear and peeled out. He knew it was true, but couldn't do anything about it now except to wait and watch.

"I'M GETTING close," Karl Reichter said to his contact in the KBG. "Someone has run the fingerprints of the *Phantom*." The *Phantom* was the name given to the leader of the group of Spec Ops who had been connected to assassinations of several of their key operatives, but no one had a clue as to his true identity.

Karl Reichter worked as a double agent in the CIA and had been funneling information to Russia for almost a decade now. The modern world assumed the Cold War was over, but in truth, the espionage battle between the US and Russia still raged on into the twenty-first century.

In the last couple of years, this mole had become obsessed with finding the leader of this illusive spec op group, meaning Zach and his team. They were deemed to be the best of the best in the CIA, which made them so hard to ever find. To make matters worse, Zach was considered a rogue SOG which was generally considered the most secretive special operations force in the United States. He'd been known to sell his services to the highest bidder...always one of the good guys, but still his clients had varied from time to time. He was as good as they came, and Reichter wanted him... badly. Getting him would be a real coup.

"I'm going to find the person who ran the prints and see if they can lead me to this guy," Reichter declared. "This person was close enough to get his fingerprints. We've never had such a good lead. I believe they can be persuaded to supply additional information like a description or better yet, his name. I will find out everything they know and then, eliminate them."

CHAPTER
11

P aul had delivered the bad news to Arianna and Lisa. There was no match on the fingerprints. What was supposed to be her ace in the hole had turned out to be yet another dead-end street. Only problem was, there were no more clues. No more avenues to pursue. Like a wave crashing on the shore, frustration and anger rushed in only to recede, leaving sadness and depression in its place. Arianna retreated within herself, trying to weather the storm of emotions that consumed her. She was finding it difficult to come to grips with the fact that her abduction might forever be a mystery.

There had been one piece of good news, however. Kevin had contacted his parents. He was alive and well and trying to make his way to Pakistan where he hoped to catch a flight home. Fighting was everywhere and moving about in the country was still dangerous. He estimated it could take him as much as a month before he could arrange transportation out of the country.

Arianna hadn't spoken to him personally but was told he was relieved to know she was safe and couldn't wait to talk to her. Also, from what she understood, he had most of the B roll they'd shot. She took some solace in knowing they might still be able to get their documentary together.

"Lisa," Arianna announced, as they sun bathed at the beach one day, "I've decided I'm going to stay until Kevin gets home, then, I plan on going back to the States and work on my documentary." Her new passport had arrived a week ago, and she'd obtained a credit card and picture ID. She now had the necessary credentials for getting a flight home.

"Before I leave however, I want Kevin to come here and see if he can uncover something I've missed. I just can't leave without making one more effort to solve this mystery. The answer must be here on the island. Besides, he probably could use a little R & R after the ordeal he's been through. Of course, all of this depends on if Kevin agrees. If he does, you don't have any problem with him staying at our place, do you?"

Lisa turned over to get sun on her back. "He'll have to sleep on the couch, but otherwise, he's quite welcome." She brushed some sand off her towel, then added," You know, Arianna. I don't want to get all mushy, but I'm really going to miss you when you go home."

The two of them had grown quite close. Lisa had turned out to be a true friend and Arianna would miss her as well. "We need to stay in touch," she said, "and, of course, you'll have to come visit me in the States."

She had also found friends at the club. She felt particularly close to Andre, the lead singer and manager of the club's band. He'd become like a big brother to her… a gay big brother, but nonetheless, someone she felt like she could lean on when she was down. She didn't know if it was because of her talent or if he was trying to cheer her up, but he had invited her to sing with the band, having learned of her singing background in college. Nothing big. Just a couple songs in the last set, but she was looking forward to her debut performance. For this reason and others, she would miss the new life she'd begun to forge here on the Isle of Costa Luna, but at some point she knew she had to put a period and move on.

"Ari, sweetie," Andre said, sun bathing nearby, "if you want my advice, you'll give up your quest to find this phantom abductor. I know you want Kevin to come here and give this one more shot, but after that, you need to get on with your life. It's like you're obsessed with this, and it's making you a very dull girl."

"Why, thank you so much, Andre, for that wonderful compliment," Arianna chuckled. Then turning serious, she said, "I know you're right, but how is one supposed to forget going to sleep in one place and waking up in another, half way around the world? That's not exactly an everyday event in someone's life."

"I don't know, love," he said. "Maybe you should try getting laid."

Arianna spit her drink all over her lap. Coming from a gay man, this sounded especially funny. It wasn't a bad idea though. It had been a long time.

"You tell her, Andre," Lisa chimed in. "Do you know how many cute guys she's turned down at the club lately? God, Arianna, you've been so caught up in this abduction thing, you've passed up a zillion chances to meet someone."

"Come on, you guys. You know trying to find my kidnapper is important to me. Give me a break. Anyway, none of those guys at the club were my type."

It was mostly true. In fact, she hadn't met her type in a long time, but then, that was the problem. She didn't know what her type was. She had known, at least at one time she thought she knew the perfect guy for her, but that was a painful memory now. So as she'd always done, she lost herself in her work. She found staying busy was the perfect balm for a restless soul. For now she would continue working and enjoying her new friends while she waited for Kevin's arrival.

LATER IN the week, Arianna stopped by the club to pick up her check. On her way out, she was greeted by a man wearing a white shirt, khaki pants, and dark sunglasses.

"Excuse me, Miss," Karl Reichter, mole with the CIA said. "Are you Arianna Garrett?"

"Yes," she answered, curious as to how this stranger knew her name. "I'm Arianna. How can I help you?"

"Agent Dan Jeffers, FBI." Reichter flashed his fake badge. "Can we go someplace quiet to talk? I have some information about some fingerprints that were sent to our lab."

Arianna was speechless. She couldn't believe what she was hearing. This guy had information about the prints. Could this be the break in the case she'd been looking for? Maybe the FBI knew more than they had originally told her.

"Hey, you ready to go?" Lisa said, joining Arianna, having also come to pick up her check.

"Lisa, this is FBI Agent Dave…"

"Dan," the agent corrected her. "Dan Jeffers."

"Dan Jeffers," Arianna repeated. "He has some information about the fingerprints. This is my roommate, Lisa Calder. She's been following this case with me."

"Miss Calder," Reichter said, a tinge of irritation in his voice. *Damn! Two witnesses to get rid of now.*

"Ladies, is there some place quiet we can go talk? How about that pavilion down the beach a bit? It looks like a nice, private place where we won't be disturbed."

The pavilion was a bit out of the way and rather obscure which caused Arianna to think the information the agent had must be highly sensitive. This only added to her heightened sense of anticipation.

"I wanted to meet someplace where we could be alone and not be overheard. Your place is not safe. I fear it might be bugged, plus the man you're looking for is a dangerous man."

"Does that mean you've identified the owner of the finger-prints?" Arianna looked at the agent who seemed a bit nervous and had a slight facial tick. She was the nervous one. She didn't know what he had to be nervous about. She'd just learned a dangerous man had bugged her house and was after her. If anyone should be anxious, it should be her.

"Yes, I think so," Reichter lied. "He is an international fugitive. You might be in grave danger. But first things first. How did you happen to meet this guy?" He pulled out a notebook to take notes.

"Well," Arianna said, noticing a black dagger tattoo on his inner wrist as he opened the notebook, "you see, I'm a journalist who was on assignment in Kervistan about a month ago. I have no memory of how I got to this island. I don't know the name of the man that brought me here."

Reichter stepped back a minute, a surprised look on his face. "But the room key and money with the prints? You had to be at least close enough to get this man's fingerprints. Perhaps you had a little romantic tryst with him in a hotel?" the agent asked, probing for more information.

"Not likely. I must have seen him. I know there is a connection somehow. I might recognize him if I saw him again. He had some interest in me, that's for sure."

The agent stared at her, becoming agitated. These weren't the answers he expected to get. Also, he didn't know if he believed her. It was a wild story, but he was confident it had to be the *Phantom* since Fasi was assassinated the very day she had been abducted. She must have seen something she shouldn't have or else he would never have brought her out of the country, if in fact that is what happened.

"You say you're a journalist. Is it possible you've captured something on film that may shed some light on this?" *God, having a picture of this guy would be too good to be true.*

"My partner has all the footage we shot, but he's stuck over there. We could have film, but I'm not aware of it."

"Ah, yes! So what is your friend's name and the name of the company you worked for?" Karl asked.

Arianna hesitated. Something about this guy bothered her. He seemed extremely interested in her case, but so far he'd had more questions than answers. "His name is Kevin Baxter, but going back to what you said earlier, you said this guy was a dangerous person, so does that mean you know who he is or not?"

Reichter fidgeted with his notebook, his nervous tick becoming more pronounced.

"I understood all the information about him was classified, "Arianna continued, "so you must have special clearance to check his file.

Who is this guy?" Also, she was curious. Why would a real FBI agent be sharing classified information with her? Something wasn't right about this guy or was it just her imagination.

"You ask a lot of questions, Miss Garrett," Reichter said. "That could be bad for your health, and... oh, shit!" He snapped his notebook shut, startled by something he saw in the distance. Getting up, he bolted out of the pavilion. "We'll talk more later," he yelled back over his shoulder, as he dashed down the street and into one of the hotels on the beach.

Arianna spun around to see two men moving up fast, apparently chasing after the agent. "Whoa! What in the hell is going on?"

Lisa stood there with her mouth wide open. "That FBI agent looked like he was running for his life. Did I see that right? Were those two guys really chasing him?"

"That's what it looked like to me. Wow! This is wild!" Arianna said, still staring off in the distance. "Maybe I should just leave well enough alone. For all I know, he could have been my kidnapper, just trying to see if I can identify him. The more I dig into this, the scarier it gets. These are dangerous men."

"Well, let's get the hell out of here before anything else happens," Lisa said, hurrying toward the car.

Arianna hustled along behind her. "I'm going to call Paul and tell him what just happened. I'd like to hear his take on this." She tried calling him, but there was no answer.

"Keep trying," Lisa said as they sped down the street toward home. "We need his advice about what to do."

"I don't mean to make light of this," Arianna said, "but as scary as this situation today is, I think I must be getting close to solving the mystery. All this action leads me to believe that I'm going to meet my abductor soon."

"I hope not," Lisa said. "The FBI agent said your kidnapper is a dangerous international fugitive. I don't think I want to know who he is now. If this is what it's going to be like, you're better off not finding him. Of course, like you said, maybe this guy today was your abductor? He could have been lying about who he was, you know.

Maybe the next time the guy will kill you instead of just drugging you. I think it's dangerous to know his identity. Maybe we'll both get killed. Maybe...."

"Lisa!" Arianna snapped, seeing that she was starting to freak out. "Relax! We'll go home and wait until we can talk to Paul. He'll know what to do. In the meantime, we need to stay calm. Take a deep breath and relax."

"You're right," Lisa said, exhaling deeply. "I need to calm down. We'll talk to Paul, and he'll guide us through this. Everything will be all right. I need to relax."

"DAMN, WE just missed him," Juan said to Zach, describing the scene on the beach. "If we'd gotten there five minutes earlier, we would have had him. He disappeared into one of the hotels, and we couldn't find him. We didn't really get a good look at him."

"I don't know what the girl told him if anything," Zach said when he heard what happened. "Just the fact that she saw his face is enough to get her killed. He's not going to leave those women around to blow his ten year cover as a double agent."

"So what do we do now?" Tony asked.

Zach stared out the window of his office. He didn't need this complication in his life. It had seemed so simple in Kervistan. Get the girl out of there. Save her live. Give her some cash, and she'd be on her way home. That should have been the end of the story. Now, it had all changed.

"We need to pick her up and bring her here," Zach said. "We'll keep her out of sight until we can personally find this mole and eliminate him. When he's dealt with, she can go safely on her way with no fear for her life."

"Aren't you afraid she'll recognize us?" Tony asked.

Zach continued to stare out the window of his office. He had a beautiful view of the Caribbean Sea from the first floor of his seaside mansion. It was so peaceful and calm here. This compound was his haven from the violence of the other world he lived in. Now, he knew it would change. No matter the complication, he hadn't brought that girl half way round the world to safety only to throw her to the wolves. He'd do what he must to keep her safe once more.

Zach turned and said, "Yes."

Tony and Juan just stared at him, not moving.

"Okay," Zach said, irritation just under the surface. "We had long beards and wore turbans so not much of our face was visible, but yes, I know this is still risky. There's always a chance she can recognize us, but do you guys have a better idea? This is not a game for Christ's sake. People in our world play for keeps. They'll snuff these two out and not give it a second thought. Is that what you want?"

"No. No. We get it," the men said, talking over each other.

Tony knew Zach well enough to know his mind was made up. "You're right, Zach. We're with you. I'll get the men together, and we'll work out a plan to bring her here."

"Them. Get her roommate, too. She saw his face also."

"Yes, both women. What do we tell them?" Juan asked.

Zach shrugged his shoulders. "What can we tell them? Not the truth for sure. We tell them nothing. They won't have a clue about what is going on, but that can't be helped. Now, get moving. This guy won't wait very long before he comes back for them. We need to grab them fast."

"Roger, that," Tony said. "I'm on it."

CHAPTER

12

The sun was setting as Lisa's yellow Volkswagen came to a sudden halt in the carport. "Still no word from Paul," Arianna said, dropping her cell phone back into her purse. "Damn it! We really need to talk to him."

"Yeah, I'll feel much better once we hear what he has to say." They jumped out of the car and rushed into the house, locking the door behind them. "It's getting hard to tell the good guys from the bad. I think we could be in a lot of danger, but I'm not sure why. I just have an eerie feeling about all this."

Arianna double checked to be sure the door was locked and then picked up the phone on the desk and examined it. "The FBI agent made it sound like we're in real danger, and he told us our house might be bugged. How in the hell do you tell if someone bugged the phone?"

Lisa shrugged her shoulders. "Beats me. Maybe it will have something that looks like a small microphone in it?"

Arianna opened two beers and offered one to Lisa. "I think we should look around and see if we can find anything that looks like a recording device. I'll check here in the kitchen and living room. Why don't you have a look in the bedrooms and bathroom?"

After searching for about twenty minutes, Lisa came back into the kitchen. "Nothing. I didn't find anything I thought was a bug."

"Me either." Arianna grabbed another beer. "Just to be on the safe side, don't use the house phone. I can't tell if it's bugged or not."

Lisa plopped down on the sofa and pulled her feet up around her. "Well, me either. I could take the entire phone apart, piece by piece, and I wouldn't know a bug if it bit me."

Arianna checked her cell phone once more, but still no call from Paul. She moved over and sat down across from Lisa. "I don't know why anyone would want to bug our house anyway. I'm a just a simple journalist from Milwaukee. I don't know anything that could be of any interest to anyone. Actually, I'm a victim. I'm the one who was kidnapped and brought to this place, so why are all these things happening around me?"

Lisa finished her beer and went to the kitchen for another. "Maybe if we had more time to talk to the FBI agent, he could have cleared all this up for us."

"If he actually was an agent," Arianna said. "For all I know, he could be the guy who abducted me, and he doesn't want the FBI to find out who he is. Him running off like that was kind of strange, don't you think? But if you believe Paul, my kidnapper's identity is classified, so why would he worry about being identified?"

"Don't ask me," Lisa said, coming back to the sofa. "I'm as confused as you. Since your kidnapper's prints are classified, he must be a government agent, but why would a government agent kidnap you? And, if he's a government agent, then there could be other government agents chasing him, but what possible reason in the world would they want you? You're not leading some secret life that you're not telling me about, are you?"

Arianna laughed. "Hardly. You know I've been thinking. Why would this man today contact me about this matter unless he was looking for the kidnapper, too? The strange thing about that is, why contact me? I'm the one trying to find out who the kidnapper is. If I knew who he was, I wouldn't have contacted them in the first place. Something's not adding up here."

For a moment, they just sat there and stared at each other, not speaking. Finally, Arianna said what they were both thinking, "We don't have a clue what's going on, do we?"

Lisa shook her head. This circular conversation was going nowhere and with so little information, all they could do was continue to take wild guesses.

"So, how about going to the police?" Lisa asked, again.

Arianna knew it was time. In hindsight, she probably should have gone to the police the first morning she woke up in the Cass Hotel. This situation was not getting better. In fact, it was getting more complicated by the minute.

"As soon as Paul calls us back, I'll talk to him about going to the police. I don't want to rush ahead here and get him in trouble."

Lisa let out a long yawn. They'd been talking for hours with nothing resolved. "Boy, I'm starting to crash. Those beers relaxed me, but this is emotionally draining. I'm going to bed."

"Me too," Arianna said. She checked the door one last time to be sure it was locked. "I'll wake you up if I hear from Paul. Try to get some sleep. I'm sure things will look brighter in the morning."

CHAPTER
13

A hand covered Arianna's mouth, and a knee pressed into her chest, pinning her to the bed. She tried to yell for help, but the only sounds out of her mouth were muted little moans.

"Shh!" the intruder said, putting his finger to his lips. "I'm not here to hurt you, but you have to come quietly with me."

Fighting off the fog of sleep, Arianna blinked rapidly and willed herself fully awake. She didn't for a moment believe this guy was not there to hurt her. She fought to stay calm even as she struggled to quell the panic welling up inside of her.

In the dim light of the bedroom, she could barely make out the form of the man hovering over her… his face not covered, but his features indistinguishable. He slowly removed his hand from her mouth and lifted his knee from her chest, bringing momentary relief from the crushing weight. But this relief was fleeting, for as he threw back the covers of the bed, a new sense of vulnerability swept over her. The thin material of her pajama top revealed the clear outline of her breasts, and the skimpy bikinis she slept in barely covered her bottom. Suddenly, she felt precariously exposed and imminently susceptible to being ravaged.

Grasping her wrist, the intruder pulled her out of the bed and wrestled her toward the door. Grabbing a lamp off the nightstand,

Arianna swung it at the assailant with all her might. As he deflected the blow, she bent down and bit the hand holding her, affecting a momentary release.

"Son-of-a-bitch," he cursed, as he snatched her back with his other hand. Pressing her against the wall, he held her there at arm's length. He alternated between sucking the blood off his hand and shaking it in an attempt to stem the pain. Letting out one last son-of-a-bitch, the man threw Arianna over his shoulder and headed out of the bedroom.

"Let go of me!" Arianna yelled as she thrashed about and beat the man's back, the blows having absolutely no effect. The next thing she knew, she found herself in a heap on the living room sofa. Quickly righting herself, she turned to find Lisa sitting next to her.

"Oh, my God, Arianna! Who are these guys and what do they want?" Lisa asked, leaning close to her.

Arianna grabbed a throw pillow, hugging it for security and to cover what her revealing pajamas failed to. She looked around the room and saw three Hispanic men huddled in the kitchen area, whispering softly to each other. She thought they were speaking in Spanish but wasn't sure.

"Are you okay?" she asked Lisa.

Lisa sat there immobilized with fear, not answering.

Arianna shook her. "Now, listen to me, Lisa. We have to keep our wits about us. I have no idea what these men want, but don't panic. We'll get through this together. Do you hear me?"

Lisa nodded slowly, her eyes still transfixed on the men in the kitchen.

Arianna watched as the intruder from the bedroom searched through their purses, dumping all the contents into a duffel bag. Next, he grabbed Lisa's computer and put it in the bag with the other belongings. Looking toward the men in the kitchen, he held up a lone cell phone, which he then tossed to one of them.

Waving the phone, this man approached the sofa. "Which one of you ladies owns this phone? I assume you both have cell phones, so who's phone is this and where is the other phone?"

Arianna shook her head. "There is no other phone. Right, Lisa?" she hastily added.

The man smirked. "Okay, we'll do this the hard way then." He swiped the screen with his finger, and opened the settings app to locate the number for the phone. Using his own phone, he dialed the number and let it ring. Finally, voicemail picked up and said, "Hi! This is Arianna. Leave a message."

He scowled at Arianna, then looked at Lisa and said, "Your phone? Where is it? You're wasting our time."

Before Arianna could even stop her, Lisa blurted out, "In the car. It's in my car."

Arianna cursed under her breath. She would have continued to deny the existence of the other phone, but it was too late now. These intruders had both of their cell phones, computer and all their personal identification.

"What do you guys want?" Arianna asked. She wondered if these men were here to simply rob them or if they had something more sinister in mind.

No one answered at first. Finally the guy with the phone said, "You two are in danger so we're taking you to some place safe."

A chill ran down her spine. This did not sound good. She looked at Lisa, who had a petrified look on her face.

"What danger? The only danger I see is coming from you," Arianna said.

"No, not likely," the man replied, not breaking stride as he rummaged through Lisa's desk, continuing to look for what, she wasn't sure. "Your friend at the beach today," he finally said. "You do remember that guy, don't you? He wishes to do you great bodily harm."

Her mind started whirling with possible connections and scenarios. How did they know about the FBI agent, and how had they found her and Lisa? Were these the two guys chasing the agent today?

He also said the agent was a dangerous man, but he at least had met them in broad daylight in a public place. On the other hand, these men had broken into their house in the middle of the night, were robbing them, and she didn't know what else they had planned. At the moment she feared these intruders more than the man on the beach. Something Lisa said earlier popped into her head... something about not being able to tell the good guys from the bad. Of course, maybe they were all bad, in which case, she and Lisa were caught in the middle of a very dangerous situation.

She had no more decided this group was there to do her harm, when the man who had hauled her out of the bedroom, came up from behind and dumped a couple of robes on the sofa. Arianna stared at them like she'd never seen a bathrobe before. *Why would he do anything so chivalrous as to bring us something to cover up with?* At this point, confusion reigned supreme in her mind.

"So, who are you guys anyway and what do you want?" she asked again, as she slipped on the robe.

Another long pause. Finally, the man in front of her said, "Who we are isn't important. Just follow instructions, and you'll be fine. We're not here to hurt you, but you need to do as you're told, and right now, we need you to come with us."

We're not here to hurt you. That was the second time she'd heard that tonight. She didn't believe him either.

"I'm not going," Arianna said, standing up. "I'll go to the police if I'm in danger. They'll keep me safe. Since you want to keep me safe, you don't have any problem with that, right?"

She moved toward the phone, but the man who brought her out of the bedroom stepped in front of her, blocking her path.

"Look, Miss," the other man continued, his demeanor now deadly serious. "You can either come quietly, or we'll gag you and carry you out that door. But one way or the other, you're going with us tonight."

"I think we need to do what they say," Lisa said, getting to her feet and urging Arianna to follow.

Arianna shook her head defiantly. "No. Lisa, it's not safe. We can't go with them. Don't do it."

Then, as if there had been an invisible signal, everyone sprang into action. The man, who was talking, took Lisa by the arm and escorted her out the door. Next, with all the precision of a trained fighter, the man from the bedroom dumped her face first onto the sofa before she even had time to offer the slightest resistance. He put his knee in her back and pushed her head between the cushions. Pulling the belt off her robe, he used that to gag her. Finally, he took some cable ties from his pocket and tied her hands behind her back, then pulled her to her feet.

"Once again, we'll do this the hard way," he announced as he hustled her toward the door where she came face to face with the third man for the first time.

Arianna looked at him and paused a moment, thinking for a fleeting second there seemed to be something faintly familiar about this guy.... maybe his piercing dark eyes. She wasn't sure. As they stared at each other, a strange feeling washed over her. She felt flushed and anxious. She shuddered and wished she could pull her robe together in front, since her breasts could clearly be seen through her skimpy pajamas. Her hands being tied behind her back made that impossible.

Shaking off his stare, Arianna knew she had to focus on the moment at hand. Kicking out at him, she let out an angry scream through her gag.

"Hey! Hey!" the man holding her said. "You need to be nice, or you're really not going to like what I do next."

Arianna continued to kick and thrash in an attempt to get away from the guy holding her, and so once again, he hoisted her up over his shoulder and proceeded to a waiting SUV. Dumping her in the back seat beside Lisa, he slid in next to her, and they sped off into the night.

ZACH HAD watched the entire scene as Juan carried the girl out of the bedroom over his shoulder, her beautiful derriere prominently displayed. She'd put up quite a bit of resistance and had taken a nice chunk out of Juan's hand.

He also noticed she had not been afraid to stand up to Tony as he questioned her about the phone. The other roommate was obviously scared to death, but not this girl. In a way, he marveled at how she handled herself. This same moxie had likely brought her to Kervistan on a dangerous assignment. But tonight, he had no time for this foolishness, so he had signaled for the group to move out, and Tony and Juan had sprung into action. The dark haired girl had gone easily with Tony, but the blond needed to be restrained. Juan wasn't taking any chance on getting injured again.

When he came face to face with her at the door, it had been the moment of truth. The first hurdle had been crossed when she showed no sign of recognizing him. As they stood looking at each other, he felt the same pang of attraction as the first time he'd seen her. No one could have imagined finding this beautiful little imp, hidden under that burqa.

Her shimmering, blond hair, wild and tasseled from being wrestled out of bed, framed the delicate features of an angelic-looking face. She had a nicely tanned complexion and azure blue eyes that sparkled like diamonds, but were spitting fire at the moment. And, oh, the fact that her pajamas hid very little of her trim, well-rounded body, only made his attraction that much stronger.

What a beauty, but the angelic face was all a façade. This girl was a little hellion! He knew she wouldn't understand what was happening, and there was no way she would accept what she considered to be a kidnapping. It didn't matter. There was a target on her back. He'd gotten her into this. He'd get her out of it. In the meantime, as he did with all missions, he would keep his emotions in check and get the job done.

SANDWICHED BETWEEN Juan and Lisa with her hands tied behind her back and mouth gagged, Arianna found it impossible to put up any resistance. She had tried to kick the seatback in front of her, but Juan had put his leg across hers, pinning her feet to the floor. She sat helplessly trapped and watched the city lights disappear as the SUV sped to a part of the island she'd never been to before.

Tony turned and looked at Arianna from the front passenger seat. "We'll take the gag off and untie your hands," he said, "but I'm warning you not to try anything. I'm not in the mood for any more of your tantrums tonight."

Juan had a skeptical look on his face, but he reached over, cut the cable ties, and untied the gag.

Arianna rubbed her hands and flexed her fingers to restore the circulation. "You could let us go, you know? That would solve both of our problems. What do you want with us anyway?"

Tony shook his head and looked over at Zach who stared straight ahead as he steered the Escalade toward his seaside mansion. This would be the future home for these two women until the CIA mole was eliminated.

"Miss Garrett, that is your name right? Arianna Garrett," Tony said, looking directly at her. "Well you see, Arianna, you and Miss Calder, Lisa, are in more danger than you know so we're going to look after you for a while."

Arianna stared at him, trying to absorb what he was saying. It just didn't add up in her mind. How do you claim to be saving someone when you break into their house in the middle of the night and virtually kidnap them? No one had purposely hurt her, but one thing was certain. She and Lisa were being held captive by these men.

"So, who are you guys?" she asked, again.

Tony fumbled in the glove compartment, not answering. Finally he said, "I'm Tony. The guy beside you is Juan, and this is Zach behind the wheel."

"No, I mean. Who are you guys, really, and what do you want with us?" These men were professional *somethings*. She just didn't know what that something was yet.

"I told you. We're just some people who don't want to see you get hurt, and that's all you need to know for now."

Arianna drew her feet up, pulled her robe around her, and rested her head in her hands. She was emotionally drained and struggling to fully understand the situation she was in. If these men really wanted to protect them, why didn't they just take them to the police? Assuming their lives really were in danger, hadn't they heard of witness protection programs? And if they were on the up and up, they'd be doing something besides whisking them away in the middle of the night. She had a very bad feeling about this.

When she looked up, her eyes met the driver's as he glanced at her in the rearview mirror. His stare riveted her to the seat and caused her pulse to quicken. *Who is this guy?* She couldn't explain it, but for some reason, she had the distinct feeling he influenced more of the events than it seemed. She didn't know why she thought that. He hadn't said a single word the whole evening and had stayed in the background. Tony was clearly in charge so why was her attention drawn to this guy? But most confusing of all, was that under different circumstances, she might have even been attracted to this handsome abductor. *Oow! Get a hold of yourself. This is no time for flights of fancy.*

"We need a couple more things from you ladies tonight," Tony said, breaking into her thoughts. "I need you to jot down your passwords and PIN numbers for your cell phones and computer. We're going to need to get into your accounts. We can get them on our own, but it would make things a whole lot easier if you'd just write them down for us."

"Are you kidding me?" Arianna snapped, the stress causing her to run completely out of patience. "There's no way we're giving you that information."

Tony glanced at Zach who continued to stare straight ahead. Tonight was not the time to explain the reason behind their abduction or how they planned to successfully orchestrate their disappearance. He understood their apprehension, but he couldn't do anything to allay their fears. He needed those codes tonight.

"Ladies, as I was saying," Tony continued, "if you would just jot down your passwords, I'd appreciate it." He handed a notepad and pen to Lisa.

"Don't tell them anything, Lisa," Arianna cautioned. "You give them your password, and they can hack into all your personal information. Don't do it."

Despite Arianna's caution, it was obvious Lisa was too scared to resist. She jotted down some codes and then, passed the notebook back to Tony.

Tony looked at it, and obviously pleased, said, "Thank you, Miss Calder. Now, Miss Garrett, if you would be so kind as to do the same, I'd appreciate it."

Arianna could feel everyone subtly watching her. She saw the driver glance at her in the rear view mirror, almost daring her to resist. She snatched the pad and pen out of Tony's hand, not really sure what she would do. God! She was not going to cooperate with these guys. But how could she not? If they were sinister enough to kidnap them in the middle of the night, what else might they do to get information they really wanted? Not that it mattered. She was sure they had the expertise to hack into her accounts without her cooperation. She imagined their plan was to rob her blind, then... well, she wasn't sure what the end game was.

Summoning all the courage she could, she made a decision. Anything they would get, they would have to get on their own. It would not be coming from her. So, she began to slowly print her response... *Go-To-Hell!* finishing it with a flourish and an exclamation point. Leaning forward, she handed the notebook to Tony saying, "Here you go, Tony. Let me know if you need any more information."

Tony looked at what she'd written and shook his head. He tipped the book slightly so Zach could also see what Arianna had written also.

"Ah! Miss Garrett," Tony said, more amused than angry. "You certainly do know how to make things more complicated, don't you? Are you always so difficult or are you just doing this for our benefit?"

Zach glanced at her in the rearview mirror once more. He didn't know this girl all that well, but he was pretty sure he knew the answer to that. Likely, this was but the first of many rebellious moves she'd make. Time would tell, but at this point, he'd bet money on the fact that eventually it would take more than mere words to illicit her cooperation.

CHAPTER

14

They turned onto a side road and traveled a short distance until they came upon a security gate already in the process of opening. Zach powered down his window and greeted the guard coming out of the gatehouse.

"Evening, sir," the guard said, peering into the back seat. "Mission accomplished I see." Looking at Juan he said, "Looks like you got the best seat in the house."

Juan just glared at him. "Could we just move on, Zach? I need to see Doc and get this hand looked at. Probably going to need a damn tetanus shot."

"Whoa! You must have tangled with the wrong person tonight," the guard quipped, bringing a smile and a chuckle from Zach and Tony.

"Screw you, guys," Juan said. "Some of us have had a better evening than others, depending on who was doing all the heavy lifting." He gave Tony a hard shove in the back causing him to lurch forward.

"Hey!" Tony snapped, regaining his balance. "Don't take your bad night out on me."

Arianna thought all of this must be a reference to her, and she took a momentary delight out of knowing she'd been able to put at least a small chink in their armor.

"Later," Zach said to the guard and continued on up the drive.

With the windows down now, Arianna could hear the ocean in the distance. In only a matter of seconds, the driveway opened up and looming in front of them was a large two story mansion. Yard lights illuminated a perfectly manicured lawn, bordered by blooming flower beds and palm trees. Balconies, overlooking the sea, lined one side of the house, and on down the drive stood a separate building which looked like a guest house or possibly servant quarters.

The SUV pulled up beneath a portico brimming with tropical plants and hanging ferns, wafting gently in the breeze. They came to a stop beneath several steps that led up to a double-door entrance.

Arianna was shocked by her surroundings. She had never expected to be going to such a magnificent place as this. In her mind, she had visions of being taken to some rustic fisherman's hut on a dirty, deserted beach. The longer the night wore on, the more confused she became.

The front door opened and a servant made his way to the vehicle. "Good evening, sir," he said to Zach and took the keys from him. Zach acknowledged him with an imperceptible nod and proceeded to the house. At the doorway, he stopped to speak to an older woman in a black servant's uniform, and then, he disappeared inside.

"Follow me," Tony said to Arianna and Lisa, offering his hand as they exited the vehicle. Lisa accepted the offer, while Arianna ignored his outstretched hand.

As they entered the house, they found themselves in a large, open foyer with a grand circular staircase that rose to the second floor. Contemporary, light and airy, the interior was done in all neutral and off-white colors. Straight ahead, Arianna could see into a spacious living room with a wall of windows and doors that led out onto an elaborate pool area.

To the right of the foyer, double doors opened into a sumptuous dining room, complete with a dazzling crystal chandelier and a beautifully polished dining table that could easily seat a dinner party of twelve or more. Several sets of French doors opened onto a patio covered by a balcony above.

Breaking into her thoughts, Tony turned to the girls and said once more, "Follow me."

He led them down a hallway into the kitchen at the back of the house. Not surprisingly, the sparkling, white kitchen was equally spacious with multiple preparation areas as well as double ovens, double sinks, and the usual variety of appliances one would find in a kitchen designed for entertaining. In contrast to the large expanse of the kitchen, nestled away in the corner, was a small cozy dining nook which Arianna thought must be where the servants dined.

"Okay, ladies," she heard Tony say. "I'd like you to meet Pilar. She is in charge of all the servants and the complete running of this house. Pilar, this is Arianna and Lisa."

All the women stared at each other but didn't speak or acknowledge one another directly. Arianna wondered if this servant wondered what these two strange women were doing, standing in her kitchen in their bathrobes at two o'clock in the morning. If she was surprised by any of this, she didn't let on. *She must be in on this too, or maybe this happens all the time around here.*

Tony continued, "Pilar is going to be your special hostess while you are here. She'll see that you have what you need to be comfortable during your stay."

Looking right at Arianna, but speaking to the servant, Tony said, "Now, Pilar. I think you should know that Miss Garrett here, Arianna, is not exactly a happy camper. You might say we've had a little trouble with her this evening. However, I'm sure that she is not going to give us anymore problems."

If he expected some kind of retort, it was not forthcoming. Arianna just stood there glaring at him.

"So you see," Tony went on, and though addressing both of them, still looked right at Arianna, "as long as you behave yourself and do what Pilar tells you, this won't be so bad. And one more thing, just in case either one of you gets any ideas about doing something stupid, like trying to leave or call for help, Carlos here, will be nearby to intervene."

So quietly that no one had noticed, a new man had entered the kitchen and had seated himself in the nook directly behind them.

"Well, Pilar, unless you have any questions then, I'll leave you to get acquainted with your new charges."

Her only response was to shake her head and say, "Good night, sir." Turning to the girls she said, "Come with me."

She led them through a large pantry and down some steps into a lower level hallway where the servant's quarters were. Using a key from her pocket, she opened a door and invited the girls to enter. Inside the small but neat room, were two twin beds, a nightstand, lamp, dresser, and a TV.

"There are fresh towels and toiletries in the bathroom. I see you have your own nightclothes. However, if you need anything else, just knock on the door, and Carlos will come and wake me."

With that she moved to the nightstand, unplugged the phone and took it with her as she proceeded to leave the room. Pausing by the door she turned and spoke again. "Try to get some sleep. You are safe. No one will bother you." Then, she left.

What would she know or did she know the kind of evening they'd had? One thing for sure, she had correctly sensed the anxiety she and Lisa felt as to whether they were safe. After having been rudely wakened once already this night, the possibility of another unwanted intruder loomed large in Arianna's mind. She heard the door lock behind Pilar. Kidnapped. No doubt about it, Arianna thought. They could call it what they wanted, but it was a pure and simple kidnapping.

Letting out a deep sigh, she sat down on the bed. "I keep thinking this is a bad dream and that any moment now I'm going to wake up, and this will all be over. How in the world did we get mixed up in this anyway?"

Lisa slumped down on the other bed. "I'm so scared. I can't stop shaking. What do you think these men want?"

Arianna let out another long, nervous sigh. "I have no idea. I've been trying to figure this out, but I just don't get it. I've asked several times, but they refuse to say what they want with us."

Lisa pulled a blanket up around her. "These men have been pretty rough, but so far they haven't hurt us although they still could. We know they're going to hack into our accounts, so at a minimum, they're crooks. And look where they brought us. You know it's never a good thing when you can identify your kidnapper's face and where they live."

"I thought about that, too," Arianna said, shifting on the bed. "That seems very odd. Why would they bring us to their home? We can lead the police right back to this place, of course, that's only if we get out of here alive."

"Oh, God, Arianna. Don't even say that. I'm scared enough already."

"Oh, I'm sorry. I didn't mean to scare you even more. They said they were trying to keep us safe, so I'm sure they wouldn't kill us. But I'm not going to wait around to find out what they have in store for us. If I can find a way out of here, I'm going. I'll go to the authorities and tell them everything I know. I'm done trying to figure things out on my own. This is bigger than both of us."

Lisa got up and checked the door. It was definitely locked. "I wish I could lock the door from this side, too. I'm afraid someone may come into our room while we're sleeping." She plopped back down on the bed. "You were really brave tonight, Ari. I was proud of how you stood up to these guys, but you need to be careful. I don't think these men play around. I saw a gun in Tony's waistband."

"Yeah, me too, but I'm not going to make this easy for them."

The girls talked until they were talked out. Lisa nodded off first, and Arianna made her way to the bathroom to freshen up a bit before going to bed. Slipping off her robe, she looked into the mirror. Her hair was sticking up everywhere, and her eyes had dark circles under them. And oh, dear! Her pajamas. You could see her breasts right through the gauzy material, and when she checked the side view, it was obvious that her bottom was barely covered. She could only imagine how much cheek she'd shown draped over Juan's shoulder. And to think, these guys had seen all of this. Especially that quiet one… Zach.

The way he had looked at her had unnerved her enough, but now, knowing that he had practically seen her naked, made her feel… made her feel…what? What exactly was it she was feeling about this guy and about the part of him practically seeing her naked? Surely not…flushed? Tinged with excitement? *Oh! For God's sake, Arianna. Stop it!*

Tired. That was it. Yes, she was so tired she wasn't thinking straight anymore. She finished up in the bathroom and stumbled out to her bed and fell in. She was bone tired, but fought off the sleep until she could fight it no more. Slowly she drifted into an uneasy slumber.

"I'M AFRAID it's going to be a long night, guys," Zach said to Tony and Juan who had joined him in his office. "We've got some loose ends to tie up, and we need to take care of them tonight."

A servant came in and set a pot of coffee on the desk. "Anything else, sir?

Zach waved him off.

"How's your hand?" Tony asked, turning to Juan.

"I think I'll live, but what the hell. It took all the patience I could muster to keep from clobbering her. If tonight is any example, she's going to be handful."

This brought a smile to everyone's face. It wouldn't be so funny except that Juan was a trained killing machine. Under normal circumstances he could have dispatched with this girl in an instant and come away without a scratch on him.

"Okay, let's get to work," Zach said, pouring himself a cup of coffee. "We're going to be up all night the way it is. Juan, get me a full dossier on these two. We need to know where they work, who their relatives are, friends, etc… as much background as you can get."

"Tony, get someone at the Agency to hack into their accounts… computer, cell phone, Facebook, twitter, all of them. You have the one girl's code. Get someone working on the blond's… Arianna's code.

Find out who they're talking to, who they're tweeting, and friends with on Facebook. Have someone monitor their communication so they can communicate back. If it's a phone message, text back. Keep a running dialogue going so it appears they're still around and everything is normal in their life."

Zach took a sip of coffee and ran his hand through his hair. "Uh…have someone phone in a message to where they work and make an excuse for why they suddenly aren't around…family emergency or something like that. If we work this right, no one will even know they're missing. As long as it doesn't take us too long to get this CIA spy, I'm pretty sure we can pull this off. They'll be staying in touch with everyone without really staying in touch."

"While you guys are working on this," Zach continued, "I'm going to talk to Veritas about setting up a couple of decoys. We need to smoke this mole out so we can nail him. I need him to keep thinking he's on the trail of these two women. I'll work out the details once I talk to someone at the Agency."

Tony stifled a yawn, then stood up and stretched. He was struggling to stay awake. "Okay. Let's get going on this. The sooner we get the ball rolling, the sooner we can turn in."

Zach nodded. "And one last thing. Juan, send someone back to the house to gather some of their clothes and personal effects and bring them here. Then, have them move the girl's car too. Put it in storage somewhere for now. And guys…"

Juan and Tony turned to look at Zach. "Let's wrap this up fast. I don't want these women around here for too long."

CHAPTER

15

Arianna woke with a start and a feeling of panic. It took her a moment to calm her breathing and get her bearings as to where she was and why. She looked at the clock and could see it was almost noon. Considering the circumstances, she couldn't believe she had slept so long and so soundly. Slowly she began to recall the events of the night before...the break-in, kidnapping, her kidnappers, *him*. Only Lisa saying good morning broke her reverie.

"Morning," she mumbled back. Looking around the room, she was surprised to see a couple of boxes sitting just inside the door. Knowing that someone had been in the room while she slept was yet another jolt to her already skittish nerves.

She rummaged through the boxes and saw that they contained a jumble of some of their clothes, an assortment of personal effects, and the contents of their purses, minus their cell phones, of course.

"Wow! I never heard them come in the room, did you?" Arianna asked.

Lisa shook her head. "That's spooky."

Wondering if they were still locked in, she tried the door. To her surprise, it opened. Peeking tentatively into the hallway, she saw no one but heard sounds coming from the kitchen above. Closing the door, she stood immobilized as she pondered what to do next. Finally, she said, "Well, I guess we should get dressed and venture out to see what the day brings?" Grabbing some clothes from one of the boxes, she headed into the bathroom.

"Wait for me," Lisa said, afraid of being alone. Snatching some clothes out of the box, she scooted in behind Arianna. First one showering and then the other, the two women dressed and moved toward the bedroom door.

"You ready for this?" Arianna asked, scrunching her wavy, blond hair into place.

"Still pretty nervous," Lisa said. "I'm afraid of what might happen next."

Arianna turned and gave her a reassuring hug. "Everything is going to be all right, Lisa. Just be brave, and we'll get through this together, okay?" Stepping back she squared her shoulders, took a deep breath, and exhaled sharply. "Okay. Let's do this." She led the way down the hall, up the steps, and into the kitchen.

Noticing the women's arrival, Pilar greeted them with a single word, "Ladies."

Barely moving their lips, they mumbled back, "Morning."

Almost immediately Arianna's attention was drawn to the view seen through the expanse of windows in the back of the kitchen. In the full light of the beautiful, tropical day, she could see, what in the dark of night, had been hidden from them. This house sat high on a bluff that overlooked the sparkling, blue Caribbean Sea.

As if drawn by a magnet, she moved out the backdoor, past a man standing guard and onto a covered veranda. The outside dining area had a large rattan dining table and matching chairs with seating for eight. It also featured a BBQ grill, outdoor kitchen, and a seating area with wicker loveseats and sofas, adorned with overstuffed cream and pastel cushions. A fire pit in the center of the area made a cozy gathering place for the occupants of the house.

Transfixed by the beauty of this island paradise, she hadn't heard Lisa come up behind her until she spoke. "Man! Can you believe this place?"

Arianna shook her head. She had been in some luxurious homes before, but none as magnificent as this.

Her attention was drawn to water cascading over the edge of some rocks in the massive pool that snaked around the property. A spectacular waterfall formed the opening to a secluded grotto, nestled beneath the natural rock formation. Chaise lounges, deck chairs, and patio tables with cream-colored canvas umbrellas ringed the perimeter.

On out toward the ocean, a cement rail ran along the edge of the bluff with a built-in viewing area perched in the middle. To the right of this, a large staircase provided access to the beach below. And finally, on down toward the far end of the property, lay two tennis courts, a basketball court, putting green, and a stable.

"Wow! Talk about a playground for the rich and famous," Lisa said. "This place looks like party central?"

"Yeah, this is unbelievable, but right now, I'm more concerned about finding a way out of here than how beautiful it is. I see a tall wrought iron fence that wraps around the side and front of the property," Arianna said, pointing toward the house. "That means the only way out in that direction is through the security gate, which is manned. You've got the ocean all around the back so unless you're a fish, no way out there. Hmm….maybe down along the beach? Maybe we could walk out of here. This is an island, after all. Eventually it has to lead back to civilization."

"Ladies," Pilar said, interrupting their conversation, "if you're done admiring the view, I have lunch prepared for you."

If Pilar had overheard any of their conversation concerning avenues of escape, she said nothing. They followed her back into the kitchen and had a seat in the dining nook.

"Where are those men who brought us here last night?" Arianna asked.

At first it didn't seem like Pilar was going to answer. Finally, she replied, "Gone on business, I suppose."

A young, black maid approached the table. "Good afternoon, ladies. My name is Stella." She set a plate with a chicken salad croissant and a ramekin of fresh tropical fruit in front of each of them. "What would you like to drink? We have tea, lemonade, soda, or water."

Arianna's mouth dropped open. If it weren't for the fact they were being held against their will, one might have thought they were merely vacationing in some posh resort.

"Pilar," Lisa said, while cutting her sandwich in half, "I was wondering…who are those men that brought us here, and what do they want with us?"

Once again Pilar was slow to respond. "You two ask a lot of questions." She set two glasses of tea in front of them. "But I do not discuss the business of my employer. All I know is that you are to be under my supervision for the time being."

Arianna sensed that this lady knew a lot about her employer's business and could tell them many things. The problem would be to get any useful information out of her. Trying a different tact, she asked, "So, Pilar, how long has your employer been in the kidnapping business and do you babysit his victims like this very often?"

If she hoped for a reaction to her sarcastic remark, it didn't happen. "Finish your lunch, ladies," the housekeeper replied. "I have work to do. Please rinse your dishes and put them in the dishwasher, and then follow me."

It was clear Pilar was not going to be waiting on them anymore than she had to, and it even looked like they would be asked to pitch in and help. Lisa dutifully complied, rinsing her plate and carefully placing it in the dishwasher, while Arianna clunked her dishes in the sink, then turned and walked away. There was no way she was lifting a finger around here.

"Miss Garrett. Let us understand something," Pilar said. "You either need to come along with me so that I can supervise your whereabouts or you will be locked away in your room. What is your preference?"

Well, since she put it that way, the choice was simple. Locked away, she had no chance to escape, so she would go along with Pilar.

Before she could answer however, Lisa jumped in and said, "We're going with you."

"Very good, then," Pilar responded. "Follow me."

CHAPTER
16

The girls followed Pilar down the hall into the foyer and ascended the circular staircase to the second floor. Carlos, the guard, trailed nonchalantly behind them. Greeting two other maids along the way, they walked down a long, wide hallway where Arianna counted about six bedrooms. This seemed curious since other than Pilar, the servants, and the tagalong guard, she had not seen another soul the entire day. She wondered again, where her abductors had gone.

They entered a bedroom, a man's Arianna guessed by the masculine decor. The room was furnished with rich mahogany furniture, and a peek inside the walk-in closet revealed all male clothing. Two sets of French doors opened onto a balcony that ran along the entire length of the bedroom.

Pilar handed her a set of sheets. "I think the time will pass more quickly if you stay busy. Perhaps you might make the bed."

Arianna looked at the sheets, back at Pilar, and then, pitched them onto the bed.

"Look, Pilar. Don't take this wrong, but you might as well understand something. You work for Tony or whoever your boss is, and you have to do these chores. But I'm being held here against my will. I'll tag along with you if I must, but I'm not going to be doing any housework, so don't ask." With that she went out onto the balcony, plopped down on a chaise lounge and made herself comfortable.

Tony? Pilar thought. Is that who she thinks owns this place... is in charge around here? Oh, was she in for a huge surprise. But she thought she understood how Arianna had gotten that impression. She had been Zach's nanny since he was born, and even as a little boy, he had been a person of few words. Because he'd probably let Tony do all the talking last night, the girl had assumed Tony was in charge. Oh, well. So be it. She was sure that at the proper time, Arianna would learn the truth.

"You'll have to forgive her, Pilar," Lisa said, gathering the linens. "She's not taking this very well. Actually, I'm not either, but I don't mind helping out. Here. I'll make the bed."

Arianna sat on the balcony looking out to sea as Pilar and Lisa went about setting the room in order. As she looked around, she noticed a phone on a table at the far end of the balcony. Hmm! This could be the opportunity she'd been looking for.

She glanced back into the bedroom and didn't see Pilar any-where, and Carlos was reading a magazine just outside the bedroom door. This was her chance. She picked up the phone and dialed 911, but instead of ringing, she got a busy signal. Thinking this was the kind of phone you needed to dial a nine to get an outside line, she hung up and tried again. But just when she thought her call was going to go through, she heard a beeper going off and saw Carlos jump to his feet and head her way.

He came dashing out onto the balcony through one set of French doors while Arianna scrambled back into the bedroom through the other, still holding the phone and hoping her call might go through. Her hopes were dashed as the guard jerked the phone jack out of the wall. Frustrated at the failed attempt to call for help, she winged the phone at the guard, missing him but cracking a pane of glass in the French door instead.

Seeing Carlos coming for her, she turned and scurried back onto the balcony through the opposite door. As he came toward her, she threw some potted plants at him and then dashed back into the bedroom, knocking over everything in her path. Seeking refuge, she ran into the bathroom and locked the door behind her. She didn't know if he would hurt her or not, but she liked her chances better in a locked bathroom.

Stella and another maid, hearing the ruckus, came running. Their initial look of horror soon turned into amusement at the sight of this highly trained guard, standing in the midst of a completely destroyed bedroom, banging on the bathroom door. Nothing like this had ever happened around here before, and they found it quite amusing. Pilar stood by impassively, perhaps a bit amused herself, but hiding it well. As usual, Lisa once again froze with fear.

Carlos rattled the door, trying to open it, while shouting, "Miss, you need to come out of there!"

Uh, oh! She leaned against the bathroom door. *What have I done now?* No one had tried to hurt her so far, and she'd certainly given Juan ample reason to if he had so desired. Pilar had said no one would hurt her, but she feared she might have just crossed the line.

"No, I'm not coming out until you go away," she yelled through the door.

"I'm not going to hurt you. But you have to come out of there. Open this door!" Carlos demanded.

She stood there, feeling a bit panicky, not sure what her next move should be. The only thing she was sure of was, she wasn't going to unlock the door.

"Sir, she's locked herself in your bathroom," Carlos said as he talked to Zach on his cell phone. "What do you want me to do?"

Zach thought to ask which girl, but he already knew which girl it was. "What the hell do you mean, she locked herself in the bathroom?"

He filled Zach in on the failed 911 call and the wrecked bedroom. "All I tried to do was stop her, but she ran into the bathroom and locked the door. How do you want me to handle this, sir?"

Zach knew what he wanted to tell the guard to do with her but resisted. Instead, he told him to get her out of there, and then, lock her back in her room in the servant's quarters. If she was going to keep trying to create havoc like this, he had no choice but to lock her up. Maybe a few hours of *real* captivity would cool her enthusiasm for escaping and make her a more compliant guest.

"Yes, sir," the guard responded and snapped his phone back into its case on his belt. Returning to the door, he leveled a couple high kicks at the door and it came crashing open. "Let's go," he said to Arianna, who had backed into a corner. He grabbed her arm and pulled her out of the bathroom. He then briskly escorted her down to her room in the servant's quarters with her kicking, screaming, and dragging her feet the whole way.

"Ooow! Damn you!" she screamed after he left. Moving to the door, she banged, kicked, and shook it to no avail. She didn't really expect it to come open, but it was a good way to release some of her frustration. Flinging herself onto the bed, she pounded her fists into the mattress. This whole ordeal was really starting to get to her. Resigned to the fact the locked door meant she was going nowhere, Arianna lay there mulling over her situation late into the afternoon until she finally drifted off to sleep.

"ARI. ARIANNA. Wake up," Lisa said.

Arianna woke with a start and was happy to see it was Lisa shaking her. "Whew! What time is it?" she asked.

"A little after six. Are you okay?"

Arianna sat up and pushed her hair back off her face. "Yeah, sure," she said, as she shook herself awake. "Carlos didn't hurt me, but I'm really mad at myself for blowing that opportunity."

"Arianna, sweetie, you know I love you, but I have to ask, what the hell were you thinking? You're lucky he didn't clobber you or something."

Arianna stood and stretched. "Yeah, I guess I was kind of pressing my luck, but so far no one's laid a hand on us. They're trying 'to keep us safe', remember? I don't think they're going to hurt us."

"I'm not so sure, but maybe you should try a different approach. Maybe we can talk our way out of here. Especially you. You know you have a charming way about you. I think if you changed your tactics, you could have these men eating out of your hands in no time."

Well, it was a thought but somehow she didn't think any of the men she saw last night were the "eating out of your hands" type. She began pacing. It had only been a few hours, but this small, window-less room was beginning to drive her crazy.

"Have you seen any of those men from last night?"

"I helped Pilar around the kitchen all afternoon. Tony came through once and glanced at me, but didn't say anything. He just nodded and walked on by. I tried asking Pilar some questions, but that's useless. She won't tell me anything."

"If she knows anything," Arianna said. "What about Juan or that other guy, Zach? Did you see him?"

Before Lisa could answer, there was a knock on the door and Pilar entered with a tray of food. She set the tray down and said, "This is for you, Miss Garrett. Miss Calder, your dinner is waiting in the kitchen."

"You mean, Arianna is stuck here, but I'm free to leave?" Lisa asked.

"Yes, of course, that's exactly what she means," Arianna interjected. "Evidently I'm being punished for trying to escape."

"Or perhaps destroying the bedroom," Pilar hastened to add.

Arianna just glared at her. She didn't care about the bedroom. Whatever happened served them right.

"I think I'll eat down here too, then," Lisa said.

"Miss Calder, come with me, please." Pilar opened the door and stared at Lisa, indicating she was to exit the room with her. A guard stood watching just outside the door.

Knowing it was probably useless to resist, Lisa followed Pilar out of the room. Looking back, she shrugged her shoulders and shook her head. "I'm sorry. I'll see you later tonight, Arianna."

Arianna waved her off. "I'll be fine. I don't want to see any of those guys anyway."

After they left, she stared at the food on the tray and set it aside, too angry to eat. If they thought keeping her locked away was going to deter her from trying to get out of this place, they were wrong. But today had certainly taught her an important lesson. She realized she would have to be a lot smarter the next time. She'd bide her time and when they least likely expected it, she'd make her move again. The next time however, she would be successful.

ARIANNA PACED back and forth. Having slept all afternoon, she had more energy than she knew what to do with. She snapped on the TV, thinking maybe she might see her face on the news in a missing person's segment. Of course, who would report her missing? Her mom was accustomed to not seeing her for months on end, so she wouldn't know she was missing. Kevin was out of the country and out of contact. André at the club might wonder where she was, but these men planned to hack into her phone. They could easily text him and make some excuse as to why she wasn't around. He'd never be the wiser. In fact, she suspected that was why they were so anxious to get their passwords and PIN numbers. She had to admit, it was an ingenious strategy.

Lisa returned to the room around ten o'clock. Carlos stepped inside at the same time and retrieved the tray of uneaten food, then left.

"Hey," Arianna said, looking away from the TV. "You were gone for quite a while. Everything all right?'

"Yeah, interesting evening. After dinner, Tony came up to me and invited me outside to talk. I didn't know what he wanted, but I figured it was more of a command than an invitation."

"Yeah? So what did he want?"

"He asked me a lot of questions about the FBI agent. He wanted to know everything about him... what he looked like, what he said, what we said, anything I could remember."

Arianna shut the TV off and turned toward Lisa. "And what did you tell him?"

Lisa plumped up the pillow on her bed and sat back. "I didn't know what to tell him. Not sure if the FBI agent is the enemy or these men are, I was afraid to say too much. I was afraid not say anything at all though." Then, suddenly her face clouded over, and she began to tear up.

"Hey, what's the matter?" Arianna asked, coming over and putting her arm around her.

"I don't know," Lisa cried. "I told him just about everything I could remember. "I don't know if I should have or not, but I totally caved. This pressure is getting to me."

"Don't worry about it, Lisa. I doubt we know anything that is worth knowing. Anyway, if you had refused to talk to him, it could have gotten really ugly. So don't worry about it."

"It was kind of strange, though," Lisa said, drying her tears and getting up. "Tony was actually pretty nice, kind of friendly even. He asked me a lot of questions. He was curious about you and your kidnapping, but there wasn't much to tell. I told him you had no idea who kidnapped you. He also asked me several questions about myself...some I thought had nothing to do with this situation. Pilar and Stella have been decent, too. I can't explain it, but I actually had kind of a... pleasant evening."

Arianna frowned. "Wow! That is strange. I guess it's better than having a scary evening or a totally boring evening like mine."

"I'm not as afraid as I was in the beginning. I know I'm not free to leave, but this is feeling less and less like a kidnapping all the time."

"Really?" Arianna couldn't believe what she was hearing.

"Yeah, but you'll have to see for yourself, so hopefully, they'll let you out in the morning."

"Sure," Arianna said, looking skeptically at Lisa. "Maybe they'll let me out in the morning."

THE AGENCY had sent two women to serve as decoys. They had arrived early in the morning and had situated themselves into Lisa's house, hoping the mole would think it was the two girls and attempt to contact them once more. Word had come down a man had been spotted, staking out the house. Zach and Tony armed themselves and made their way back into the city, looking to grab him. Unfortunately, the alleged mole turned out to be a utility worker sitting in his van, filling out reports.

They returned home late in the afternoon with the mole still at large. On the way back, Zach got the call from Carlos about Arianna. Tired from no sleep the night before and pissed about the thwarted attempt to get the mole, he was ready to blow a gasket when he saw the carnage in his room. He'd just finished a stressful mission in Kervistan, and this was supposed to be down time for him and his team... time to unwind and relax before they went on the next assignment.

He understood the girl's frustration. They'd purposely kept the women in the dark as to their identity and as to the reason they were being held captive, so it was logical that she'd want to escape. She thought they were the enemy, but it didn't matter. She wasn't going anywhere for the time being. He now realized however, that soon, very soon, he would have to personally step in and get this girl under control before she could create any more havoc in this normally quiet refuge, he called home.

CHAPTER

17

Arianna tossed and turned all night. Anxiety coupled with an abundance of sleep from the day before, prevented her from dozing off more than an hour or two. At six in the morning, she rose, checked the door, and found it unlocked. *Did that mean she was free to go?* She could only hope. She grabbed a quick shower and came out of the bathroom just as Lisa was getting up.

"Morning, Arianna. Pilar came by while you were in the shower. She said breakfast would be at seven, and that we should both come up when we're ready. Guess you're free to go now."

It was welcome news. She'd had all she could take of this room. "I've already showered so I think I'll go on up. Do you mind?"

Lisa waved her on.

Arianna made her way to the kitchen. For the first time since she'd been brought here, she saw her abductors who were having breakfast out on the veranda. She was hoping no one would see her as she hung back in the corner, so she jumped when she heard Pilar. "You must be very hungry. Would you like something to eat?"

"What I'd really like is to drop a bomb right in the middle of that group out there. Pilar, please. We're being held against our will. Can't you help us?"

"Miss Garrett, sometimes things are not always as they seem. Perhaps you have this situation sized up wrong."

"I doubt it, and please, just call me Arianna. But what part could I possibly have wrong? I'm being forced to stay here and so far, no one has given me a good reason as to why. I don't care who these guys are any more. I just want to get as far away from this place and these men as possible."

Pilar pulled a pan of muffins out of the oven and set it on the counter. "All I can tell you is that if my employer has decided it is necessary to keep you here for your own safety, I'm sure he knows what he is doing. Despite what you think, this is not a normal occurrence around here."

"But that's just the point. Who is Tony to decide what is best for me? I'm perfectly capable of taking care of myself. I sure don't need his help."

"Tony?" Pilar said in surprise. "That's who you think is in charge here?"

"Yeah, I mean. Sure. He....," but then something about the look on Pilar's face told her that wasn't right.

"Who then?" she asked, even as it hit her like a ton of bricks. "Him!" she gasped and spun around to look out at Zach and then back at Pilar who just stared at her. "Zach? This place? All this is his?" she asked, motioning around.

Pilar nodded.

"But he didn't say a single word the other night."

"That you knew of," Pilar interjected, as she continued to prepare breakfast.

It was a stunning revelation. Having previously channeled all her anger at Tony, Arianna had to rethink the entire situation. "So tell me something, Pilar. All this kidnapping, manhandling, restraining me, locking me away stuff...whose idea would that be?"

"I'm afraid that I have said too much already," Pilar answered, suddenly hesitant to say more. "It's not for me to discuss Zach's business. I can tell you with one hundred percent certainty Miss, uh... I mean, Arianna, that nothing went on the other night, before, or since you've arrived that wasn't authorized by Zach, and let's just leave it at that."

She picked up two plates and handed them to her and Lisa who had come into the kitchen and joined them. "Here, ladies. Help yourself to the breakfast bar on the veranda." She then walked off.

"What was that all about?" Lisa asked, having caught the tail end of the conversation.

"Did you know this is Zach's house… that he is in charge around here?" Arianna asked.

Lisa looked surprised. "No. You could have fooled me. I thought Tony was in charge. Either way. Zach? Tony? We're still stuck here. But, hey, let's go get some breakfast."

Arianna paused a moment, not sure she wanted to go out there. Lisa locked arms with her and said, "Come on, Ari. You haven't eaten since yesterday. You can't stay in here forever."

Moving outside with Lisa, she stood at the breakfast bar looking at the men at the table. She took special delight in seeing Juan with his hand wrapped where she'd bitten him. Zach was the first to look up and make eye contact with her. For one intense moment their eyes locked, sending nondescript but electrifying messages to each other. Arianna forced herself to look away, thinking she would incinerate if she stared any longer.

The rest of them men noticed Arianna and the veranda suddenly got very quiet. Surprised to see her, no one knew quite what to expect. It was Carlos that broke the silence when he jumped up and threw himself in front of Juan. "Don't worry! If she takes even one step toward you, I'll protect you, bro." The veranda broke out in laughter with Juan feigning indignation and shoving Carlos away.

Had she not been so furious at being made fun of just now, she might have completely swooned at how handsome and charming Zach looked. *No. How could this be?* She refused to allow any thoughts like that to enter her head. Letting her temper block out any positive thoughts toward Zach or any of her captors, she was sorely tempted to wing a bowl of fruit at Carlos when Lisa stepped in.

"Okay. Let's set that over here," she said to Arianna, heading off a potential disaster in the making.

Arianna rushed back into the kitchen and scrunched back in the corner of the nook where she could not be seen. She could feel the tears welling up in her eyes but refused to cry. She was glad she provided them with something to laugh at because she didn't find any of this funny... just totally frustrating.

Pilar came up and handed her a plate of food. "Here, Arianna. You need to eat something. You'll feel better when you get some food in your stomach." Trying to console her, she continued. "They don't mean any harm. They're poking fun at Juan as much as at you. I'm afraid you've created quite a bit of excitement by injuring him and nearly destroying Zach's bedroom. I don't believe anything like that has ever happened around here before."

Then, suddenly becoming very serious, she said, "I must caution you, however, Arianna. I would not press my luck. There is a limit to how much will be tolerated."

"And then what? They'll shoot me?" Arianna asked. "These men are supposed to be keeping me safe. Not hurt me. Remember?"

"Just the same, Arianna—" She was interrupted by a servant before she could finish.

She had not eaten in twenty-four hours and was famished. She devoured the scrambled eggs and bacon Pilar brought her and washed the food down with a large glass of juice. Her stomach now full, she felt refreshed and in much better spirits. Moving out of the corner she had sequestered herself in, she dared to peek out at the group still finishing their breakfast at the dining table. She noticed Lisa was off to the side, sitting on a sofa, talking to Tony. She was smiling and it looked like she was enjoying herself. How could that be? These men had abducted them. Why would you be having a friendly conversation with them?

"You know," Pilar said, coming to her side, "you've been cooped up for two days now. You need to go out and get some fresh air instead of sitting in here." Seeing the skeptical look in Arianna's eyes, she prodded further. "It's okay. They won't bite. Maybe you could help Stella bring in the dishes off the breakfast buffet, for instance?"

Though ambivalent about how she felt, Arianna moved outside and ambled over to the breakfast bar. Zach glanced over at her, a nondescript look still on his face. He was beyond handsome, but that didn't take away from the fact that he had orchestrated this entire kidnapping plot. All her displaced anger toward Tony now flowed toward Zach, making him the next person she wanted to wound around here.

She began to gather some dishes and help Stella clear the buffet when Juan approached to refill his plate. "You see this bite mark?" he said, flipping the bandage back on his hand. "You wouldn't think a little thing like that could do much damage, but thanks to you, I had to get a tetanus shot and take some strong antibiotics to fight infection."

Arianna looked at the wound then up at him. "I think it serves you right for attacking me in the middle of the night. I hope you're not expecting an apology."

"No, I'd have been scared too, so I don't hold it against you." He flipped the bandage back over the wound and pressed it into place. "A word of advice, however. You might want to think twice before you try that again. The next guy might not be as tolerant as I was."

Arianna shrugged her shoulders. There was nothing she could say. He was probably right. He could have done her real bodily harm had he so desired.

Putting one last dollop of scrambled eggs on his plate, he continued. "Despite what you think, we're just trying to help you. You might try to cooperate more. We're really not the bad guys here."

"So you say, but it doesn't seem that way to me. Who are you guys, and why are you trying to help us? I didn't even know I was in danger and needed help."

Juan grimaced and continued to fill his plate, not answering.

"And it doesn't help when you guys won't answer any of my questions. That's why I don't believe you. Anyway, I don't want to be here. I can take care of myself. I can go places where no one can find me if I have to, not to mention all the police protection I can get."

Juan chuckled and shook his head. "I know this must be hard on you. But here's the bottom line, Miss Garrett..."

"Arianna. Call me Arianna."

"Okay, Arianna. First, I get it. I know you don't understand the danger you're in, but trust me, it's real. Secondly, there's no one else that can help you. And lastly," he said looking directly at her, "be careful. I wouldn't press my luck too much and continue to bank on your host's benevolence, hospitality, or patience." He reached across the table and brushed her cheek with his knuckle and gave her a wink and a smile.

Arianna recoiled slightly, but gave him a faint smile back. He was nicer than she thought, but it was the second time today someone had told her not to press her luck. What luck? She had no luck. If she'd had any luck she wouldn't be here. And what benevolence, hospitality, and patience? She hadn't seen any of that, either.

After Juan left, she proceeded into the kitchen and was drying some dishes when Zach came walking through and stopped to say something to Pilar. As he talked, he glanced over at Arianna. Finishing his conversation, he turned and walked right up to her.

Her heart began racing in her chest, and for some reason, it was hard to hold his gaze. He had coal, black eyes that seemed to look right through her. Much to her dismay, she felt herself start to blush. She hated him so why did she feel she was about to swoon? She was a bright, confident woman. Why had her nerve abandoned her? She felt paralyzed in his presence.

Zach opened his mouth to speak, but hesitated.

Arianna looked at him, blushed and looked down at the pan she was drying, then up again, then looked away. Anxious to mask the nervousness he caused in her, she let the pan slam down on the metal preparation table, took a step back, and glared at him.

He smiled faintly, shook his head and walked away, having never said a word.

She let out a ragged sigh of relief as soon as he left the kitchen, sure that she'd been holding her breath the whole time. *What was that all about and what was he about to say?* She could only imagine. Oh!

He infuriated her. Like she said earlier. He was the next person she wanted to wound around here.

If Pilar had not seen the entire scene with her own eyes, she wouldn't have believed it. It was a first. This girl had Zach totally baffled. He had been completely speechless. It looked like he couldn't decide if he wanted to kill her or kiss her. It tickled Pilar to watch these two play this cat and mouse game. Could it be Zach had finally met his match in this girl?

CHAPTER

18

N ot imprisoned, yet not free. Arianna and Lisa once again found themselves trailing along with Pilar as she set about on her daily chores. Moving down the hall toward the foyer, Arianna caught a glimpse of Zach and some of the men gathered in his office. They looked serious as if discussing important business, and she wondered again, just what their business was. As usual, a guard tagged along behind them. It seemed they still didn't trust her any more than she trusted them.

This time as they entered Zach's bedroom, she viewed the room with renewed interest. First of all, she noticed that the bed had only been slept in by one person, and a cursory check of the rest of the room didn't reveal any signs of a female presence. No woman's clothing in the closet. No picture on the night stand. No extra toothbrush or woman's toiletries left behind from an overnight stay. But with Zach's good looks and great wealth, she was positive there had to be a woman in his life. She just didn't see the evidence of it at the moment. *But, oh, why was she even wondering about this?* She hated him so it irritated her that she was giving this any thought.

She learned Pilar had taken it upon herself to personally attend to Zach's room, a habit acquired from years of picking up after him since boyhood. Otherwise, she spent more time supervising rather than doing actual physical labor concerning the running of the house.

They helped Stella straighten another bedroom, which turned out to be Tony's. Although not as large as Zach's, it was just as richly appointed. Four remaining bedrooms were used when entertaining out-of-town guests. Juan and Carlos lived in the large guesthouse located behind the pool. Other than this bit of general information, neither maid was too anxious to talk about the occupants or goings on of the house.

Pilar plumped the last pillow and looked around the room with satisfaction. "I think we are finished for today. Everything seems to be in order. Ladies, I'm retiring to my office to attend to some ordering and paperwork. Perhaps you might like to go for a stroll on the beach for a couple of hours."

Hmm! Yes. It was a perfect idea. Just the opportunity Arianna had been looking for... her chance to explore possible avenues of escape that existed on the beach. The only problem was "Lurch", as she had taken to calling the new guard who was never more than a few feet away.

"Just don't get lost," was the only thing the guard said, however, when informed of their plan to take a walk on the beach.

"You mean you're not going with us?" Arianna asked.

"Why? You don't plan to swim out of here, do you?"

Arianna rolled her eyes at him. She would if she could, but no, what a ridiculous thought. Before he could change his mind, Arianna grabbed Lisa's arm and took off. Together they crossed the lawn and headed down the staircase leading to the beach.

At the bottom of the steps, they were surprised to see a small beach house... something that hadn't been visible from above. Curious, they stepped up on the front deck of the house and checked the door. Finding it unlocked, they ventured inside and discovered the dwelling had a kitchenette, bathroom, and cozy living room with a fireplace. Done in all natural fabrics, Arianna guessed the quaint little getaway was used for cookouts or romantic evenings on the beach.

They opened a well-stocked frig and helped themselves to a couple of beers. Sun, sand, and a beer. What a perfect combination. Leaving the beach house, they walked along the shore, feeling halfway free. The further they went, in fact, the more Arianna wondered if it was possible to just keep on going... keep on walking to freedom.

After a while, Lisa said, "Shouldn't we start back now? We've gone a long way."

"Lisa, think about it. This is an island. If we keep on walking, we might be able to walk right back to civilization."

"I don't know, Ari. If that were the case, why wouldn't the guard have come along with us?"

"I have no idea, but he didn't. Look. Down there. Look at that outcropping of rocks. I think we can climb up those rocks to the top of the bluff and escape. We have plenty of daylight and could be long gone before anyone notices." She looked around and saw no one.

"Are you sure?" Lisa asked. "This seems too easy to me." She stopped and looked nervously down the beach.

"You don't have to come, if you don't want to. All I ask is that you don't go back to the house until I've had time to get away."

"No. If you're going, I'm going, too. You're not leaving me behind."

NEITHER GIRL could have known they had been under surveillance from the moment they'd first set foot on the beach. In the line of work Zach was in and considering his wealth, it had become necessary to have around-the-clock protection for himself and his property. He had enemies both known and unknown, and the problem with a waterfront residence—there was no way to put a fence on the beach. You needed a physical presence to monitor for unwanted visitors. A guard, sitting in a camouflaged hut on the bluff above, had been observing their walk the entire time.

"Base, this is base one. Over," the guard radioed.

"This is base. Go ahead, one," Zach responded.

"We have a problem. It looks like these two are planning on walking right out of here. Over."

"Well, stop them and get them back here. Radio Manny and tell him to get his ass on the ATV and get down there. Over."

"Roger that, base."

The guard put in a call to Manny, the second guard on duty, hoping he could intercept the girls before they reached the rocks. Stepping out of the hut, he yelled down at them. "Ladies, you need to stop and return to the house."

Arianna was startled to see a guard high on the bluff above. "Listen, Lisa. I'm going to make a run for those rocks. He's too high up to jump, so there's no way he can get down here and stop me. I can climb to the top of the next bluff and be long gone before anyone can reach me. You stay here, and I'll send help back once I get to a phone."

The guard could see that Arianna was continuing on down the beach so he radioed Zach once more.

"Base, the one girl isn't stopping. Manny's on his way, but not here yet. It won't take her long to shimmy up the rocks at the edge of your property and be out of here."

The guard was taken aback by what he heard next over the radio. All he could do was sputter, "Yes, sir. No, sir. No you didn't stutter. I copy. Right away, sir!" With that, he yelled down at Arianna, "Miss, I'm asking you one more time to turn around and come back."

Arianna ignored him and kept on walking. Just a bit further and she'd be there. She wanted to sprint, but she needed to save all her energy until the very last moment.

As it turned out, it wouldn't be necessary. She had walked no more than an additional ten feet, when a hail of bullets from the bluff above burst in the sand in front of her. She froze, paralyzed with fear.

"Oh, my God, Arianna!" Lisa screamed. "Stop before they kill you."

She stood motionless, afraid to take another step. *They really wouldn't shoot her, would they?* Another round of bullets peppered the beach in front of her. They seemed to be coming closer and closer or at least the sand was spitting more furiously back into her face.

"Ahhhhh! Okay! Stop! I'm coming back," she yelled, rushing back to where Lisa was standing and hugging her for reassurance. It was a frightening experience, and they were both shaking. As they stood contemplating their next move, a guard on an ATV came rolling up.

"Ladies, you need to come with me. Beach time is over."

What could they say? Another attempt to escape foiled. They began to walk silently back toward the house. The guard followed closely behind them on the ATV, talking to someone on the radio. With every step, Arianna began to do a slow burn. *Damn! So close. Just a few more steps.* Guess they'd be locking her away again. Maybe both of them. At least she'd have company this time. When they arrived at the steps to the house, the guard grabbed her by the arm, having decided it was his job to personally escort her the rest of the way.

"Let go of me, you idiot. I can walk by myself." She kicked sand at him and resisted his attempt to physically escort her up the stairs. She wasn't going to argue with bullets, but by now she'd figured out no one was going to hurt her, and she intended to use that knowledge to her advantage. Despite her best efforts to free herself from his grip, he held on and escorted her all the way to the veranda where Zach, Tony, and Juan were waiting. She jerked her arm away and swung back around trying to hit him, but missed.

Unwilling to give Zach the satisfaction of letting him know she knew he was in charge, she looked straight at Tony as she spoke. "Well, you've finally stooped to a new low… trying to shoot me. They almost killed me down there. So glad you're trying to keep us safe," she said. "Of course," and now half looking at Tony and half looking at Zach, she continued, "maybe you aren't really the one who told that guard to shoot at me. Just like maybe you're not really the one who decided to kidnap me in the middle of the night and lock me up here." Finally, turning to look squarely at Zach, she snapped. "Maybe it's your silent partner over here who's too much of a coward to do his own dirty work. You and your stupid help can go to hell!" With that she kicked over a small deck table right at Zach.

It happened so fast, Arianna never saw it coming. Zach grabbed hold of her and yanking her along behind him, walked briskly to a chair and placing his foot on the lower rung for leverage, threw her over his knee.

"Ahhh! What are you doing? Oh, my God! Let go of me," Arianna yelled, in total shock.

With her feet unable to touch the ground, and his hand pressing into the small of her back, she could only flounder around with no real target to strike and nothing to grab onto except his leg. Without a moment's hesitation and with all the force he could muster, Zach rained down several smacks in a row to her unprotected bottom before setting her down with a thud.

Instantly her hand lashed out to slap him, and just as fast, Zach grabbed her arm before she could make contact.

"Oooow! You bastard!" Arianna snapped, still attempting to kick and fight him.

In a blink of an eye, she found herself once again, up ended over Zach's knee. Kicking and screaming, she continued to call him names and struggle for all her might as he once again smacked her bottom with his open hand as hard as he could. Slowly she came to realize that the more she resisted and the more names she called, the harder he spanked her.

Finally realizing that all her thrashing about and name-calling was getting her nowhere, she began to beg and plead for Zach to stop. Reduced to tears, she not only begged and pleaded for him to stop, but found herself *apologizing* for her behavior. She didn't care. She'd say anything to make this all end.

As abruptly as he had started, Zach stopped and set her down with a thud. This time, however, it didn't even cross her mind to lash out at him or let loose with any expletives.

He snapped her close to him and holding her so tight she could barely breathe, he spoke quietly into her ear. "I speak when I have something important to say so heed my words, Miss Garrett. Your life is in danger because you were in the wrong place at the wrong time. If I don't protect you, an assassin will find you, and he *will* kill you, so you're not going anywhere until I say so. In the meantime, let's get something straight. This is my house. My rules. My way. And you *are* going to behave yourself. Is that understood?"

Arianna stubbornly bit her lip and looked away.

Enraged at her continued insubordination, Zach took her chin in his hand and turned her head so she would have to look him in the eye. "Do you understand?" he repeated sternly, glaring at her and daring her to defy him one more time.

Damn him! He was demanding her complete acquiescence. She tried to look away but the pressure on her chin prohibited that. Given no choice and afraid not to answer, she spat out the word, "Yes."

But by the way he continued to glare at her, she knew that that wasn't the exact response he wanted. One thing she'd just learned about Zach Acevedo was that he was a tough taskmaster who was quite accustomed to getting exactly what he wanted. Now, totally succumbing to his will, she begrudgingly whispered the response she knew he was waiting for. "Yes...sir."

Nodding his approval, he turned his attention to Lisa, pointing in her direction and snapping his fingers, indicating that she should come over to where they were standing.

Slowly she moved over to Zach and waited fearfully.

"So far," he said to her, "you've been cooperative so I don't have any problem with you. But if you *ever* even think about escaping or helping your friend here in one of her escapades, you'll be in for the same treatment. Do you understand me?"

After what she'd witnessed, oh, God, did she ever. "Yes, I promise. There won't be any more trouble," Lisa said in a small, quaky voice.

"Good." Then looking once again at Arianna he asked, "Have I made myself perfectly clear, Arianna?"

Ooooow! She knew what she *wanted* to say, but for the first time in her life knew she couldn't... wouldn't say anything but what he expected. So once again, she dutifully responded, "Yes... sir."

He continued to stare at her for a moment as if assessing the sincerity of her response. Evidently satisfied with her reply, he let her go with a jerk.

She ran into the house, down to her room, and flung herself on the bed. Pulling a pillow over her head, she cried bitterly.

Lisa came into the room only seconds behind her. "Oh, Arianna. I'm so sorry. Are you all right?"

"All right?" she asked, sitting up and pounding her fist into the pillow. "How could I be all right? I've just been totally humiliated not to mention it hurt like hell."

"I know, Arianna, but no one seemed to think it was funny or anything. I think they were all kind of stunned."

"They were probably happy. They probably thought I had it coming. Oh, I hate him. That bastard!"

"Shh! Don't say things like that. It makes me nervous to hear you say that even in private."

"Well, he can stop me from saying it out loud, but he can't stop me from thinking it." Tears were flowing freely now. "But I know he meant every word he said, so if I try to run away or anything, I'm sure he'll do the same thing again if he catches me. What a barbarian! He must have been raised by wolves. And the worst thing is, as much as I hate to admit it, I'd rather die than have this happen again, so he's won. Damn him! Damn him! Damn him!" she said, pounding her fist into the pillow with each expletive.

Lisa tried to console her, but she was not to be consoled. Score round one for Zach, but she knew Arianna too well to think that this would be the end of her resistance. Regrettably, she feared there would be more fireworks in the future.

CHAPTER

19

Arianna was well out of the picture when the men walked over to Zach and gave him a high-five. Juan summed it up best when he said, "What took you so long? You should have done two days ago. Would have saved us a lot of hassle."

Zach couldn't disagree. What a handful she'd turned out to be. Not anymore though, at least not while she stayed here. He thought he had sufficiently made his point clear concerning her behavior.

"I give her credit though," Tony said. "She's fearless. Not surprised. Anyone with enough guts to travel to Kervistan for a story has to be fearless. Don't meet too many women like her."

"Fearless *and* beautiful" Juan added. He looked back at the house as if remembering the way she looked. "I'd love to have a go at her, but she's too much for me to handle." He went to the wet bar, grabbed a beer and offered one to both Zach and Tony. "How 'bout you, Zach? You think you could handle all that?"

Zach did a double take. "Me? What the hell you talking about?"

Juan and Tony gave each other a knowing smile and tried to camouflage a snicker.

Shooting them a dirty look, Zach sat down on the wall surrounding the veranda and propped his foot up on a chair. "I don't know what the hell you're talking about. I already have a girlfriend, remember?"

Oh, yeah. They knew. Zach always had a girlfriend, *and* it always ended the same way. Women were crazy about him, but he always tired of them and moved on. They were all beautiful, but judging by the rate at which he moved from one girl to the next, it was obvious it took more than beauty to win Zach over. Despite the crazy circumstances of how he met Arianna, Juan and Tony both thought they saw something in her that was different. Beauty, brains, *and* moxie which could match Zach's own, strong, indomitable personality. They had a hunch Zach recognized it, too. It was hard to tell with him. He always held his cards close to his vest.

Zach gave them a look that said this discussion was over. "It looks like this illusive mole has gone deep undercover. We probably tipped him off the day we tried to run him down at the beach."

"Yeah, and he could lay dormant for months while we sit here babysitting these two." Tony took a swig of his beer. "I can't see that working out too well."

Zach shook his head. *God forbid!* He wasn't prepared to deal with that complication.

"What about interviewing Arianna and Lisa again? Maybe they can give us a better description about what this guy looks like," Juan said. "Something we can send to the Agency that might pinpoint who this mole is."

"Correction," Tony interjected. "We never interviewed Arianna. I believe we decided it would be futile to ask her any questions and expect to get a straight answer. Maybe now that she's had an 'attitude adjustment', she might be more amenable to answering some questions. What do you think, Zach?"

Zach shrugged his shoulders and moved over to the table. "Worth a try. Juan, go ahead and question her. I'll be standing by if the going gets too tough," he said with a sly grin.

"Fuck you!" Juan shot back with a smile. He was never going to live down being bitten, trying to restrain Arianna that first night.

"In the meantime," Zach continued, "I've got an idea for plan B. Something I hope will bring this guy up for air again. Let's use Arianna's partner, Kevin, as a decoy. We'll leak it back through the

Agency that he has some photos from Kervistan of the men who assassinated Fasi."

"Go on," Tony said, his interest peaked.

"A fake photo with my print on it arrives at the Agency just like before. It gets flagged as classified, again, and is dismissed, but not before the mole picks up on its existence. He believes it's the real deal and decides to hunt Kevin down to get that picture and any other photos he might have."

"Bingo!" Juan jumped up and smacked the table. "And we're there waiting for him. Poof! No more mole. No more danger to these girls. Mission accomplished. What a brilliant idea!"

Tony nodded his approval. He tipped his beer toward Zach in a congratulatory salute. "Yeah, great idea. I think this will work."

Zach pitched his empty beer bottle into the trash and got up to leave. "I'll get with Veritas and finalize the details. We'll need his help within the Agency to initiate this. In the meantime, Tony, find out where Kevin is and get his ass home. Have our people use their influence to cut through the red tape to get him out of that country. Let's keep him in the dark about what's going on. He can't know he's a target."

"You don't think her partner really has any pictures of us, do you?" Juan got up to leave, also. "I only saw him shooting pictures once, and we lifted that camera and destroyed it."

"And I don't remember Kevin taking any pictures of us when we hitched a ride to town with them," Tony added. "I wonder if they took any pictures we don't know about."

"Don't know when they would have done that," Zach said. Had anyone taken a picture of them, his team would have never let that camera or film leave the country, no matter what it took to destroy it. "For now, let's just worry about whether this mole believes Kevin has pictures of us or not. If he doesn't believe this story, then this plan is DOA." He started walking into the house. "Everybody get moving on this, or you're right. We'll be babysitting these women for months."

ARIANNA WAS sitting uncomfortably in her room when there came a knock at the door. She was afraid to open it. Afraid it might be *him*. She didn't care if she ever saw *him* again. But then, why would *he* knock? Being the bore that he was, she was sure he'd just come barreling in. Gathering her courage, she slowly opened the door and was relieved to see it was Pilar with dinner.

"I appreciate how nice you've been to me," she said, as Pilar set the food down. "Even this thing today... well, you tried to warn me, but I guess I was just too stubborn to listen."

"I do trust you got the message and don't plan on making any more problems, Arianna. Zach is no man to trifle with. He absolutely will not tolerate you disobeying him."

"Oh, I got that message loud and clear. By the look on his face, I could see he meant every word he said. Well, not to worry. I'm not going to put myself through that again. The way he acts... I don't see how he can have any friends, much less girlfriends. If he does, it's probably just because of his money. It sure wouldn't be because of his personality."

Pilar chuckled to herself. "I have known Zach all his life, and I can tell you, he has many loyal friends. And girlfriends? Ah! There would never be any shortage of those."

"Well, they must be crazy. How anyone could like a man like him is beyond me."

Yes, Pilar thought it probably was. Arianna had never really seen the true Zach. Well, in time, she hoped things would be different... she liked this girl and hoped she'd be around here for a long time.

IT WAS dinner time of the second day of a self-imposed exile, when Lisa informed Arianna no more food would be brought to the room. If she wanted to eat, she would have to come upstairs.

"Oh, gee! Let me guess whose idea this is," Arianna said.

"It's time anyway, Arianna. You can't stay down here forever. You have to face those guys sometime or go hungry."

She hated being manipulated like this. She was sure this was *his* idea, but what choice did she have. She'd have to eat sometime, but not tonight. She'd hold out one more day.

When she woke the next morning, she noticed Lisa's bed had not been slept in. As she lay there, pondering the significance of her absence and calculating her own next move, Lisa came into the room.

"Hey, are you all right?" Arianna asked. "Where were you last night?"

Lisa continued on into the room. "Well, uh, I know you'll find this hard to believe, but uhm, I was with Tony."

"Tony! Like sleeping with Tony?" she gasped, sitting up abruptly.

Lisa nodded slowly.

"But I don't understand. I mean, okay, I know he's good looking, but he's the guy... these are the men who broke into our house a week ago and kidnapped us. Are you sure you know what you're doing?"

"Noo.... yes. I mean, I hope so. Oh, I don't know, Arianna." Lisa sat down on the bed across from her. "Tony and I've been talking the last couple of days. Nothing serious. Just small talk. The more we talked though, the more it became apparent there was an attraction. So, last night after dinner, we had a couple of drinks. One thing led to another, and I ended up spending the night with him."

Arianna sat in stunned silence.

"Oh, God, Ari! I hope I haven't done something stupid," Lisa said, suddenly unsure of herself. "I can't explain what happened. It's not like he forced himself on me or anything. He was a perfect gentleman. I wanted him as much as he wanted me."

Arianna felt like she was in some kind of altered universe... like Alice in Wonderland who had fallen down a rabbit hole. "Wow! So do you trust him? Lisa, we don't even really know who these men are."

Lisa fidgeted with the corner of the bedspread. "I know, and no matter how many times I ask him who he is and why they're trying to help us, he won't answer. I'm not afraid of him, though. It seems we're in more danger than we realize, and I believe them when they say they're trying to help us."

Yes, Arianna had been mulling this situation over herself for the last two days and was warming a bit more to the idea that these might be the good guys and not the enemy.

"Zach told me I was in the wrong place at the wrong time and that an assassin was out to kill me. You know, I feel like this is all connected back to Kervistan. That warlord was killed shortly after I was there. Do you think someone thinks I have pictures of the assassin who killed Fasi or maybe that I was a witness? If that's the case, then we're in way over our heads."

"Oh, my God," Lisa said, shivering slightly. "It's so scary knowing an assassin is trying to kill you and me also. My nerves are about shot over all of this."

Arianna walked over to where Lisa sat. How many twists and turns would this ordeal take before it would be over?

"I know, and I apologize for being so skeptical, Lisa. Of course, you'd know if Tony wasn't honestly interested in you. What the hell! Nothing about this situation makes any sense anyway, so why not hook up with Tony? But Lisa, just be careful, okay? In case we're wrong about this, I'd hate to see you get hurt."

"I will," she answered, her spirits lifted by Arianna's quasi approval of her taking up with Tony. "Now, listen. Get dressed and come up. I'm telling you these guys aren't half bad once you get to know them."

"Sure. Especially Dick the Bruiser. What a great guy he's turned out to be," Arianna said.

Lisa knew she was referring to Zach. "Well, I know your experience with him hasn't been great, but the men and all the servants really respect him. He doesn't say much, but he notices everything. Don't hate me for saying this, but he's actually a pretty cool guy."

Arianna shot her a look which said, "Are you kidding me?" *They must have brainwashed her or is she really that gullible.* One thing for certain, her attitude about these people and this experience was vastly different than Lisa's. Dejected, frustrated, and confused best described Arianna's feelings at the moment. She couldn't remember a time in her life when she felt so out of control and completely helpless to shape her future.

CHAPTER
20

The first person Arianna saw when she entered the kitchen was Stella who immediately flashed her a big smile. "Hey! Good morning. Nice to see you out and about."

Taken by surprise at Stella's warm greeting, Arianna responded back with a wary, "Good morning."

Not skipping a beat, Stella went on. "You know. I gotta tell you. You were great the other day. I love the way you gave those guys such a hard time."

Arianna shook her head as if not understanding.

"I'm sorry what happened to you," Stella continued, "but otherwise, it was great. Gunfire. Men scrambling around. Furniture flying. We haven't had this much excitement around here in years. You'd a thought we were at war or something. We loved it."

"Stella!" Pilar said sternly, walking in at that moment. "For pity sakes! Don't be praising her. We don't want to encourage a repeat of that incident."

"Yes, ma'am," Stella said contritely, but as soon as Pilar was out of earshot, she continued. "I don't care what Pilar says, we all loved it. Don't get me wrong. We love Zach and the guys, but every now and then, it does our hearts good to see someone yank their chains. You go, girl!"

Giving Arianna a high-five, she quickly added, "Pilar's right, though. Zach's no one to mess with, so watch yourself."

Arianna certainly never expected this reaction. It buoyed her spirits somewhat to know at least she'd sacrificed her body for a good cause. She looked outside and saw Lisa sitting at the table with Tony. *What a difference a day makes!* Of course, she saw *him* too and immediately started to do a slow burn.

"Actually, Arianna," Stella said, breezing by once more, "since you and Lisa have arrived, there's been lots of excitement around here. I see those two are kind of an item now, Lisa and Tony. In fact, everyone's leaving for Miami this weekend except for Tony. It seems he's canceled his plans in favor of staying home."

"Really?" Arianna said, surprised. "Maybe he's staying back so he can keep an eye on me."

"Oh, no. I was told a 'break up' call was made to a certain young lady in Miami, telling her he wouldn't be coming this weekend. I guess the sparks really flew on the other end of the phone. Well, all I can say is good. That's one down. Now if we could get rid of another certain *lady* if you want to call her that, we'd all be quite happy."

"Stella, enough!" Pilar snapped, overhearing her comment. "I do not want to hear another word about this. We will not have gossip in this house. Now, get back to work!"

"Yes, ma'am," Stella said, but not before she whispered. "It's not gossip. It's the gospel truth."

Pilar didn't disagree. In the rich society Zach and Tony traveled in, it was hard to find a woman who hadn't been tainted by a life of money and privilege. The woman Stella was so scornful of was Lydia, Zach's current girlfriend.

She was by most standards drop dead gorgeous, but that was as far as it went. She had two distinct sides to her...the one Zach saw or rather, the one Lydia let him see, and the one the servants saw. Lydia could be oh so sweet when Zach was around, but totally rude and demanding when he was gone. The typical pampered little rich girl, none of the servants really liked it when she came to stay. Being loyal to Zach however, they never complained. They went about their business and kept their mouths shut.

Nevertheless, for now, Pilar had other things on her mind, such as getting Arianna back into the mix of things. Shoving a basket of pastries into her hands, she said, "Here. Would you take these out to the breakfast buffet, please?"

It was the moment of truth. Arianna didn't know if she could go out there or not. She didn't know if she could face Zach again after what he'd done to her. But then, she'd have to face him and everyone else sometime. She might as well get it over with.

Slowly she stepped out onto the veranda and walked over to the breakfast bar. Remembering her last entrance where Carlos had poked fun at her, she prayed this time, no one would try to make a joke on her behalf. She would just die if they did.

Her fears were unfounded, however, as the men noted her presence but did not otherwise respond. Her eyes met Zach's for the first time since *it* had happened, his expression unreadable. With great effort, Arianna worked to camouflage the anger welling up inside of her. She didn't want to give him the satisfaction of knowing how upset she was, and she was also a little afraid of acting in a way that would make him mad again.

Lisa joined her at the breakfast buffet. "Hey, Arianna. You doing okay?"

"Yeah, I guess. As long as no one tries to make a joke about what happened, I'll be fine."

Lisa looked over at the group. "Well, so far, they hardly seem to notice you."

Arianna exhaled deeply, releasing the tension, which had built up inside of her. She looked once again at Zach and slightly trembled at the thought of what he might do to her if she made him mad again. Never before had anyone evoked this feeling in her. It was strange though. Such barbaric treatment should have completely turned her against him, but curiously, unexplainably... it hadn't.

Yes, she was *absolutely* furious with him for inflicting such pain and embarrassment, but the thing was, how many men had ever stood up to her like that before? How many men had ever put their foot down and told her no? How many men had ever had enough influence over her to make her do anything she really didn't want to do? The answer was simple. None.

None of the men she'd gone with had ever denied her a thing since they were so desperate to win her favor. In fact, they'd bent over backwards to make her happy and would have humbly begged her forgiveness had they ever made her mad. Of course, she wasn't with any of these guys for one simple reason. She lost all interest when a man became putty in her hands.

But it was clear to her Zach was not like any man she'd met before. She knew without even knowing him all that well, he would never come groveling to her, never beg her forgiveness, never try to buy her affection with gifts, nor whine at her rejection. Never allow himself to be manipulated by her.

And so, despite being manhandled by him, she found herself being infuriatingly drawn to him. Drawn by his good looks. Drawn by how he stood up to her. Drawn by his power, strength, and dynamic presence. And last, but not least, drawn by a feeling she least liked acknowledging... pure animal attraction. Lust!

Arianna, get a grip! What is happening to me? She shook herself and turned away, trying to block out all of these feelings. *I must be losing my mind. If I don't get away from here soon, I'm afraid of what will happen next.*

IN THE beginning, lifting a finger around this place was the last thing Arianna intended to do, but now she'd come to believe it wasn't such a bad idea. Staying busy helped her pass the time, and she also found she enjoyed the company of Pilar, Stella, and the other hired help who stopped by the kitchen for coffee. And by the way the servants were treating her, you would have thought she was some kind of hero. Stella had not lied. She'd created quite a stir, but an interesting stir. Evidently, everyone loved the excitement she brought to their otherwise routine days.

It was about eleven o'clock when Zach came into the kitchen. Once again he spoke briefly to Pilar and then, walked over to Arianna. He stopped and leaned back against the counter, folding his arms across his chest. Seemingly not in any hurry to speak, he studied her for a moment. Arianna's pulse quickened, and she felt flushed. Fidgeting with a towel in her hand, she looked up at him and then down, then back before finally looking away. She wished whatever he was going to say—or do, he'd hurry up and get it over with.

Unlike their previous encounter in the kitchen, this time Zach wasn't at a loss for words. Speaking softly but with an air of authority that couldn't be ignored, he said, "I'm going to be gone for a few days, and I want to make something perfectly clear. If you cause even the slightest disturbance while I'm away, when I get back, you'll sorely regret it. Do you understand?"

Arianna shuddered at this frightening thought. She continued to look away, trying to avoid giving a response. What a futile idea that was. Having decided to lay down the law, Zach would settle for nothing but a spoken acknowledgment to his directives as concrete evidence of her compliance to his will.

When she didn't respond, he stepped forward and lifted her chin, forcing her to look him in the eye. "My patience with you is wearing thin so I suggest you answer me before I completely lose my temper."

Begrudgingly, she responded, "Yes," and then even more reluctantly added, "sir."

He stared at her a moment before continuing. "And just so you're clear, this is the last time I will wait for an answer. If I wait again, it will be at your expense. Now, is that understood as well?"

Ohhh! You bastard! He was not going to cut her even an inch of slack. She was definitely learning that once you got on his bad side, there was all hell to pay. Stomping her foot, she exhaled deeply, looked at him as he expected, and replied, "Yes, that is perfectly clear...sir."

An amused look crossed his face at how she was still maintaining a subtle air of defiance, but otherwise satisfied she got the message and would behave, he turned and left.

Arianna made sure he was long gone before she let the pan she was holding crash down onto the counter. "Oooh.! I hate him!" Tears welled up in her eyes, and she stood there steeped in frustration and anger. "I'm sick of this place...of him...of this whole ordeal. I want to go home."

Pilar walked over and put her arm around her. "Shh! I know, but it will be all right. It will just take some time. As soon as he sees you are not going to cause any more problems, he will not be angry with you."

Arianna shook her head back and forth and dabbed at the corner of her eyes. "I find that hard to believe. He hates me now because of all the trouble I've caused, and he's not going to be nice to me ever... not that I care."

"No. That's not true. You need to be patient. It will all work out. You'll see."

It was curious though. Hate her? No. Pilar suspected it was just the opposite. Ironically, his current treatment of Arianna, far from being an indication he hated her, told Pilar the opposite. That's because she knew if Zach disliked Arianna even a little, never mind hated her, he would have absolutely nothing to do with her. He wouldn't even waste his time getting mad at her. Furthermore, long ago he would have sent her to some other location to stay until this was over. So the fact she still remained in his house, spoke volumes to Pilar.

Normally Zach wasn't this strict and demanding. He was kind and thoughtful. But right now, Arianna saw the side of Zach he wanted her to see. The intimidating side. The angry, domineering side that would keep her in check and prevent any further disturbances. So far, she had complied. If she hadn't, she would have been gone despite any growing attraction toward her. Zach never let his emotions override his judgment. Never. But at this moment, Pilar didn't know how to explain any of this to Arianna...wasn't sure, given the present circumstances, she even cared what Zach thought. All she could do was stand back and watch this love-hate relationship play out and hope for a happy ending.

CHAPTER

21

Not every mission goes as planned. Winging his way to Miami on his private Gulf Stream, Zach had nothing but time to think about the current state of affairs. It was never supposed to be like this. She was *supposed* to wake up in that hotel a month ago and go home. She hadn't. Every soldier knows getting emotionally involved can compromise the mission. Arianna was getting to him and that was trouble. It wasn't supposed to go down like this.

As he settled back with a Jack Daniels and Coke for the long flight, he thought back to seeing her on the patio at breakfast this morning. Only a concerted effort on his part had kept him from gawking at her like a lovesick schoolboy. She was strikingly beautiful and her face had a radiant glow from her day on the beach. The simple, cotton sundress she wore, clung seductively to every single curve of her nicely rounded body, causing a stir within him that verged on embarrassment.

Even from a distance he could see how her cobalt, blue eyes sparkled mischievously, as she desperately tried to camouflage the little imp being held *very* precariously in check within her. No surprise. He knew he could illicit her short-term compliance but could never completely stifle the unbridled passion or spirit for living that simmered within her, nor did he want to.

However, beyond his obvious attraction to her physically, he struggled to understand exactly what he was feeling about Arianna. He'd had many relationships in his life, but so far none had lasted. Invariably every woman he'd dated all too readily tried to transform herself into the person they thought he wanted them to be. Nothing caused him to lose interest faster than when a woman became putty in his hands.

Arianna was a different story. He was certain she would never mold herself to try to please him, but he found this quality intensely appealing. You'd have to be on your toes to keep a step ahead of her, but he relished the challenge. For him, it was all about the chase, and Arianna's elusive, untamed quality drew him to her like a moth to a flame.

The flight attendant asking him if he wanted another drink jarred him back to the present. He was on his way to Miami to spend the weekend with his girlfriend, Lydia, who he hadn't seen in almost two weeks. Whether it was because of the current situation at home or something else, he wasn't looking forward to their reunion as much as he usually did, which even at that, had been less than exciting lately. He liked her, but he knew he didn't love her. She was beautiful and had proven to be a satisfying partner in bed, but that was how he would sum-up their relationship. Satisfying… not exciting or thrilling…just satisfying.

"We're landing soon, Mr. Acevedo," the flight attendant said. "May I clear your tray top?"

Zach waited as she cleared the glass and cocktail napkin in front of him, then he buckled up in preparation for landing. When the plane came to a stop, he looked out and saw Lydia waiting for him. Gorgeous and shapely, she was the daughter of wealthy investment banker, Randal Calhoun, who lived in an exclusive suburb of Miami.

"Zach," Lydia squealed, when he exited the plane. She ran up and threw her arms around him and gave him a passionate kiss. "I thought you'd never get here."

He returned her kiss, escorted her toward the waiting limo, and they climbed inside.

"I've invited a few close friends to our house for dinner and drinks tonight," Lydia said, stopping to straighten Zach's collar, "and tomorrow is the pro/am golf tournament at the club. Thanks to Daddy, you're paired up with the current US Open Junior champion. Daddy said you two will probably win the tournament."

Zach frowned. Randal Calhoun had never hidden the fact he wanted him to marry his daughter. He probably thought making a huge monetary donation to the foundation, assuring he was paired with the best player in the tournament, would be a good way to enhance his daughter's chances of snagging him. Little did he know how much Zach hated it when people used their money and power in this manner.

"What? You're not pleased?" Lydia asked, seeing the frown on Zach's face.

"Do I look pleased?" Zach snapped, shifting in the seat. "Tell your father, thank you, but ask him not to do that again."

"I thought you'd be excited. Daddy did it for your sake, you know?"

"No, your father did it for his sake, not mine." Annoyance radiated off him.

"Oh, Zach, I'm sorry," Lydia said, snuggling up next to him and putting on her best pouty face. "Please don't be mad at me." Her face clouded over, and she looked like she might cry.

"I'm not mad at you." Zach put his arm around her. "Your father meant well. Thank him for me when you see him." He didn't want to get into an argument.

"Oh, good" she said, her mood suddenly changing. She wrestled herself around and positioned herself on his lap. She planted little kisses on his face and pressed her breasts into his chest. "I hate it when you get mad at me," she cooed and leaned in for a kiss.

At first Zach returned the kiss and ran his hands up and down her body. It had been a couple weeks since he'd seen her, so it didn't take much to get him excited. But something didn't feel right. It wasn't clicking with him at the moment. He broke off their embrace and moved her off his lap.

"You're no fun," Lydia said, miffed at being rebuffed.

Zach leaned over and gave her a kiss on the forehead. "Later, baby," he said, and pulled out his cell phone to check his messages.

But despite the shaky start in the limo, the weekend turned out to be enjoyable. Randal Calhoun hadn't been wrong. Because Zach was a scratch golfer, he and the young golf pro easily won the tournament.

The only blight had been when he'd run into Tony's now ex-girlfriend, Susan, at the dinner dance at the country club. She was distraught about the break-up and had peppered him with questions as to why Tony might have dropped her.

"Zach, please," she begged. "I need some answers. He's not answering my calls anymore. Is there another woman? I miss him so much".

"Susan, I'm sorry for your pain, but you have to take this up with Tony. I'm not going to get involved in Tony's business." He could sympathize with how she was feeling, but there was no way he would be disloyal to Tony and meddle in his affairs. Truth be known, this break-up had been coming for a long time. Lisa entering the picture had just accelerated the process. Tony, like all the rest of the men on his team, was a one-woman man. With Lisa in the picture now, Susan would be out.

During the time away, he'd checked with Tony to get reports on events back home, especially about *her*. He was very happy to hear she had not made one single attempt to leave or cause any disturbances. He was really hoping he wouldn't have to make good on his threat of dire consequences should she step out of line.

"You won't believe what Arianna's been up to," Tony told Zach on one such call.

"I'm afraid to ask."

"No. No. I mean, damn, she's been working outside with the grounds crew—her idea. That's what she wanted to do. I didn't see any harm in it, so I okayed it. She even helped clean the stables yesterday."

"You're kidding?" Zach's mouth dropped open.

"No, I'm not, and I must say all the help is in love with her. She's very charming and quite the little entertainer."

Zach was silent for a moment. "Okay, but keep your eyes open. She's a devious little thing. Wouldn't surprise me if she was trying to get one of the staff to sneak her out of there."

"Wow! Hadn't thought of that angle. I'll ask the maintenance supervisor, José. He'll know if she's up to something."

"Good idea. I have a quick face-to-face meeting with Veritas in the morning, and then, I'll be home later in the afternoon. In the meantime, don't let your guard down."

"Roger that. See you soon."

WHEN ZACH arrived home, he found the servants scurrying about preparing for the arrival of weekend guests and for the upcoming party taking place at his estate. When he and his team were home from a mission, they let their hair down and partied hard. The presence of the two girls at the compound had added a wrinkle he hadn't planned on, but invitations had gone out a month ago. There was no cancelling the party now. Adaptations would have to be made.

"Welcome home," Pilar said as Zach came through the kitchen.

He gave her a quick hug, grabbed a sandwich and a beer, and headed out to the pool.

"Hey, Zach," Tony said as he approached the pool. "Welcome home."

He returned the greeting and leaned down and gave Lisa hug, taking her by surprise. Juan and Carlos with their respective girlfriends were also there. However, it wasn't any of these people he was looking for. He caught sight of Arianna on a riding mower cutting the lawn down by the tennis courts.

She was wearing a bathing suit top and shorts that showcased her body beautifully. This time there were no pajamas partially concealing her breasts as she jiggled along on the mower. Her sun-streaked, blond hair was gathered up in a loose ponytail on top of her head with several undisciplined strands falling rebelliously down her neck.

As he continued to watch, his pulse quickened. Something stirred within him, and he felt a strong attraction toward her that surprised even himself. How long had it been since he'd felt this way about someone? But he cautioned himself to take a step back. She was still an unknown quantity, and anyway, the last time he'd spoken with her, they'd been strong adversaries. Not exactly the right ingredients for a potential relationship, not to mention another minor problem. He had a girlfriend... supposedly... probably, and she would be arriving in a few days.

BEFORE ZACH returned, Lisa had begged Arianna to join them for a swim, but she had waved off the offer and kept mowing. Everyone was coupled up and she felt out of place. She didn't know Zach was home, and, in fact, had no idea when he was to return.

The pool looked better and better to her as the temperature rose. She decided to take Lisa up on her offer. As a teen, all her teachers thought of her as a quintessential angel, but in reality, no prank was too daring nor any scheme too outrageous for her to try. The plain truth of the matter was, when she was around, you could count on exciting things happening.

Making her way to the pool unnoticed, Arianna climbed up through the artificial rock formation to the diving board high above. Poised there in a royal blue bikini that highlighted her smooth, dark tan, she undid her ponytail and shook her hair loose. Shapely and trim, she had the body of someone who obviously took excellent care of herself. A body that had probably caused more than one man to lose all reason when it came to her.

From the edge of the diving board, she whistled sharply through her fingers to get everyone's attention. With all eyes on her, she moved to the back of the board, turned and paused. She raised her hands dramatically over her head and pointed her toe like an Olympic diver. Flashing a big smile, she walked briskly forward, and in one fluid motion, came up into a handstand at the end of the board.

Holding this position for one *long*, breathtaking moment, she kicked up and out of the stand, and propelled herself semi-gracefully down into the water below.

Rising to the surface, she thought she was coming up in behind Juan who she intended to dunk. Instead she found herself face to face with Zach. Shocked and surprised to find him there, she flopped backward below the surface, swallowing a mouthful of water. Choking and gagging, she floundered her way to the side of the pool and quickly popped out to the sound of whistles and people yelling, "Bravo! Encore! Encore!"

She looked back and saw Zach leaning on the side of the pool, nonchalantly sipping a beer and watching her towel off. Her pulse quickened and she felt flustered. Despite calls for an encore, she quickly grabbed her shorts and rushed back to join the lawn crew.

She was obviously not expecting to see Zach in the pool, and it had startled her. How odd! In a way, she was actually happy to see him...glad he was home. The only thing she couldn't figure out was why. He was the enemy. And even more curious was trying to figure out how she could have enough nerve to do that dive off the high diving board, but become flustered and weak in the knees whenever she came face to face with him. It wasn't fear, but something about him was really getting to her.

"Well, Zach, I must say. You have a real way with women," Juan joked as Arianna rushed off. "Did you see the look on her face when she saw you? She looked like she'd seen a ghost. Way to impress the ladies there, bro." He gave him a slight shove. "You're a real Romeo."

"Yeah, evidently," Zach mused and shoved Juan back. But before that, for the first time, he'd seen the side of her that had won everyone's heart this week. She really was quite an entertainer. That move on the high diving board was gutsy as hell. God, she was fearless, and man, he was losing it when it came to her.

Not every mission goes as planned, and this mission was coming off the rails... *fast*.

CHAPTER
22

Arianna hated doing housework. She also hated doing nothing. Weeding flowerbeds wasn't her preferred outdoor activity, but it was better than sitting idly, thinking about her current predicament.

Juan approached as she finished weeding the last section of flowers. Despite their rocky first encounter, these two had begun to build a friendship. To Arianna's surprise, she'd discovered he was really a gentle, caring person, not at all like the brute she'd met the first night when he had wrestled her out of bed and kidnapped her. He came now to tell her she was wanted in Zach's office.

"Don't worry. He won't bite," Juan said, seeing her apprehensive look.

"Sure. So why am I not looking forward to going in there?" She felt like a naughty school girl summoned to the principal's office.

Juan offered his hand to help her to her feet. "Come on. You'll be fine. Anyway, I seem to remember you're pretty good at handling yourself in tough situations," he said with a wink.

Arianna chuckled. True, but standing up to Zach took a whole new kind of courage. They stopped in the kitchen long enough for her to wash her hands and towel off her face before proceeding down the hall to Zach's office. As she entered, she found Lisa, Tony, and Zach waiting.

Zach's desk sat prominently in the center of the office in front of a large picture window through which you could see miles and miles of ocean. On the opposite wall was a floor to ceiling stone fireplace with a seating arrangement in front of it. Arianna thought this must be where they huddled when they planned such dastardly deeds as their midnight break-ins and kidnappings.

"Thanks for coming," Tony said, motioning toward a sofa. "Please, have a seat. Would you like something to drink?"

"No, thank you," she said, sitting down. She looked expectantly at Lisa, trying to read her expression… wondering what this meeting was all about. Lisa shook her head and shrugged her shoulders. She seemed as puzzled as Arianna as to why they had been summoned to Zach's office. She glanced over at Zach who was standing behind his desk, looking out the window.

"Well, as you've probably heard," Tony began, "we're hosting a large party this weekend. The circumstances of you two being here is a complication we hadn't planned on, but the invitations have gone out already, so there's no calling this off. We've invited you here to discuss the plan for the weekend." He paused and looked at Zach to see if he should go on.

Zach walked over and sat down across from the two women. Seeing he was going to take it from there, Tony moved to the background.

"As far as your situation is concerned," Zach began, "nothing has changed. You still cannot leave." Then, looking specifically at Arianna, he added, "And creating some kind of scene this weekend in hopes of finding a way out of here, would be a bad idea."

He shifted in his seat slightly before continuing.

"You have two options. One, you can give me your word you'll keep quiet about who you are and why you're here, in which case, you can move freely about as you have been. The second option is, I can lock you away in a place where you won't have an opportunity to talk to anyone. I just need to know which option you prefer."

"No worries about me," Lisa quickly added. "Arianna, you're good, too, right?"

Ignoring Lisa's question, Arianna looked directly at Zach. "You know. I've been wondering. Who are you guys, and how long do we have to stay here?"

Zach looked down, picked some lint off his pants, and then looked up again. "I can't answer that."

"Can't or won't?" Arianna asked.

Zach got up, walked to the window, and stared out to sea.

"Just as I thought. The answer is, you won't. I think there's a lot you could tell us, but you *won't*." Arianna got up from the sofa and started to pace. "I don't think I need your help anyway. I don't want your help. I want you to let us go. We'll leave… well, I'll leave… Lisa might want to stay, now. But, I'll leave, and we can forget all about this. I won't go to the authorities, I promise. You'll never see or hear from me again. That's one way to solve the problem for this weekend. This could be the third option. I vote for option three." She walked back to the sofa, sat down, and waited for Zach to answer.

Zach continued to stare out the window. *She didn't get it. There was no worry about her telling anyone. People at the Agency could quash any story she would tell, preventing him from ever being implicated, never mind charged with any crime.*

He turned from the window and started to walk toward her but stopped and leaned back on his desk. "There is no option three, Arianna. You were in the wrong place at the wrong time, and that's put you in a dangerous position. The FBI agent you met on the beach… he's not an FBI agent. He thinks you can lead him to someone he's looking for… someone he wants to assassinate."

He waited a minute for this information to sink in. "He wants information you can't give him because you don't have it, but he doesn't know that. Right now he doesn't know where you are, so you're safe. And what you said a minute ago about me not hearing or seeing from you again would probably be true. That's because you'd be dead if you left here."

Arianna's mouth dropped open. She looked at Lisa and saw a shocked look on her face that matched her own. Something in Zach's voice said every word he spoke was true.

"W…what is it I'm supposed to know that I don't?" she asked.

That I kidnapped you in Kervistan. That I assassinated that warlord, Fasi. Or how about that I… we, all the men here—work deep undercover for the CIA as paid mercenaries. No big deal. Just a bunch of information that could get you killed. Zach sighed and walked toward the sofa, ignoring her question… a question he would never answer.

"But there's something else you should know," Zach said. "This guy's tapped your mother's phone waiting for you to call and also staked out her house, hoping you might come home. If you were to show up there, it would be the kiss of death for both of you."

"My mother?" Arianna said, springing to her feet. "Is she all right? Oh, my God! What have I gotten her into?"

"Your mother is fine," Zach said, noting Arianna's mounting distress. "I sent some men to watch over her. She has a twenty-four hour guard around her, but she isn't aware of it. So far she has no idea what's going on."

Looking toward Lisa, Arianna asked, "Her parents, too?"

Zach nodded.

She sank back down on the sofa, stunned. Her heart thundered in her chest, and she fought to stay calm as the full gravity of the situation sank in. All of these men were big time players in a game where the stakes were very high… phone taps, surveillance, counter surveillance, kidnapping, *murder*. She put her head in her hands, fighting back the tears welling up in her eyes. She'd never been so afraid in her entire life. She finally got it. A death sentence was hanging over her head.

Silently Zach sat down on the coffee table in front of her. It had been a long, slow deterioration. So strong and spirited in the beginning, the stress of the past month had finally taken its toll. Reaching forward, he gently took her hands in his.

Arianna looked up, shocked to see it was Zach tenderly holding her hands. Her first instinct was to rip them away from the man who had held her against her will and inflicted such pain on her. But at the same time, a feeling of warmth and security washed over her as he held her hands in his.

"We haven't found this guy yet," Zach said, "but we will. When we do, we'll take care of it so you won't have to ever worry about this again. You'll be free to go when that happens."

For a moment she was frozen in his eyes. His touch calmed her... reassured her that she would be all right. But as suddenly as he had taken her hands in his, he released them and walked back to the window.

"In the meantime, Arianna, you're safe, and your mother is safe, too. Now, do I need to say any more about the party this weekend or do you understand what's at stake?"

"No," Arianna whispered. Composing herself, she rose to leave. "I understand. There won't be any problems this weekend. Is there anything else or may I go?"

Zach shook his head and waved her on.

She walked toward the door but paused a moment before leaving. Turning and looking back at Zach, she said quietly, "The FBI agent, the guy at the beach... he has a tattoo."

Zach spun around from the window, startled by what she said.

Tony jumped to his feet. "H...he what? Are you sure?" Tony asked.

"His left wrist. You can see it when he turns his hand over. A black dagger."

"She's right," Lisa said. "I forgot all about that. This should help you find this guy, right?"

"Absolutely!" Tony exclaimed. "Damn! This is exactly the break we needed to identify this man."

Zach gave Arianna a nearly imperceptible nod of appreciation... a subtle gesture weeks ago, she would have totally missed. But day-by-day, she was learning more and more about this quietly imposing stranger who had swept into her life that first fateful night. With that she turned and left.

ARIANNA RUSHED through the kitchen past Pilar and Stella and headed down to the beach. She started to run and kept running until she was exhausted. Sinking to her knees, she sat there staring out to sea. Time had a funny way of changing one's perspective. A month ago, she was obsessed with finding her kidnapper. Now, knowing someone was trying to kill her—Lisa, and both of their families as well—her kidnapping didn't seem so important anymore.

It was late in the afternoon when she returned to the house. She nodded and walked silently past the group who were lounging on the patio. Lisa caught up with her and followed her down into their room.

"You were gone a long time this afternoon. Everything all right?" Lisa asked.

"I think so. How about you? Are you okay?"

"Not really. I'm petrified," Lisa responded. "Really scared for you, though. I wonder what it is you're supposed to know, that you don't know."

Arianna shrugged her shoulders. "I've wracked my brain trying to think what it is. I have no idea, and I can't think about it anymore, or I'll go crazy."

"I guess we should feel lucky we have Zach and Tony looking out for us."

Arianna nodded slowly. Her head hurt, and she felt numb. She really didn't know what she thought anymore.

"Lisa, I'm so sorry I caused you to get mixed up in this situation. You should have never befriended me that first day at the Cass Hotel."

"Don't be silly," Lisa said. "You had no way of knowing what was going on, and you needed a friend. I don't regret a thing."

"You're kind to say that," Arianna said. "You've been a great friend."

"I feel the same way. Now quit worrying about it. Let's let Zach and Tony handle this. I trust them." She gave Arianna a big hug.

"And hey! About this weekend," Lisa said, changing the subject, "I guess this party is going to be a really big deal… seventy-five to a hundred guests. Tony had several dresses sent out for me to try since I obviously didn't arrive prepared for this occasion."

150

"Nice," Arianna said, happy to change the subject. "When do I get to see them?"

"Soon, but you know, Arianna, you could go to the party, too, if you asked."

"No, that's all right. I'll pass."

"Well, uh, I was thinking," Lisa stammered, "that, well, Zach seemed very concerned about you this afternoon. Did you ever stop to consider that maybe he might kind of like you?"

Arianna spun around and looked at her like she was crazy. "Have you been in the sun too long? Had too much to drink maybe? You're kidding, right? We go together like the fox and the hound. What a silly idea!"

"I'm not so sure, Arianna. I think I detect something here. Don't ask me why. Call it women's intuition or whatever."

"No," Arianna said, shaking her head in disbelief. "That's okay, but I think I'll hang around in the background with the servants this weekend. I'd like to keep my distance from these people, and when this is over, I want to walk away and forget about anyone and anything associated with this whole situation... not you, of course, but everything else."

"Are you sure?" Lisa pleaded. "We could have so much fun if you'd come to this party."

"I'm quite sure. Anyway, you'll be with Tony, so what more could you want? But right now I have to go clean vegetables and do some prep work for the party. I promised Pilar I would do that, so I better get hopping, or I'll never get everything done."

With that she hurried upstairs, totally dismissing Lisa's suggestion about attending the party, and especially the part about Zach liking her.

CHAPTER

23

Arianna was still tired when the alarm rang Friday morning. She'd been up long after midnight cleaning vegetables and making canapés for the upcoming party. Trudging into the kitchen, she saw Stella, who along with several temporary staff workers was busy preparing for Saturday's big affair.

"Good morning," she mumbled to Pilar who was pulling a pan of biscuits out of the oven. Pouring herself a cup of coffee, she savored the aroma a moment before taking her first tentative sip of the hot liquid.

"Thanks for helping with the prep work last night," Pilar said. "That was a big help."

"I hope I never see another carrot stick as long as I live," Arianna sighed. She reached for the basket of biscuits. "Here, I'll take those out to the buffet."

Arianna stepped out onto the veranda and glanced over at the table where Zach and the rest of the group were having breakfast. A beautiful, young woman she'd never seen before was sitting next to Zach. She appeared to know everyone, and it didn't dawn on her who this woman might be until she leaned over and gave Zach a kiss on the cheek as she got up to leave the table.

Of course! She knew Zach must have a girlfriend, but she was shocked to finally come face to face with her. Perfectly coiffed and manicured, this woman was gorgeous.

Arianna noticed her own hands, callused and scratched from working outdoors, her fingernails short and unpolished. She had quickly tied her hair up in her usual wild ponytail, and she couldn't remember the last time she'd applied any make-up. All of a sudden, she felt very inadequate and completely out of place.

She was also feeling something else. Something she didn't want to acknowledge...a twinge of jealousy. She tried to stifle that feeling and chastised herself for having such a ridiculous thought. After all, what did she care about Zach's girlfriend? He could have a dozen girlfriends for all she cared. She was just biding her time until she could go home and put this whole ordeal behind her.

Lisa saw that Arianna had arrived and came over to talk to her. As they were talking by the breakfast bar, Lydia approached.

"So, Lisa, that's your name, right?" Lydia said, looking at Lisa. "We need to talk." She handed Arianna an empty juice pitcher, believing her to be one of the servants. "Here. Refill this."

"Lydia," Lisa began, "this is Arianna, and she's not...."

Arianna interrupted her. "I'd be happy to refill that for you. Is there anything else you'd like?" She didn't care if Lydia thought she was one of the servants or not. Without comment, she took the pitcher and made her way into the kitchen.

When she returned, Lydia took the pitcher of juice from Arianna, and taking note of her for the first time, asked, "Are you new here? I don't think I've seen you before."

"Yes, you might say that," Arianna responded.

"Oh," Lydia said, and continued to stare at her as if something didn't seem to fit. Then, shaking off whatever thought had momentarily crossed her mind, she took the juice and returned to the table.

Lisa was seething. "God, what a bitch!" she whispered. "That's Zach's girlfriend, you know?"

"No, but I figured as much. She's very pretty."

"Humph! She let me know in no uncertain terms that Susan, Tony's ex-girlfriend, is her *best* friend."

Seeing that Lisa was becoming worked up over this, Arianna said, "I know, but just relax and don't let her get to you. Once she goes back and tells Susan how much Tony's in love with you, that'll shut them both up."

"You're right," Lisa said, calming down. "She's not worth getting upset over."

Arianna grabbed a muffin and some grapes and proceeded to go back into the kitchen. She noticed Zach was not sitting at the table any longer but instead was leaning on the ledge that enclosed the veranda. It seemed he wasn't paying much attention to Lydia, but then, since he wasn't a very demonstrative person, she didn't know if this meant anything or not. He could be completely in love with this woman, but given his demeanor, would never show it. *But oh, what am I dwelling on this for? Zach was a mean, brutish man who spanked me. He's no one I would ever be interested in!*

ARIANNA STAYED busy all day helping the servants prepare the pool and patio area for the party. They pruned the flowerbeds, hung baskets of ferns, washed windows, mowed lawns, and strung and checked party lights.

A good deal of her time was also spent readying the inside of the pool house. Just like the main house, this area was luxuriously appointed including his and her dressing rooms and showers. During the week, the space on the ladies side was a workout area with a large assortment of state of the art fitness equipment. For the party, the machines had been rolled into storage and the area had been transformed into a lounge area.

Comfortable sofas and chairs looked out over the pool through a magnificent floor to ceiling window. Nestled in among hanging ferns and large potted plants stood a five-tier water fountain, which would provide a relaxing atmosphere for the ladies to enjoy during brief respites from the party.

Of special interest to Arianna was a stage just outside the pool house, complete with a very expensive sound system. She learned there was to be a performance by a live band, followed by dancing to the music of a DJ.

Several cabana bars ringed the pool, and the bar keeps were busy stocking the shelves with every assortment of wine, beer, and liquor anyone might like. The guests would dine on grilled filet mignon steaks, bacon wrapped and served with sautéed portabella mushrooms, accompanied by a choice of grilled shrimp or Maine lobster.

Even though she didn't plan on attending the party, she found herself getting excited for the first time since her ordeal had begun. She would help the servants serve appetizers, food, and drinks, but she hoped to find time to hang around in the background and enjoy the entertainment.

Zach and his male guests were off playing golf, while Lydia and some of the female guests spent the afternoon lounging by the pool. Lisa decided to spend the day working with Arianna and helping Pilar in the kitchen.

"Arianna, if you would join me, I'd feel much more comfortable at the pool, but I don't want to be around Lydia by myself. Tony thinks I'm being too paranoid about this," Lisa told her. "He assured me they would accept me as his new girlfriend, but not if I was going to shun them."

"Boy!" Arianna said. "He sure does not understand women. Susan was Lydia's best friend, and there's no way she's going to welcome you with open arms."

"Maybe you could join me. You know Zach doesn't care, and frankly, I need the company."

"No, you'll be just fine. Now, go on over there. The guys will be back from golf soon, and everyone's going to hang out at the pool. You have to be with Tony."

Later in the afternoon, Arianna was stowing the last of the cleaning supplies in the tool shed, when José, head groundskeeper, approached. "Arianna, why don't you go join those young people at the pool? A beautiful girl like you should be over there having fun, not working around here like a common field hand."

Arianna smiled. "Oh, you, sweet talker. Now, why would I want to hang out with any of those guys when I can be here with a handsome fellow like you?"

"Ah, senorita," he said, kissing her hand gallantly, "You flatter me, but Miss Arianna, you work too much. It is time to go play."

Arianna looked over at the pool. Zach and all the men were back from golf and, of course, Lydia was there, sitting on the side of the pool, looking quite prim and proper. Something about Lydia's holier than thou image caused Arianna to change her mind about joining the group.

"You know, José, on second, thought, I think I will join them. Keep watching. You're not going to want to miss this."

Peeling off her shorts, down to the swim suit she wore underneath, she made her way up to the high diving board in the pool. Walking out onto the platform, she whistled loudly to get everyone's attention just as she had before. With all eyes on her, she smiled and waved as she once again assumed the dramatic Olympic "ready" position.

She proceeded to turn a cartwheel and then, sprang high into the air off the board. She did a cheerleader, "touch your toes splits" move, and with a loud Tarzan yell, came screaming down toward the water. At the last minute, she balled herself up into a cannonball and hit like a tidal wave, sending water drenching everyone on the side of the pool, especially Lydia Calhoun with her perfectly coiffed hair and flawless make-up. Jumping out of the pool, she was met with cheers and a big round of applause, and also by Lydia, fuming at having been drenched.

"Oh, I'm really sorry, Miss Calhoun," Arianna said upon seeing how mad she was. "Could I get you a towel?"

Lydia glared at her as she tried to push her water soaked hair back off her face.

Arianna started to walk away, but not before pausing in front of Zach. Feigning innocence she said "I just wanted to cool off before I quit work for the day. I hope you don't mind, sir."

He smiled slowly, and then said, "Not at all. I trust you've cooled down now."

Arianna thought she had the situation well in hand until Zach, subtly looking her up and down, allowed his gaze to linger momentarily on her breasts. Gone in an instant was her poise and cool demeanor and in its place came the proverbial blush and rapid heartbeat he so easily elicited from her. Their interlude may have gone on much longer had it not been for Juan, who came up behind Arianna, hoisted her high in the air, and threw her screaming into the pool.

Zach was still watching her fight for her life as Juan sought to dunk her when Lydia came up beside him.

"Really, Zach. I had no idea the hired help was allowed to swim with the guests. Don't you think you should say something to her? And the by the way she is so shamelessly flirting with Juan, she should be reprimanded or better yet, fired."

Flirting with Juan? Her original archenemy? Not hardly. I think for the first time since I met her, she just flirted with me.

"Yes. I should say something to her," he told Lydia.

It wouldn't be what she thought he would say, however. Arianna had appeared on the scene and in a matter of minutes, energized the entire group. Tony, now, high above on the diving board was about to make his own Olympic dive. Arianna had dropped the gauntlet, and one by one, all of the men would take up the challenge to top her dive. Their egos wouldn't let themselves be outdone by a girl.

Another loud whistle, the infamous fake Olympic starting pose and Tony was off. And though his attempted jackknife had started well, he hit the water in a big belly flop. This brought on more whistles, hisses, and boos, followed by additional dares for more dives from anyone brave enough to try.

Such excitement she'd brought to the group! But what complications she was bringing to his life right now, Zach thought as he stood next to Lydia. Disaster seemed be looming on the horizon. *Maybe I should have locked her away for the weekend.*

But then he realized locking her away wouldn't address the real problem, which was she'd gotten into his blood. Even if she were out of sight, she wouldn't be out of mind. He decided he needed to get himself in check before something bad happened. So he turned his attention to Lydia by grabbing a towel to dry her off. Hopefully with a little tender loving care from him, he could soothe her ruffled feathers and salvage the weekend. He wasn't sure if this would help, but he had to try.

CHAPTER

24

S aturday dawned bright and clear, a perfect day for the party. The kitchen was bustling with activity as the temporary help scurried around preparing food for the evening's affair.

Arianna passed Zach coming through the kitchen. They looked at each other, but neither one spoke, causing Pilar to wonder what was to become of these two. The attraction between them was obvious, at least to her, but it looked as though they had decided even the simple act of speaking might be letting down their guard, and in doing so, unleash the river of feelings they stubbornly denied since the day they met. And so the cat and mouse game continued.

"Where is everyone this morning?" Arianna asked, noticing the veranda was empty.

"Oh, I think the men are off playing golf," Stella answered. "And as for her *highness*, well, she's sleeping in, waiting for breakfast in bed."

"And who might her *highness* be?" Arianna asked, thinking she already knew.

"That would be Miss Calhoun," Stella smirked. "She's a beautiful woman, but she always breezes in here all high and mighty. She's about the most ungrateful thing I've ever seen. She don't act that way in front of Zach though. No way he'd still be with her if he knew what she was like when he wasn't around. Just sayin'."

"Arianna! Hey," Lisa said, as she came bursting in. "I'm so glad you're up. Here. Come with me. You've got to see the dress I'm wearing to the party, and oh, have I got some great news to tell you."

Lisa pulled Arianna upstairs to Tony's room where she spent all of her nights now. A large assortment of rejected dresses and lingerie lay scattered everywhere. Lisa reached down and picked up a black cocktail dress adorned with sequins across the bodice. Shucking her T-shirt and shorts, she quickly put it on. She stepped into a pair of black strappy sandals and twirled around. "So? What do you think?" she asked.

"Wow!" Arianna said. "You look stunning, and I love the neckline. Have you modeled this for Tony yet? "

"No, I'm waiting until the party tonight," Lisa said. "But wait. There's more. Don't move."

She went into the bathroom and in a moment, came back strutting a pair of diamond stud earrings and a matching open-heart diamond necklace.

"Well?" she said, looking expectantly at Arianna.

"Oh, Lisa. They're beautiful! Tony got those for you?"

"Yep," Lisa answered, beaming. "You know, he's so good to me it scary. I'm so in love with him. I don't know what I'd do if we ever broke up."

"Well, first of all, I'd say to stop worrying about it. Tony is a great guy, so relax and just enjoy yourself. He's not a schmuck like your last boyfriend."

"You're right. But, oh, wait! I almost forgot to tell you the other exciting news. Guess who's performing tonight?"

Arianna shook her head. She had no idea.

"André! His band is playing."

"No! You're kidding?" Arianna said, excited. Then, suddenly frowning she asked, "But aren't they worried because he knows us?"

"Didn't seem so." Lisa changed back into her regular clothes.

"Hmm! Why not?"

"Well, according to Tony, André called your phone, so they sent him a text, as if it was you writing, of course. The text said we had to disappear for a while because you were being stalked by your ex-boyfriend who had threatened to kill both of us. They told him we were going to drop out of sight and would contact him when it was safe to return. From Andrés response, he was surprised and shocked, but he didn't question it."

Arianna had to admit. These guys were good. It seemed they'd answered a lot of her calls, pretending to be her. It dawned on her probably not too many people had even given her disappearance a second thought, never mind thinking to go looking for her. She suspected in their line of business, this was standard operating procedure, whatever their line of business was exactly. So, Arianna Garrett, Lisa Calder, Jane Doe... didn't really matter who saw them at the party. They were just another face in the crowd.

"Of course, you can't tell André the real story about why we're here," Lisa continued, "and to be on the safe side, ask him to keep our whereabouts a secret. He will, won't he?"

"Oh, I'm sure he will. He's like a brother to me, and I trust him completely."

She'd be only too happy to go along with the stalking story. The last thing she wanted was to bring someone else into this mess and put them in danger like she had her mother and Lisa and her family. She'd say whatever she needed to say to keep André in the dark.

IT WAS late afternoon before Arianna finished setting the last table and went down to her room to clean up and change for the party. Guests wouldn't be arriving for two hours, so she had plenty of time to get ready.

Before dressing, she took a long, hot bath to soothe the sore muscles acquired from the last few days of manual labor. Unlike Lisa, she wasn't wearing a new dress and jewels to the party. She decided to help the servants out, and so Stella had found her a uniform to wear. She'd become friends with most of the staff and felt at home working alongside them. This would be her way of being at the party without *being* at the party.

For the first time since she'd arrived, she applied some make-up. With a touch of color on her cheeks, some mascara, and light lipstick, she looked fresh and radiant. Her blond hair shimmered from being streaked by the sun, and she wore it down, parted on the side, and scrunched into place. Yes, it was a bit on the wild side, but she really didn't want any beauty shop, "fixed" look. Hair that was a bit unruly and sassy, just like her, suited her best.

Finally, she slipped into some slim, black Capri pants and a white dress shirt with a pleated bodice...the basics of the servant's uniform. The third piece was a red silk vest with three buttons in front and an adjustable strap across the open back. She topped the ensemble off with a black bow tie and stepped in front of the mirror to check herself out. She had to smile. It wasn't as stunning as the cocktail dress and jewels Lisa was wearing, but for a servant, she thought she looked damned good.

When she came into the kitchen, Stella made a feeble attempt at a whistle but blew mostly air. "Wow, Arianna. You look too good to be working as a servant. You know, you don't have to do this. You can change and go to the party like all the rest of the guests."

"Well, not quite," Arianna said. "You see, I have nothing to change into that would be suitable for this occasion, but thank you anyway, Stella. This is what I want to do. There's no way I'm going to this party with everyone all coupled up and me by myself, not to mention, this group is way out of my league."

Stella shook her head in dismay. "Oh, hush, Arianna. No offense, but sometimes you are just plain stupid. Dressed up or not, I think you'd be the prettiest lady at the party, but here." She handed her a tray of hors d`oeuvres. "Since there's no changing your mind, take these out there. Come back when you need more."

THE AROMA of steaks on the grill permeated the air and at the cabana bars, the bartenders were busy serving up cocktails. Most of the guests had arrived, and by the sound of all the laughter and chatter, it seemed the party was off to a good start. Also, by the looks of all the glitzy cocktail dresses and jewels, it looked like there were a lot of high rollers in attendance.

Arianna moved through the crowd and came upon Zach standing with Lydia, Lisa, and Tony. She almost swooned at how handsome he looked, dressed in a black sport coat, gray slacks, a crisp, white dress shirt, and a thin black tie. His jet-black hair was slightly mussed, and he held her captive with his blackberry eyes as she stood among the guests at the party. Surrounding him, was a bevy of female guests who had swooped in upon him, hoping to catch his attention, despite the fact Lydia stood velcroed to his side or that their own mates were somewhere nearby. She wished them luck. She was sure Lydia kept, or at least tried to keep, Zach on a very short leash.

"Appetizer, anyone?" she asked.

"Please," Lisa said and stepped close. Whispering, she said, "You look amazing. I can hardly stand you masquerading as a servant though."

"Thank you, Miss Calder," Arianna said loudly, before whispering under her breath. "Don't worry about me, Lisa. I'm fine. You just relax and enjoy yourself."

She did her best to avoid looking at Zach, who hadn't taken his eyes off her since the moment she'd appeared. As quickly as she could, she moved on.

After she walked away, Lydia turned to Zach and snipped, "I thought you were going to fire her after yesterday's escapade. She's just doesn't know her place."

Lisa glared at her, but Zach did not respond, turning his attention instead to other guests who had begun arriving.

When André arrived, Tony escorted him over to the side of the veranda, away from the crowd, where Arianna was waiting.

"Arianna!" André cried, picking her up and twirling her around. "God, you little fool. Why didn't you just come to me and tell me the truth about this stalker boyfriend? I would have helped you. I've been so worried about you, darlin'. I thought someone had kidnapped you again."

Arianna's heart caught in her throat. "No. No. Nothing like that." She looked over at Tony. "We're hiding out here from, uh, my stalker boyfriend. Trouble seems to find me no matter where I go," she said with a nervous chuckle.

"Well, you're as beautiful as ever, but what's with the servant's uniform?" André asked, stepping back to look her over. "It's so not you."

Arianna laughed. "It's a long story. I'm dateless, and there's no way I'm going to go to this party with everyone else coupled up. For kicks, I decided to help with the serving. It gives me something to do, and it's not much different than waiting tables at the club, so I don't mind, really."

André gave her a puzzled look. "Sure, if you say so, but anyway, what bad luck for you and Lisa. Don't know how it happened but if Zach Acevedo is protecting you, you have nothing to worry about. He's the wealthiest man on this island, and I hear he has connections all over the world. I'm not sure how he got involved, but that's fortunate for you. Not to mention the guy is absolutely gorgeous. I'll trade you places anytime you want, darlin'."

"You're bad," Arianna said, amused. "Sorry to disappoint, but I'm afraid he's taken."

"By you?" André asked. "Oh, God! What a lucky girl!"

"No, definitely not by me. Heavens no! Anyway, you *absolutely* cannot tell a soul you saw me here. No one. Not even my mother, not that you would ever talk to her, but no one. We can't tip my ex-boyfriend off in any way about where I am. He's obsessed with me and quite dangerous. Do you promise?"

"Arianna, of course. You have my word. I swear," he said, crossing his heart. "Not a soul."

"Thank you! Now go get set up. Your audience awaits."

Hugging her once again, he rushed off.

CHAPTER
25

After dinner, the guests settled back in preparation for Andrés first performance. Arianna poured herself a tall scotch and water and found a secluded place to sit and enjoy the music. She hadn't done any singing or performing since college, but music was an integral part of who she was. Nothing stirred her blood more than hard pounding, loud music. André had a beautiful singing voice, and the band played a nice mix of songs ranging from contemporary to retro. It felt good to just relax and let the music, aided by the tall scotch and water, take her to a happy place where there were no kidnappings, murder, or espionage.

After the first set, André came over to where Arianna had sequestered herself, a cheeky grin on his face. Lisa was tagging along behind him looking rather smug herself.

"Hey, darlin'," André began. "I have a great idea."

"Yeah," Lisa chimed in.

"Oh, no. Why am I getting bad vibes about this?" Arianna asked.

"No really. You see, I was just thinking how great it would be if you sang with us tonight," André said.

"Yeah," Lisa agreed. "You practiced with the band, but never got to perform because we had to leave abruptly. I'm dying to hear you sing."

"Oh, I don't know. First, of all, I don't think Zach would like that idea, and secondly, I haven't practiced or anything."

"I already asked Zach," Lisa said. "It did take him by surprise, but after he thought about it a minute, he said he didn't care. I can't think what it would hurt. I doubt anyone is going to go running out of here telling your ex-boyfriend they saw you. They don't even know him, or… ahem, anyone else that might be looking for you."

"Anyone else?" André asked, a frown crossing his face. "Is there someone else looking for you guys."

Lisa shot Arianna a nervous look. "No, of course not. Just a figure of speech… no, no one else, of course."

"Hmm!" André paused a minute. "Well, anyway, as far as you being out of practice, I don't think that will be a problem. It'll all come back to you once you start singing."

"And what do you propose I wear? You know, servant's attire isn't exactly the going rage."

"True, but we can figure something out as soon as you agree to sing. What do you say? Ever since we practiced, I've been dying to perform this set with you, darlin'. Please," André begged.

"Yes, please," Lisa pleaded.

What a novel idea, Arianna thought…actually stepping out of kidnapping mode… survival mode… and doing something *normal*. Something she enjoyed doing before this all began. But maybe that was exactly what she needed… a chance to be normal again.

She looked at André and Lisa's anxious faces before finally responding. "Okay, I'll do it."

"Yesss!" André and Lisa said in unison, high-fiveing each other.

"Good. Let's go," André said. He led her over to the stage.

"Okay, we've got to pull this together fast." Arianna ducked behind some tall music cases at the back of the stage. She had an idea about how to transform her servant's attire into something suitable for performing.

She removed the vest and slipped off the white dress shirt and her bra. Next, she put the vest back on and cinched it tight around her waist by adjusting the strap in the back. Using the black bow tie, she twisted her hair up into a loose pony tail, giving herself a youthful and trendy look.

"Wow! Very nice!" André said as she stepped back onto the stage.

The V-neck of the vest plunged just low enough to show a bit of cleavage, and the open back added a nice touch of sex appeal, while the tight Capri pants finished the look. Servant to diva in less than five minutes. Borrowing a bright shade of lipstick and some blush from Lisa, she completed her stage makeup-up and was ready to go.

"You look fabulous!" Lisa said. "You're going to shock the hell out of these guys. I can't wait." She gave her a big hug and rushed off to join Tony.

Arianna knew she had a good voice, not necessarily great, but one that had a unique quality which people enjoyed. The entertainer in her, however, was the thing that inspired her to perform because she had no desire to make a living as a singer. Like other things of her youth, she had left this aspect of her life behind.

For this performance, she was singing mostly duets with André. What topped off all of her performances was her ability to sell the song. She looked good. She moved well, and she exuded sex appeal. Truth be told, the women in the audience probably wished they could emulate her and the men probably wished they could be with her. When you had this going on, you didn't have to be the best singer in the world.

Eye contact while performing was important as well. The more eye contact you made with an audience, the better to draw them into your performance. Tonight was rough, however. Zach's eyes never left her for a second. She did her best not to look at him. Tried. Really tried. It didn't work, and of all the times for their eyes to meet, it happened during the Lady Antebellum duet, "Need You Now".

It's a quarter after one
I'm a little drunk
and I need you now.

It was an intense moment. It was also irritating. Why, oh why, couldn't she be singing something like Miley Cyrus's, "I Came in like a Wrecking Ball" or maybe, Lady Gaga's "Bad Romance"? Anything except a song about love, desire, and need when their eyes met.

"GOD, I think I'm in love," Parker Zales said, gawking at Arianna. Parker had been one of Zach's close friends for years. "But didn't I just see her waiting tables earlier? Too cheap to hire separate help, are you, Acevedo?"

Zach just shook his head. *If he only knew...*

As the performance ended to rousing applause, Parker said, "Come on, Zach. You gotta introduce me to this girl. What do you know about her? Is she single, I hope?"

Zach shrugged and escorted Parker toward the stage. Lisa reached Arianna first and engulfed her in big hug almost bowling her over. "You were great! Everyone absolutely loved you."

"Whew! Thanks, but I was really nervous tonight."

Tony leaned down and surprised her with a kiss on the cheek. "I had no idea you were such a good singer. I thought diving was your forte," he said with a wink.

Arianna shook her head as a sly grin played across her lips.

Out of nowhere, Juan swooped in and gave her a big bear hug.

"Put me down, you dog," she said, weakly protesting.

"Hey! Hey! Let me in here," Parker insisted. Looking at Zach, he elbowed him in the ribs and said, "Well?"

Zach winced from the jab, and said, "Arianna, I'd like you to meet Parker Zales. He owns a chain of five star hotels, so if you're ever looking for a singing gig, give him a call."

"Pleased to meet you, Arianna." He stepped forward and air kissed each side of her cheeks. "I loved your performance, and you can work for me anytime you want."

"Why, thank you. That's a very generous offer."

"For an amateur, you have potential," Lydia piped in. "Maybe you should give up your job as a service employee and try to make a career of singing. If I were you, I'd leave here and take Parker up on his offer."

"Why, thank you, Miss Calhoun," Arianna replied. "I'll keep your advice in mind."

"And now, Arianna," Parker said, "if you have any energy left, I'd be honored if I could have this dance."

She glanced at Zach, not sure whether he was okay with that or not.

"Well, Acevedo?" he asked. "Certainly you're not going to make her work right through her break, are you? Never mind. Here. Forget about him." Parker took Arianna by the hand and led her out onto the dance floor.

As they slow danced to the ballad playing, Parker did his best to convince Arianna she should spend the rest of the evening with him.

"I'm very flattered, Parker, but I'm afraid I'm involved in another relationship, but thank you very much."

"Are you sure? I can show you a really good time. I'd love for you to be my guest on my yacht... no strings attached, of course."

She had experience with guys like Parker. They thought their money could buy them anything. She had no time for men like him. Giving him a kiss on the cheek, she said, "You're very sweet, and I appreciate the offer, but I'm afraid I'm tied up at the moment."

Parker struggled to hide his disappointment. "Well, if you happen to change your mind, I'll be here all evening, and I'm not leaving until tomorrow afternoon." He kissed her hand and led her over to where Zach and Lydia were dancing.

"Hey, buddy," he said, tapping Zach on the shoulder and looking at Lydia. "I can't let the night get away without dancing with this lovely young lady, too. Here. You dance with your star attraction while I see if I can't steal your woman away from you."

Before anyone could decide if this was a good idea or not, Parker twirled Lydia on down the dance floor with her protesting to no avail as he whisked her away.

Zach and Arianna stood there staring at each other, immobilized with indecision. Finally, Zach stepped forward and put his arm around Arianna's waist and took her hand in his, laying it gently on his chest. Still, they continued to stand there, looking at each other for what seemed like an eternity before finally beginning to dance.

Arianna could hardly breathe, and her heart was pounding in her chest. She did her best to calm herself so Zach wouldn't notice how rattled she was, but it was futile. Of course, he noticed. He always noticed everything.

His hand touched the bare skin of her back, and suddenly her whole body was on fire. Leaning close to her ear, it seemed he was about to say something, but then, changing his mind, he pulled back and sighed heavily.

Arianna looked up at him and fought to hold his gaze. Feeling her cheeks redden, she lowered her head and looked away. Her pulse was racing wildly, and she didn't know if she could take much more of this closeness.

Leaning down again, Zach whispered, "I'm sorry about what you've been through."

His remark shot through her like a bolt of lightning. She looked up at him, searching his face for the meaning to what he'd said, looking for the sincerity behind the words.

"I'm responsible for all this, and I'm sorry," Zach said.

Arianna was too dumbfounded to speak.

Zack slid his hand slowly down her back to a new position and pressed her more tightly to him. Once again, the touch of his hand against her bare skin took her breath away. But more than that, something else was beginning to affect her. It was the *niceness* coming from him... a *niceness* that was causing her defenses to melt away.

This could not be, she thought to herself. She didn't want to like him. She didn't want him to be nice because when he was nice, she had no reason to be angry with him. Without a reason to be angry, she could easily see herself falling for him, and that scared her. All of a sudden, her closely guarded feelings were unraveling, and she felt like she was losing control.

Zach's heart was racing, too. As he held Arianna in his arms, the fresh scent of jasmine and freesia teased his senses. Her soft, silky skin was just begging him to caress it, and as her breasts pressed into his chest, he felt himself becoming aroused. When the music finally stopped, he couldn't make himself let go.

They stood there for a moment looking at each other, both trying to say something, neither one finding the words. Unable to stand it one more moment, Arianna pushed abruptly away from him and rushed off.

She had to get away. Being so close to him in such an intimate manner was unbearable. She went to the nearest bar and grabbed a bottle of scotch and headed for the beach. She wanted to get away from this party, this place, these people. *Him!!!* Wanted to go somewhere and think… and drink… and drown all of this out.

CHAPTER
26

A rianna sat on the front porch of the little beach house sipping scotch and listening to the sound of the surf rushing in and out on the shore. This peaceful, calming setting was in sharp contrast to the riot of emotions raging in her head. Zach scared her so much. To be precise, it wasn't him, but rather her feelings toward him that scared her because as she'd stood there in his arms tonight, she could no longer deny the fact that she was in love with him. But any acknowledgment of those feelings, she feared, would take her on a journey she felt hesitant to go on.

Up until this point, by simply focusing on her anger, she'd done a good job of denying the attraction. Now, with the anger dissipating, she had nothing to hide behind and was forced to come face to face with her suppressed feelings.

She went into the beach house in search of more ice. Filling her glass, she turned to leave when she saw him standing in the doorway. Not knowing why he was there, at first she was afraid she'd done something wrong, so she moved cautiously toward the door.

"Zach! I, uh, guess I should be back helping with the party, but I didn't think you'd mind if I came down here for a while." She tried to skirt past him and go out the door.

"I don't," he said, putting his hand on the doorframe, blocking her exit.

Puzzled, she looked up at him and asked, "Well, uhm, is there something you need from me or came to tell me?"

"Yes," he said. Reaching down, he took the drink glass from her hand, threw it out the door, and then, kicked the door shut with his foot. Taking her by the shoulders, he pressed her into the wall.

Arianna gasped and her heart lurched in her chest, but before she could utter a single word of protest, he leaned forward as if to kiss her, and then hesitated. Stepping back, he studied her face a moment, ran his knuckles gently down the side of her cheek, and traced the outline of her lips with his finger. Lifting her chin, he leaned in and tenderly kissed her.

Arianna made a feeble attempt to push him away as ambivalence pooled with desire. In only seconds however, she was lost in his kiss. Relished it. Eagerly returned it as the kiss quickly turned from tender to deep and hungry.

Zach ran his hands up and down her body, fondling her breasts, his thumbs thrumming across the hardened nipples. He let out a soft groan and slipped both of her arms above her head and leaned into her with the full length of his body, pressing his knee between her legs while sealing her to the wall with his kiss.

He released her hands from over her head, only this time instead of trying to push him away, Arianna immediately began clutching his shoulders, arms, and back... anything and everywhere on his strong muscular physique.

Once more, his hands roamed up and down her body. She squirmed as if trying to get away, shaking her head from side to side, saying no, though everything inside of her screamed yes. If she thought he'd unnerved her before with just a look, it was nothing compared to the torrent of passion he was unleashing now with the touch of his hand.

Slowly, he undid the three buttons of her vest, but made no move to take it off. Instead he let his fingers trail across the swell of her breasts, edging their way down her firm, flat navel to just inside her pants, on into her panties... kneading, caressing, then, out again.

He pushed her pants down low on her hips and let them rest precariously there. The sensation of being half exposed as her pants hung loosely below her navel was intoxicating, and she could see that he was as measured in his lovemaking as he was in all the other facets of his life.

He once again pinned her arms above her head and held them there while he kissed her deeply. Her chest heaved, and she knew that at any moment her breasts would fall out of the vest. The more she heaved the more the material slipped away. The more the vest slipped away, the more the excitement built as her breasts became more and more exposed and so the more she heaved and squirmed.

Just the thought of this excited her beyond what she could have ever imagined. She wanted, yet didn't want, to be naked before him. It was such an exquisitely exciting feeling, she thought she would incinerate at any moment.

And sure enough, the vest fell away, revealing her nice, firm breasts. He gently brushed his knuckles across the taut nipples and watched her as she watched him continue his long slow seduction, seemingly helpless to stop any of it. Then, he leaned down and taking first one, then the other breast in his hand, lifted them to his mouth and gently suckled one puckered tip, flicked it with his tongue, nipped at it, before finally nursing greedily as she moaned with pleasure.

An inferno quelled between her legs. Her arms released once more, she alternated between clutching onto him and pounding her fists into the wall. Squirming uncontrollably in ecstasy, she felt her pants now slowly falling away with each move, hastening the moment at which she would be entirely naked before him.

She ran her fingers through his hair and down his back as he continued his full attention to her breasts. Lost in this magnificent seduction, his free hand found its way down into her panties. Down into the wet moist area between her legs. With just the touch of his hand, his fingers now probing and seeking, she felt herself slipping into oblivion. She wanted him more than she'd ever wanted anyone in her whole life.

She reached out and touched him, feeling his hard erection bulging beneath his pants. Unbuttoning his shirt and pushing it back off him, she raked her breasts across his bare chest.

It was as if she couldn't get enough of his body. His back, rippled with muscles. His biceps, hard from lifting weights... powerful thighs and firm buttocks. His strong masculine essence was like an aphrodisiac to her.

And just when she thought she couldn't stand it another minute, he pushed her pants all the way off. She stepped out of them and kicked them aside. Slowly, he kissed his way down her belly. The anticipation was agonizing as his lips moved lower toward their now completely naked target.

"No," she moaned, meaning yes and involuntarily bucked forward to meet his hungry mouth. She was about to slip over the edge, when he stopped and stood up and stepped out of his pants. Standing there fully erect, she knew he was about to enter her.

Against all reason, she cried out, "No. Zach. Stop. I can't do this."

STOP? ZACH couldn't believe what he'd just heard. She'd caught him totally off guard. She wanted him. He knew she did. She was fully aroused so what was the problem? He'd never had to force himself on a woman in his entire life, and he wasn't about to start now, though he desperately wanted her... wanted her as much as he'd ever wanted any woman before.

But now, to be turned down. That would be a real blow to his ego. How had he miscalculated this, he wondered? He was an experienced and sensitive lover who knew all too well how to satisfy a woman. Knew when a woman was right for the taking and she was. So what was wrong?

Not that it mattered. He would not force himself on her. If she said no, it was over. He would have to live with the rejection. He continued to study her, searching for a meaning to her sudden change of mind.

"Zach," she stammered, "I'm not on any birth control, so unless you have some protection, uh..."

He smacked the wall, frustrated at his lack of preparation. Frustrated that he would not be able to consummate this union tonight. God, he wanted her, but he had no condoms with him. In a way though, he felt relieved. This, he could deal with. Out and out rejection? Now, that would have been a blow to his manhood.

"I'm sorry," Arianna said, her distress written all over her face. "I shouldn't have led you on like this. I should have stopped things before they got this far, it's just that—"

But she never finished whatever she was about to say as Zach engulfed her in a kiss, his tongue probing deeply. Once again his hand found its way between her legs, moving rhythmically back and forth across the apex of her womanhood until she was again panting and squirming under his touch.

"No. Oh, nooo," she moaned, rolling her head back and forth.

But it was too late. She knew it was imminent. One thing she'd learned about Zach was he was not to be denied, and so far, whatever he had demanded of her in their brief, torrid relationship, she had given. He would bring her to climax despite her insincere protests. Her surrender would be complete.

"Oh, please. Oh! My God, Zach," she cried as she slipped over the edge. Contraction after contraction wracked her body as the spasms consumed her. Buckling at the knees, she collapsed into his arms, whispering his name over and over as she clutched onto him.

He scooped her up and carried her to the sofa. Straddling her, he stroked and pressed himself against her belly. The mere touch of his erection to her skin was sufficient to send him over the edge. With one loud shudder, he collapsed on top of her in a sweaty heap.

THEY HELD each other, waiting for their breathing to return to normal. Finally, rising on one elbow, Zach looked at her and tenderly stroked her cheek while he studied her face.

"You are so beautiful," he said. "I've wanted to tell you that since the first time I saw you."

"Ah, I'm sure I looked lovely rousted out of bed at three in the morning at Lisa's house."

No... under that burqa in Kervistan. Zach tucked a lock of hair back behind her ear, wanting to say more. Knew he wouldn't. Knew he couldn't.

Arianna could feel herself blush. She bit her lip and looked away. Oh, Lord! How had she gotten herself into this position?

Zach turned her face back toward him, thwarting her effort to avoid facing this moment of truth. "It's too bad we couldn't have met under different circumstances, Arianna. I'm not the man you think I am."

So, she was quickly discovering. She'd just seen a side of him tonight she had no idea existed.

"Well, you scared me that first night. I didn't understand what was happening. That's why I kept trying to escape."

Lifting her hand, he gently caressed it against his cheek and then, kissed her palm as he continued to watch her though he spoke not a word.

"Well, uhm, I'm also kind of used to taking care of myself," she continued, "and I didn't think I needed your help anyway."

"So I noticed," he said with a bemused look on his face, idly tracing a finger between the V of her breasts.

This closeness was almost too much for her. She would have given anything to be able to bolt about now, but she seemed to be trapped.

"Actually," she said, sighing, "sometimes maybe, well, see I'm not very used to being told what to do either, so I guess I might not have been as cooperative as I could have been."

"Really?" he asked, a twinkle in his eye. "You think?"

Oh, why am I confessing all this to him. He's hardly said a word, and I'm pouring my guts out. She just wanted to get up and leave. She *never* let anyone get close to her, and she *always* left when things started to get too close for comfort, and right now, they were definitely too close for comfort. But obviously, she wasn't going anywhere.

With all of her defenses completely gone, she meekly whispered, "Well, okay, I'm sorry. I'm sorry for causing you so much trouble. I know you were only trying to help me, and I'm grateful for your help." And then as if it was killing her to say it, she added, "Thank you."

Zach smiled ever so slightly and nodded his head. Bending forward, he kissed her gently and said, "You're welcome." He rose from the sofa, brought her a beach towel to cover up with, and then, went searching for their clothes.

ZACH WAITED on the porch for Arianna to finish dressing. By now he figured he'd been gone just long enough Lydia would be thoroughly pissed at him. Except for the scene she would cause, he really didn't care. There was no doubt in his mind. The relationship with her was over.

Arianna came out of the beach house looking radiant. He reached out and pulled her close to him, embracing her once again.

"Arianna, this is a bit complicated tonight. I didn't know this was going to happen exactly, I—"

It was her turn to interrupt him. "I know. Lydia's waiting for you. You need to go."

Stepping back and holding her at arm's length, he said, "No. It's not like that, Arianna. You have to understand. I don't go skipping from the arms of one woman into the arms of another. That's not my style. But tonight I find myself in an unusual situation. Because of all the guests, I have to go up there, and I have to go up there alone. I can't do anything to cause a scene at this party or at least I prefer not to if I can avoid it. I'm asking you to be patient and trust me until I can work this out."

"I understand," she said, lying. She didn't really understand at all what had happened here tonight or what was going to happen from this point on. "You need to go. You've been gone a long time."

Zach looked her directly in the eye. "Arianna, please trust me. I'll get this resolved quickly, and then, we can be together, but for now, I have to go."

Noticing she was shivering, he took his jacket off and put it around her. He kissed her tenderly one more time. Then, reluctantly pulling himself away, he took the stairs two at a time to the top.

CHAPTER
27

Tony caught up with Zach as he came across the lawn. "I have to warn you. Lydia's been looking all over for you, and she's totally pissed. Everything all right?"

"Arianna," Zach said, not breaking his stride.

"What?"

"I've been with Arianna," he snapped.

Tony shook his head, and a look of confusion crossed his face. "She do something wrong again?" he asked.

Zach didn't respond but instead walked to the nearest cabana bar and grabbed a bottle of beer. Only after practically draining the entire beer, did he respond. "No, I saw her go down to the beach, so I followed her."

He pulled out his cell phone and texted Juan, asking him to meet him by the bar.

"I can't explain it," he said, looking back at Tony. "She's all I've been thinking about lately. Even when I was in Miami last weekend, she kept popping into my head. Christ, Tony, I was screwing Lydia and thinking about Arianna. How bad is that?"

Tony shook his head. *Really bad*, but he didn't say.

"I followed her to the beach to, to... I don't know why for sure. But once I got near her...," his voice trailed off while he seemed to be reliving a moment in his mind. "I just couldn't resist her any more. One thing led to another and..."

He finished his beer, pitched it into the trash, and reached for another. "Damn, she's all I thought she would be and more. I'm in love with her, Tony."

Whew! This was heavy. Zach had never said anything like this before. Never! And there'd been lots of women.

Juan sauntered over to the cabana, a puzzled look on his face. "What's up?" he asked.

"I want you to go down to the beach house and bring Arianna up," Zach said.

"What? This isn't another one of those, let's surprise sleeping beauty in the middle of the night, but have a little hellion on my hands, is it?" he asked. "I mean, you better fill me in here." He looked at Tony for clarification, but Tony shrugged his shoulders, confused himself.

"No, it's not like that," Zach said. "I just don't want her down there alone. She can stay as long as she likes. I'd just feel better if I knew someone was with her."

"Damn, Zach. You're not making any sense. How much have you had to drink tonight anyway?" Juan asked.

Tony could see Zach was about to lose his temper. "It's okay, Zach. Here. I'll take care of this."

Tony walked Juan toward the steps to the beach. Unsure himself of exactly what was happening, he tried to fill Juan in.

"Well, this is all kind of new to me, too, but from what I know so far, Zach and Arianna, well, it seems they're a couple now. I don't know what or how it happened, but anyway, he obviously wants you to watch her, see that she's all right since he can't get away right now, you know... Lydia. Man, I hate to think what kind of scene she'd cause over this if she knew what was happening."

"Holy shit!" Juan said. "I can't believe it! Or yes, I can actually. Arianna is beautiful. Damn, what a lucky guy!"

"Yeah, I agree. It just kind of took me by surprise. Anyway, I guess you need to go down there and keep an eye on his new prize possession... make sure she's all right, you know?"

"Gotcha!" There was no need for further discussion. He headed down to the beach to find Arianna.

When Tony returned, Zach was now on his third beer. Something big had sure happened tonight. It had been a long time since Tony had seen Zach in such a state.

"All taken care of," Tony said. "What are you going to do about Lydia though?"

Zach grimaced. "It's over. I just have to tell her, but I can't tonight. Not with all these people around. She's not going to like it. Knowing her, she'll pitch a royal fit especially if she figures out she's been dumped for Arianna. I kind of have everything fucked up right now, don't I?"

Zach turned and looked toward the stairs leading up from the beach as if expecting to see someone. Arianna probably. "I'll straighten this all out tomorrow, but first I gotta get through tonight." He guzzled the rest of his beer and left to find Lydia.

AFTER ZACH left, Arianna grabbed the bottle of scotch and sat down on the porch. She needed a good stiff drink after what had just happened. And what had happened, she mused? It occurred to her, she might have just been used and cast aside. She had let someone make love to her, practically anyway, and then watched him leave to go find his girlfriend.

Of course, she understood it was complicated... that he didn't want to create a scene tonight, but why had she allowed herself to get so intimate with someone who already had a girlfriend? She knew better than that.

She wanted to think he hadn't just used her, but logically things didn't add up. They'd been archenemies since the day they'd met. She'd been nothing but trouble to him, and they'd not spoken more than a dozen words to each other in the three weeks she'd been there. So what could she be to him anyway?

She should have told him to get lost tonight… to go on back to Lydia. But she hadn't said anything. Didn't resist anything. Well, if he had used her, she had no one to blame but herself. She'd broken one of her own cardinal rules. *Never* get mixed up in a triangle.

So now, it was time for a reality check. Maybe it was the scotch talking, but the servant's uniform she wore… she thought it was quite appropriate really. She was *way* out of her league here. These people were mega rich. *He* was mega rich. She was just an average girl from a middle class family. One thing her senior year had taught her was, the rich were a closed society where the middleclass are not welcome.

She had dated the handsome quarterback of her high school football team, Derek Watson. They planned to get married after college. That was, until they told his parents about their wedding plans. No one ever said it in so many words, but she got the message. She was too common for their son. He was a *Watson,* and *Watsons* did not marry beneath their station… meaning her. In the end, Derek succumbed to parental pressure and broke up with her.

The memory of that experience cast a shadow over every relationship she'd had since. She never trusted anyone. Never fully gave herself to any relationship. Of course, maybe she'd just never met the right man all these years, but for whatever reason, any time things got too cozy with a guy, she took off.

She went inside to get more ice and when she returned, was surprised to see Juan waiting on the porch.

"Hey, what are you doing here?" she asked.

"I came to keep you company."

"What?"

"Zach sent me down here to stay with you."

"Zach sent you down here to stay with me?" she repeated as she sat down on the front steps to resume her drinking. "Why would he do that? Is he afraid I'm going to try to run away or something?"

Juan laughed out loud. "Oh, I doubt that. No, he didn't really say, but I suspect it's because he wants to make sure you're all right. He didn't want you to be alone."

Arianna sat there, numb. *Ah, yes. He's a little tied up right now with his girlfriend, but he doesn't want me to be alone. Of course. That makes perfect sense to me.* The scotch was starting to get to her.

Turning to Juan, she said, "Well, I'm fine so you can go on back to the party."

"No, I can't really."

"Why not? I'm not going anywhere, and I'll be fine. It's silly for you to be down here with me. Please. Go on back and enjoy the party."

"I'm afraid it doesn't quite work like that. You see, I take my orders from Zach, and if he tells me to stay with you, that's exactly what I'll do."

Arianna poured more scotch into her glass.

"Look, Arianna. I don't know quite what happened between you and Zach, but I know Zach. If he sent me down here to be with you, it means only one thing. He really cares about you. He wouldn't pull me away from the party and my girlfriend if this was just a routine matter. He'd have one of the other guards come down here, assuming he'd even have anyone stay with you. But he didn't. He sent me. That makes you top priority."

Mystified, Arianna sat there shaking her head. What he was saying? *He cares. Zach cares. Top priority?* She downed the entire glass of scotch in one swig and poured herself another.

"You should slow down with the scotch, you know," Juan said.

"Why? Did Zach send you down here to monitor my drinking, too?"

"No. Go ahead," he chuckled. "Drink all you want. But whatever you're trying to drown out with that booze, will still be there tomorrow when you wake up."

But it was too late already. As she stood up to set the record straight, everything began to swim in front of her eyes. She felt her head spinning, and then, everything went black. Juan reached out and caught her right before she hit the ground.

He carried her up the steps to the house, cutting around the back of the yard so as not to attract any attention. He did not escape Zach's gaze who had been watching the stairway for the last half hour. Zach thrust Lydia into Tony's care and headed around to intercept Juan who was just bringing Arianna in the side door and down to her room.

"Hey, what's wrong?" he asked.

"Nothing except she just had a little too much to drink and passed out. All she needs is to sleep it off."

Pilar, finishing up in the kitchen, caught up with them. "Here. Let me help," she said.

As Juan laid her on the bed, Arianna started mumbling something, but it wasn't coherent. Then, she passed out again. Pilar began to help her out of her clothes and to tuck her into bed when she noticed she was wearing Zach's jacket. She handed the jacket to him, and said, "I believe this is yours."

A knowing look passed between them.

"You can go now," Pilar said. "I'll take care of her."

With one last look at Arianna, Zach exited the room with Juan following. "I don't understand. How much did she have to drink?"

"Too much. But hey, Zach, I wouldn't worry about it. She's had three stressful weeks and a very eventful evening from what I heard. She's entitled to drink herself into oblivion if she wants. She'll be fine as soon as she sleeps it off. Question is—how are you doing?"

"Don't ask. This is turning out to be the longest night of my life, and it can't be over fast enough to suit me." Letting out an exasperated sigh, he rushed off to rejoin Lydia at the party.

THE NEXT thing Arianna knew, the room was spinning round and round. She got up and stumbled to the bathroom just in time to throw up in the stool, ferociously until she had nothing more to throw-up. Threw up everything but her memories of what had happened. Pilar who'd been catnapping on the bed beside her, came to her aid, wiping her face with a cold washcloth.

Arianna rested her head on Pilar's shoulder and sobbed, "Oh, Pilar. I can't take the stress of this anymore."

"Shh! It will be all right," she reassured her, as she held her and continued to put cold compresses on her face. "You've had too much to drink, but things will look better in the morning."

"But you don't understand what I did," she cried. "It's all a mess now. I, we... Zach. I let him..."

"Shh! It's okay," Pilar interrupted. "Don't worry about it. Zach is going to take good care of you."

"Zach is going to take care of me? How is that? He's ..." but without finishing whatever she was going to say, she leaned over and vomited once more.

Arianna's continued to throw up until she had the dry heaves. Pilar thought she should check with Zach about what to do for her, but he and Lydia had gone to bed hours ago, and she did not want to get in the middle of that. Taking matters into her own hands, she called Zach's personal doctor who came and gave Arianna something to curb the nausea and stop the dry heaves.

"When she wakes up, make sure she drinks lot of liquids, but not too much at once. She's bound to be dehydrated and need fluids. I'm also leaving some medicine to counter the effects of the hangover she's going to have in the morning."

Pilar tucked Arianna in and made sure she was resting comfortably before lying down herself. Whatever happened tonight must have been momentous. It looked like Zach and Arianna were finally together and though the road ahead may still be rocky, it thrilled Pilar to know these two were finally a couple.

CHAPTER
28

Arianna moaned and held her head. Despite having the hangover from hell, warm memories of the romantic interlude between herself and Zach washed over her. She relished the memory of his tender kiss as he held her in his strong embrace, and a shiver ran down her spine as she recalled how her body had come alive at the touch of his hands caressing her from head to toe. But now, she felt a twinge of uneasiness, and her initial happy glow dissipated. She didn't like the feeling of having made love to a man, only to find herself abandoned and alone the next morning.

There was a soft knock on the door. Her first thought was, please, don't let it be Zach. She didn't think she could face him this morning, fearing she'd see a cool, detached look on his face… one that said she meant nothing to him. She didn't think she could bear that.

"Ari, it's Lisa. Can I come in?"

"Yes, come in," Arianna said. She sat up and pushed her wild mop of hair back off her face.

"Boy, you don't look so good," Lisa said, entering the room carrying a food tray. She set it down on the nightstand and handed her a glass of juice. "Pilar told me to make sure you drink all of this. Doctor's orders. It's important to get fluids back in you. I brought you some meds the doctor left, too."

Arianna popped two pills in her mouth and washed them down with a glass of chilled orange juice. She took a couple nibbles of a piece of toast and tossed it back onto the plate.

"Pilar was amazing last night," she said. "I was sick as a dog, but she never left my side. She was like a second mom, taking care of me. I can't believe I drank so much. I'm sure paying for it today."

"Yeah, I heard you had a rough night."

"Really? So, what else did you hear?" Arianna asked.

"Enough," Lisa said with a sly smile on her face. "Is it true?"

"Is what true?" Arianna tried to stand, but felt weak and sank back onto the bed.

"Don't play coy with me. You and Zach? Is it true you're a couple now?"

"Didn't Tony tell you everything?"

"Are you kidding? He told me a little, but when I tried to get more information, we got into our very first fight. He let me know in no uncertain terms that I was to *never* give him the third degree about Zach's business again. End of story. So, come on. I'm dying to know. What happened?"

Arianna drank more juice and sat there not speaking.

"All right. What's wrong?" Lisa asked. "If you and Zach are really together, I'd think you'd be happy. Did something bad happen?"

Arianna sighed. "You could say that. I lost my head and did something stupid."

"Like what?"

"I don't know, Lisa. He followed me to the beach, and it all happened so fast. He kissed me, and I kissed him, and I, he...we just never stopped." Arianna exhaled. "What was I thinking? I mean I wanted him, and he wanted me, but... but..."

"But what?" Lisa asked, throwing her hands in the air. "This sounds great. Pardon my stupidity, Arianna, but I fail to see the problem."

"The problem is I was stupid. Do you see anyone lying here beside me in bed this morning? No. That's because Zach has a girlfriend for God's sake! The other problem is that he's wealthy, and I could never fit into his circle of friends. Anyway, we hate each other.

He hates me. He just used me, and I was stupid and let him. The term 'booty call' comes to mind."

"No, Arianna," Lisa said, sitting down beside her. "That's not how it is, I'm sure. No way is Zach the 'booty call' type. That's silly. And I'm sure he doesn't hate you, and you don't really hate him. I can tell you he looked absolutely miserable with Lydia last night. From what I saw, he barely spoke to her. I think he's going to break up with her as soon as all the guests leave."

"Oh, you are such an optimist." Arianna sat up. "Even if that was true, he's still way out of my league. Who am I trying to kid? Lisa, in case you hadn't noticed, these guys are super wealthy and Cinderella is a fairy tale. There is no prince charming in real life. Trust me. I know what I'm talking about."

"Oh, you know, Ari, sometimes I think you're too stubborn for your own damn good. You're beautiful and classy. I'm sure Zach doesn't care about anything but you. He'd be stupid if he did, and he's not a stupid man. Why don't you just give this a chance?"

Arianna got up and moved toward the bathroom. "Bad memories."

"Of what?" Lisa demanded.

"Rejection. Pain. You know. Wonderful things like that."

"So you got hurt before. Who hasn't, but you've got to take a chance on love again sometime," Lisa said, waiting for a response.

"Maybe, but the stakes are too high here," Arianna said, coming out of the bathroom and curling up in bed again.

"Oh, quit it! Now, you listen to me. This is ridiculous. Forget about all this nonsense and take your own advice. You need to relax and enjoy yourself. Zach's gorgeous. He's wealthy, and he's in love with you. What more could you want?"

Nothing really, she thought, but then she'd been there before. She wished she didn't feel this way. What did they say? A coward dies a thousand deaths. That was her. Too afraid to love again.

LYDIA COZIED up next to Zach at breakfast. "Is everything all right?" she asked.

"Yeah, sure," he said, nodding slowly.

"You were a little inebriated last night and fell asleep really fast." She leaned over and kissed him on the cheek. "When you get back from golf today, maybe we could make up for lost time, if you know what I mean," she whispered as she nuzzled his neck.

"Yeah, maybe later," he said, even though he knew there would be no later. "I have some calls to make before golf." He got up from the table. "I'll see you at lunch." He gave her a half-hearted kiss on the cheek and left.

There were no calls to be made. He wanted to find Arianna. Seeing Lisa sitting with Tony by the pool, he stopped and asked, "Have you seen Arianna this morning?"

Lisa nodded.

"So... how is she?"

"Hung over and kind of confused."

"Confused? About what?"

"Umh... you, I think."

Zach ran his hand through his hair and sighed. There was a lot more he wanted to ask, but he had no time. Several close friends had spent the night and weren't leaving until the afternoon. He had endured a pitiful evening trying to feign interest in Lydia. Though he wasn't good at pretending, he didn't want a huge blow-up with Lydia to be the last thing his guests remembered about this weekend gathering.

Now, he had eighteen holes of golf to get through plus a luncheon at the club before he could escort Lydia to the airport and break the news to her that their relationship was over. He faced several miserable hours before he could hold Arianna in his arms again, and the wait was killing him.

At lunch Lydia implored Zach to let her spend another day, but he dashed that idea in a hurry. And so early in the afternoon, she and all the remaining guests returned to the house to pack and catch their flights home.

"I still don't see why I have to leave today," Lydia grumbled.

"I told you. I have some important business I need to take care of, so I won't be here," Zach snapped.

"What is wrong with you? You are acting so strange," Lydia said.

"Lydia, please. Go pack your things. We'll talk on the way to the airport. Please. I don't want to discuss anything now."

He watched her stomp off thinking he hated living by his own code of ethics. He could have asked Juan or Carlos to take her to the airport and be the ones to tell her the relationship was over. That would have been a quick and easy way to end things. But that was not the honorable thing to do. His moral code said he needed to have the decency to break up with her in person.

While she was packing, he made a quick search for Arianna. He found her out by the pool, talking to Lisa. His pulse quickened, and everything inside of him came alive. He realized this is how it should be when you were in love. Realized he hadn't felt this way in a long time, if ever.

"Oh, hey," Arianna said, surprised to see him. "I didn't think you and your guests would be home this afternoon. I'll just get my things and get out of your way."

He grabbed her by the arm as she tried to skirt past him. "You're not in my way. We're not staying. I'm not staying, but I'll be back soon."

Arianna looked away, not responding.

"Hey, what's wrong?" His excitement turned to concern.

Summoning all of her courage, she looked at him, and said in a nonchalant manner, "You know I was thinking. I was pretty drunk last night. I vaguely remember us kind of, well, you know. I'm afraid that when I drink too much, I sometimes do something I regret the next morning. I'm sorry, but I guess what I'm trying to say is, I wouldn't read too much into last night if I were you. Now, if you'll excuse me, I need to get out of this sun. I'm feeling a little sick again."

She looked at him a moment, praying he would release her arm before her resolve to break this off dissipated. Reluctantly, he let go, and she rushed into the house. Once inside her room, she collapsed against the door, not quite believing what she had said. She was shaken and close to tears, but she told herself this was for the best. She could not get involved with him.

"Everything all right?" Tony asked, seeing Arianna rush away.

Zach stood there a bit dumbfounded. "I'm pretty sure I just got the brush off."

Lisa couldn't believe what she had just witnessed and knew she had to speak up.

"Zach, I think Arianna would kill me for saying this, but I have to tell you something. I don't think she means what she said. She's just scared of getting involved with you. She has this crazy notion you might just be using her because you already have a girlfriend. She also doesn't believe she could have any future with you because of the big difference in your economic backgrounds."

Zach's look changed from dumbfounded to incredulous.

"Well, I think the only reason any of this scares her," Lisa continued, "is because she's fallen in love with you, and she doesn't want to get hurt."

"She thinks I'd hurt her?" he asked.

"I think she got burned badly in a past relationship, so she never lets anyone get close to her." Lisa paused a moment, sure she'd said too much, but feeling compelled to finish.

"Zach, I know Arianna really well, and I probably shouldn't tell you this, but she plans to put up this wall and block you out despite the fact she loves you. She's stubborn, so no matter what she feels inside, she isn't going to risk getting hurt. She's not going to let you in, and she figures all she has to do, is wait you out, and some day, she'll be out of here and can put this all behind her."

Zach stood there shaking his head. He didn't know whether he should be perturbed or relieved.

Walking over to Lisa, he said, "Thank you. I know it took courage for you to share that." He leaned down and gave her a light kiss on the cheek, and then he left.

IT HAD started to rain as he drove Lydia to the airport. "I need to tell you something," Zach said, "and I don't know quite how to say this except to say it straight out. It's over for us, Lydia. I won't be calling you after today."

Lydia gasped. "What? I don't understand. You're kidding, right?"

"No, I would never joke about something like this."

"But I thought we were happy. Is it something I said?"

"No," Zach said, shaking his head.

"So, that's why you were acting so funny last night and today. Why? Is there someone else?" she asked, as tears welled up in her eyes.

His silence told her there was. He didn't need to say anything.

"Someone I know? Oh, wait. Oh, my God!" she moaned. "It's that servant girl, isn't it? What's her name? Arianna! Please, tell me it's not true."

Zach didn't respond, confirming her worst fears.

"Oh, damn you!" she railed. "You really know how to humiliate me, don't you? Wait until all my friends find out I've been dumped for one of your servants. How embarrassing!"

"She's not a servant. She's a journalist," Zach said evenly.

"Same thing. Journalist who moonlights as a servant. You go slumming, and I pay the price. Damn you, anyway!"

Zach was instantly furious. After that comment, he was feeling even more confident in his decision to break-up with her. He was also beginning to understand why Arianna thought she couldn't fit in with the rich. But it wasn't the money that was the problem. It was snobs like Lydia who sent the wrong message.

As they drove on through the rain, Lydia's rage turned to despair, ending with her begging him to reconsider, offering to do anything for a second chance.

He listened but had nothing to say. There was nothing he could say. It was over and there was no chance he'd be changing his mind. No chance he'd ever call her again. No chance they could even be friends.

When they arrived at the passenger drop zone of the airport, Lydia threw her arms around him and begged him to change his mind. It was a pitiful sight, and Zach was embarrassed at how undignified she was acting. Unmoved, he pulled her arms off of him.

"Please. Try to pull yourself together, Lydia. You're a beautiful woman, and I've enjoyed our time together. I don't want you to be hurt, but I'm sorry, it's over. There's nothing more I can say."

He got out of the car and checked her luggage with the skycap while she waited in the Escalade. Then, he opened the door and offered her his hand, which she ignored, instead getting out in a huff. Her mood had changed from sorrow to rage and now, indignation.

"Don't bother to see me off," she snapped. "Just go on back home to your little servant girl. You've really hit a new low, and you'll be the laughing stock of all your friends. I only regret I won't be there to witness it."

He just glared at her. He highly doubted that. Arianna was smart, beautiful and classy, so he was sure he'd be the envy of all his friends. Seeing Lydia's true colors so clearly now, he was glad to be rid of her.

She turned and stomped into the airport while he wasted no time getting back into the car and racing home.

CHAPTER
29

Arianna, in her pajamas and settled in for the evening, heard two sharp raps on the bedroom door. She opened it and was startled to find Zach standing there.

"Oh!" she said, stepping back into the room.

Zach stood in the doorway, staring at her for a moment, not speaking. Finally, he entered the room and walked nonchalantly over to a dresser. He straightened a lampshade, and then, turned and said, "I broke up with Lydia. We're no longer together."

"Oh!" Arianna repeated, as happiness warred with ambivalence. In a tone she hoped would convey total disinterest, she continued, "Well, I hope not because of me. As I said, I wouldn't read anything into last night. It was just one of those things."

Zach crossed his arms and leaned back against a dresser. "Yeah, well, I didn't," he answered, unaffected by her tone. "What would I read into last night anyway?"

"Well, well...nothing really," she stammered, surprised at his lack of reaction to her obvious rebuff. "It's just that when I drink, sometimes, uh, I get a little amorous and do things I regret the next morning."

"Really?" Taking a step toward her, Zach asked, "So, when you woke up this morning, did you find you regretted last night?"

Mustering her last bit of bravado, she lied, "Yes. I'm afraid last night was all a mistake."

Feeling his ominous presence, she took a step back, tripped, and plopped down on the bed. She scooted up to the head of the bed and clutched a pillow as kind of a security blanket.

Zach sat down on the bed next to her, his ebony eyes pinning her in place. Her heart was thundering in her chest, and she felt her courage slipping away. She was learning that standing your ground against Zach was a formidable task. She wasn't sure she was up to it, but maybe, if she could just hold out a bit longer, he might leave.

But instead of leaving, he leaned forward, snatched the pillow out of her hands, and pitched it across the room. Her mouth gaped open in shock, and he drew close as if to kiss her, but stopped just short of her lips. Teasing her with the promise of a kiss not given, he paused, testing her resolve to resist.

Her pulse raced and her breathing quickened. Their eyes met, and they held each other's gaze, neither person saying anything. Finally, Zach covered her mouth in a passionate kiss which at first she eagerly accepted.

Then, suddenly changing her mind, she made a half-hearted effort to push him away. Ignoring her, he continued to kiss her ardently, his tongue probing deeply while his hands roamed up and down her body. As quickly as he started however, he stopped.

Standing up, he pulled his shirt off over his head, revealing a revolver tucked in the waistband of his jeans. He laid the gun on the nightstand and with no hesitation, reached down and ripped open her pajama top, sending buttons flying everywhere.

Arianna gasped as he pressed her against the headboard, her breasts fully exposed and right there, his to do with as he pleased. She squirmed and tried to turn away, but found herself pinned there. He lifted one breast to his lips, circled the tip with his tongue before finally clamping his mouth around a hardened nipple and sucking greedily.

She clutched and grabbed his back and shoulders, writhing in ecstasy, as he continued to suckle first one and then the other nipple.

He slipped his hand down into her pajamas, into the wet recesses between her legs, cupping her and doing delicious things with his fingers, bringing on unsolicited moans as the heel of his hand moved steadily back and forth across her swollen center of desire. Her whole body was now teeming with pleasure.

Then, without warning, once again he stopped, taking his hand away, causing her instantaneous disappointment, as if her favorite toy had been suddenly snatched from her. She put her own hands down there as if she might continue to pleasure herself, a move Zach noted with a twinkle in his eye.

Without hesitation he removed her hands and pushed them to the side, causing an instant protest. She knew that he knew that she was fully stimulated and just his for the taking. This heady feeling was both exciting and maddening to Arianna at the same time.

Slipping out of his jeans, he stood before her, fully erect. He reached down and slipped her panties completely off, and grabbing her legs in the same motion, pulled her down flat on the bed. Arianna shuddered with desire in anticipation of his next move.

Taking a package out of his pocket, he ripped it open with his teeth, and removing the condom, smoothed it down over his hard erection. Snapping the light off, he lowered himself onto her steamy body. Burying her with a deep sensuous kiss, he slowly began to penetrate with her making no effort to resist. Completely filling her, he began slowly thrusting in and out.

Arianna was now beside herself with desire. "No," she moaned, a weak protest to her final surrender to him. "Noo... please. No, I ... we..."

"You know, Arianna," he whispered, "I hear what you say now, and what you said earlier, but I think your body betrays you. Is this what you claim you regretted last night?"

"Yes," she said, defiantly at first. Then, realizing it could mean he would stop and all this would end, she quickly capitulated. "I mean, no."

Actually, she didn't know anything anymore. This wasn't working out at all like she'd thought. She wanted to walk away from this...

shut him out of her life. At the moment however, she felt powerless to resist his advances. She wanted him, and she wanted him badly.

He pushed her legs further apart, driving himself deeper into her, taking her higher and higher with each thrust, just to the peak of climax and holding her there.

"So are you regretting this now?" he persisted, testing her resolve to resist and wanting to make his point undeniably clear… wanting to force her to admit she wanted him as much as he wanted her.

If she was to be believed, she knew she should say yes. She should protest…tell him to stop. But if this was how she really felt, why was she having so much trouble saying it? Where was her courage, her resolve to end this, her determination to shut him out? Oh, it irritated her that she had all but completely succumbed to his will.

In a voice fraught with frustration and in a last ditch effort to rebuff him, she said weakly, "Yes, this is a mistake."

"Oh, I should stop then?" he asked.

Damn him. Damn him to hell! He was not cutting her any slack. He would exact the admission he had come for, and she felt powerless to prevent it.

"Should I?" he persisted, shifting his weight as if he might withdraw from her.

"No," she said reluctantly, in a voice almost inaudible.

"No? Then tell me, Arianna. Tell me you want me."

She rolled her head back and forth, her last ineffective act of resistance. The fact of the matter was that she wanted him and would do whatever he asked at that moment.

Exasperated and frustrated, but now mad with desire, she said softly, "Yes, yes… I want you."

It was all she had to say. In quick succession, he continued to ride her until one huge climax wracked her body.

"Oh, Zach!" she screamed and clutched on to him for dear life, nearly scratching him in her exuberance and ecstasy. As each spasm contracted around his hard erection, what little control he had left, was shot, and he, too, exploded, collapsing on top of her. With one final shudder, she lay entirely spent in his arms. She didn't think she could even lift a single finger, but what a heavenly surrender it had been.

As they lay nestled together, Zach made no effort to pull outside of her, wanting to prolong this moment as long as possible. Wanting a lifetime of moments like this.

Having cracked through the first level of her tough veneer, there was still more to be resolved before their relationship could move forward. Wanting to fully flush out her feelings, Zach dared to ask, "Is this another one of those situations I shouldn't read too much into?"

He could feel her stiffen under him. He'd touched a nerve as he'd intended. "Arianna?" he said, waiting for a response.

"No... I mean yes," she answered, cursing her own ambivalence. Yes, she wanted him. Yes, she longed to be held in his embrace, but it still didn't mean they were a fit. It still didn't mean it could work between them.

"Well, I don't know what I'm *not* supposed to read into this," Zach said, "but I know what I do read into this. I hear you say one thing, but your body tells me something different. I know you like me so I'm just a bit confused as to why you're trying to shove me away. What are you afraid of anyway?"

She looked away, not wanting to answer. She didn't like these up close and personal questions.

Not surprisingly, he turned her face back toward him.

"Boy, you are stubborn. In a way, that's one of the things that draws me to you... you're stubborn, independent nature. However, right now, it's starting to piss me off, and you're going to find, my perseverance and persistence are every bit a match for your stubbornness. Just so you know, I'm not moving until you tell me why you're trying to shut me out."

Arianna had a pained expression on her face like she wanted to say something but couldn't get it out.

"You know. I don't care what relationships you've had before," Zach continued. "They weren't with me. The problem is, you've probably had too many relationships with boys. From what I've observed about you, nothing but a strong, confident man such as myself could ever hope to satisfy you. Anyone less than that, wouldn't stand a chance in keeping up with you."

Yes, that was precisely true, but she hadn't realized that until she met him. This was the key ingredient that had been missing in all her previous relationships. But this wasn't the only thing that stood between them.

"Okay," she said in exasperation. "I can't believe you don't get it. It wouldn't work for us to be a couple, so why won't you just let me go? When this is all over, I'll just go back to where I came from and that will be the end of things."

"And why won't this work?" Zach asked, his voice tinged with irritation.

Her temper flaring, Arianna slammed her fist into the bed and tried to pitch him off so she could get up and leave. This was all getting too close for comfort.

Undaunted, he refused to budge. "Why?" he demanded.

"Oh, because...because you're wealthy, and I have nothing. I saw all the high society people at your party, the high rollers you socialize with. All the Lydia's dripping in jewels. That's why it won't work. No one would accept me in the circles you travel in. After awhile, even you'd regret being with me. Now, are you happy? Is this the admission you were looking for?" And once again she tried to wrestle her way out from under him.

As he held her fast, he chuckled.

"I fail to see what's so damn funny," she fumed.

"Nothing," he said. "I'm sorry. It's just the whole idea of this money thing that I find amusing. As I said before, I'm not the man you think I am, and I can tell you with one hundred percent certainty, the difference in our economic situations makes absolutely no difference to me."

Rising up on one elbow, he looked her squarely in the eye. "Arianna, listen to me carefully because I'm not prone to making flowery love declarations, so I'm only going to say this one time. I think I fell in love with you the moment I first saw you. You're a beautiful, smart, independent woman, and all the Lydia's of the world, for all their many riches, can't hold a candle to you. You have everything I'm looking for, and your economic status is of *absolutely* no interest to me."

He bent down and kissed her gently, then whispered softly in her ear, "You're perfect for me, Arianna. I've never wanted anyone more."

It was quite a love declaration coming from a man of few words like Zach, and she was momentarily overwhelmed with what he said. Something clicked inside of her. Somehow, all the things she'd feared about a relationship with him were gone. She now looked at him with no reservations and liked what she saw. Liked it a lot and for the first time, believed happiness with him was entirely possible.

"You're sure?" she asked.

He looked at her with a faint smile on his face, and at first, it didn't seem like he was going to answer her. She suddenly realized he didn't like being questioned and re-questioned about the things he said.

Nonetheless, he replied, "I'm very sure, Arianna."

They both breathed a collective sigh of relief. All the tension that had been between them since the first day they'd met, vanished.

He gently rubbed her cheek. "You know, once you get an idea in your head, you are as stubborn as a mule."

She smiled and retorted, "Maybe, but I've also noticed that once you make up your mind you want something, you go right after it with all your might. So, I'm wondering...do you always get what you want so easily?"

"So easily?" he laughed. "This is what you call easy? Somehow, I don't think things ever come easily with you. But to answer your question, yes. Yes, I do." He kissed her once more and disentangled himself to visit the bathroom.

As she lay there awaiting his return, Arianna sighed with contentment. She really was in love with him and felt wonderful and more at peace with herself than she'd felt in years.

Turning in bed, she noticed the gun laying on the nightstand. Seeing it now, made her realize there was a lot she didn't know about this man, but she intended to change all that. She was eager to know everything about him... all about his family, his friends, his travels.... how he made his living. *Everything.*

CHAPTER

30

Zach awoke at five in the morning with his arms and legs still wrapped around Arianna. Pulling her close, he couldn't resist running his hands up and down her naked body one more time. She moaned softly and slid back into him. God! He wanted to make love to her, but what poor planning. He had no more condoms with him. He made a mental note to talk to Doc to get her set up with some birth control. He didn't like the condoms, but he also knew he wasn't ready to be a father either. Forcing himself out of bed, he dressed quietly, kissed her lightly on the cheek, and proceeded up to the main level of the house.

Pilar was beginning to set things out in preparation for breakfast as he came into the kitchen. "Morning," she said, nodding approvingly. Hesitating slightly, she added, "It's about time you came to your senses." It was a risky statement. Chastising Zach ever goodnaturedly wasn't generally the best idea.

"I'm so glad you approve," he said as a slight smile played across his lips. He poured himself a glass of juice. "She's stubborn and headstrong, you know? It could be a bumpy ride."

"Yes, sir, but every bit worth it, I'd say, and also, nothing you can't handle."

"Hmm," he mused. "Well, we'll see." He gave Pilar a hug as he left the kitchen. "She's definitely worth it."

He met up with Tony and Juan for their daily workout... a one-mile ocean swim, a three-mile run, followed by some weight lifting. Afterwards, they'd grab a quick shower and be ready for breakfast by the time the girls got up.

Arianna woke at seven... disappointed to find Zach gone, but otherwise feeling wonderful. Exciting images of last night's romantic coupling greeted her, and she felt warm and tingly all over. Humming to herself, she showered, dressed, and made her way upstairs where she found Stella and Pilar in the midst of preparing breakfast. However, they didn't interest her. She looked past these two, on out onto the patio where she saw Zach leaning against the veranda wall, talking on his cell phone. Tall and tanned, his hair was still wet and slicked back, and the black t-shirt he wore was snug and accented his broad shoulders and strong biceps. A shiver ran down her spine at the thought of making love again with this divinely handsome man.

As she'd done most days, she began to help with breakfast. This morning however, Stella rushed up and tried to usher her out of the kitchen.

"Oh, here. I'll take that," Stella said. "You go on and get yourself some breakfast."

"Okay, but just let me finish this first," Arianna said.

But Stella would not hear of it. "No, shoo. Go on, now."

A puzzled look crossed her face. She moved over to the nook where two of the gardeners had stopped by for coffee.

"Boy! What's gotten into her?" she said to the guys as she started to sit down.

Both men stood up and waited for her to take a seat.

"Well, hey, aren't you two quite the gentlemen this morning." As they all took a seat together, she continued, "I'll be out in about an hour to give you a hand. What are we working on today?"

There was dead silence as the two men looked at each other. "No. That's okay, Arianna," one of them finally said. "Why don't you take the day off?"

Arianna frowned. "Okay. Would someone like to tell me what's going on? You're all treating me like I have the plague or something?"

No one spoke and silence descended on the kitchen.

"Pilar? Is there something wrong?" she asked.

"Of course not, Arianna. Why don't you go on out and have your breakfast?"

Not satisfied with Pilar's answer, she probed further. "Stella? What is it? Why's everyone acting so funny this morning?"

"Well, let's put it this way. If rumor has it right, it seems you might have a new role in the house now. One that don't seem to go along with being kitchen help or a day laborer." Flashing her a big smile, she asked, "We can't have the new lady of the house working as the hired help, now can we?"

"What?" Arianna said, taken by surprise. Lady of the house? It was such a foreign idea; she couldn't wrap her head around it. But in a way, it made sense. The staff seemed to know everything that happened around here, so they must have known Zach had spent the night with her, meaning she was now officially his girlfriend, changing her status in the house.

"Ah, I see. And uh, is this what Zach said?" Arianna asked.

"Oh, no, but well, we can put two and two together," Stella said and winked at her.

In a way it was flattering, this preferential treatment, but Arianna felt she had to set the record straight right away. She did not want people to treat her like someone she wasn't. She liked things just the way they had been.

"I'll be right back, you guys. Don't go anywhere." With that she got up and went out to the veranda.

She hesitated momentarily in the doorway, feeling a bit odd. So much had happened in the last two days that, well, she just plain felt odd. Him. Her. Strangers to lovers in what seemed like a blink of an eye.

Zach, seeing her in the doorway, signaled her over to where he was standing. Pulling her close to him, he nuzzled her neck, and whispered in her ear, "You haven't made any mistakes lately that you regretted this morning, have you?"

Giggling, she slugged him in the arm. "Shut up! You're never going to let me forget I made that statement, are you?"

Zach gave her a kiss on the cheek and said, "No, and I guess you see what happens when stubbornness meets an immoveable object."

"Yes, yes I do, and I think the immoveable object won. But Zach," Arianna said, suddenly getting serious, "there is something that's bothering me this morning."

Instantly concerned, he frowned. "What's that?"

"Here. Follow me."

He hesitated a moment but followed her into the kitchen.

"Okay, guys. Listen up." Turning toward Zach, she said, "Please tell everyone that I am perfectly capable of taking care of myself, and that I can still work wherever I want to around here and… and that I don't want any special treatment from them?"

Zach was left to put two and two together. Obviously, word had gotten out that they were now a couple, so his employees likely were unsure as to how to treat her. A statement from him probably was in order.

"Okay. You heard her, everyone. Carry on as before," he said. "Any questions?"

They all shook their heads and said, "No, sir."

Looking back at Arianna, he asked, "Anything else?"

"Nope," she said, surprised that he had actually done what she'd asked.

He nodded slightly and turning, held the door open for her to go back outside. He took her by the hand and led her to the table, pulling a chair out next to his. Taking his own seat, he sat down, and spoke softly to her.

"You know, you don't have to change a thing for me. You're free to spend your time as you like. But you need to understand, that despite what I just said, they're going to make a fuss over you. It's their way of letting you know how much they like you, while honoring me at the same time. I'm afraid you're just going to have to get used to it."

Arianna fidgeted with the silverware, mulling the idea over. "Those people are like friends to me now. It seems odd for them to be treating me like I was someone special. As I told you last night, I'm not comfortable with this lifestyle."

Zach reached for his phone which had been vibrating off the holder on his waistband. He scanned the screen and frowned. "I suspect it will all… work itself out," he said absentmindedly, still studying the message on the screen before snapping the phone back into the case.

Rising suddenly, he said, "Sorry, Arianna, if you'll excuse me, I have to take care of something." He gave her a quick kiss and walked quickly into the house. As if there'd been a silent signal, Tony and Juan rose and followed closely behind him.

"What's up?" Tony asked as they rushed through the house and on out toward the stables where their weapons and military equipment were stored.

"Kevin Baxter, Arianna's partner, just landed in New York. He sent a text to Arianna, wanting to meet up," Zach said. "Unless I miss my guess, I'm pretty sure this mole has a tracer on her phone, so he'll be waiting to hear the details of where this meeting is to take place. We'll make sure the meeting happens and that we're there to give him a proper greeting."

Juan slid the door open to the back of the stable and punched in the code for the entrance to the security bunker that held all their weaponry and mission equipment. "Do we know if this mole even bought into the story we planted at the CIA of Baxter having pictures of us in Kervistan? If the story never got to him, or if he suspects it's a trap, he'll be a no show."

"Don't know. But that's out of our control. All we can do is be ready. The locals have a tail on Baxter, but this is our op to execute." Zach picked up a Barrett M82 rifle and checked and rechecked the scope. With a range of five hundred meters or more, this guy would never see it coming. They could take the mole out and be gone without leaving a trace.

"Roger that," Tony said.

"We need have our gear packed and ready for transport by ten hundred hours. Veritas is sending a helo to pick us up here on the island. They'll take us to a US base where we'll hop a military plane bound for New York."

"Does Baxter know what's going on?"

"Negative," Zach said as he threw more equipment into his duffel bag. "He'll be kept in the dark just like Arianna and Lisa. He can never know of our existence or involvement in this."

"Speaking of kept in the dark, are you planning on saying good bye to Arianna?" Tony asked.

Zach just stared at him, meaning the answer was no.

It was a good question though. He'd had several girlfriends, but none had been allowed to live here. They understood that he "traveled" a lot and had accepted his long absences as part of the relationship with him. There were no questions asked. No explanations given, and it had worked out well in the past. The same was true for the rest of the team- Juan, Tony, and Carlos. When they were home from a mission, girlfriends came for visits, but no move-ins were allowed. The men all lived a true bachelor existence. A couple of men on the team through the years had married and moved on, but for the single guys, separate residences was the rule. It seemed now with Arianna and Lisa forced to stay here, things might become a bit complicated... another reason to wrap this up quickly.

Tony and Juan both shook their heads and smiled.

"What?" Zach asked, seeing the smiles on their faces.

"Something tells me," Tony began, "Arianna's not going to like that. Have you even had a chance to talk to her about any of this... how we live? How you'll be coming and going? Sometimes gone for months at a time with no contact... anything?"

Zach threw the last bit of gear into his duffle bag and zipped it up, not answering.

"Jesus, Zach. She's going to flip out," Tony said. "There's no telling how long we'll be gone... and not a word from you. Not a clue where you're at."

"Okay! I get it," Zach snapped. "Look! This all happened so fast there's been no time to talk any specifics. What I do for a living isn't exactly pillow talk. She's just going to have to deal with it for now. We've got a job to do, so grab your shit, and let's move out."

CHAPTER
31

Home sweet, home. That's all Arianna thought about as she ran along the beach during her midday workout. The whole dynamic of her life here had changed now that she and Zach were a couple. But this change caused her to be extremely anxious for her life to go back to normal. She wanted to see her mom...wanted her to meet Zach. She wanted to work again, and shop, and travel and, and... have a normal dating relationship with Zach. Whew! She paused to catch her breath. Plain and simple. She wanted her former life back with Zach as a part of it.

Lisa met her at the beach house and brought a picnic lunch Pilar had made for them. She poured a glass of merlot and helped herself to some humus and pita chips.

"Any idea when Zach and Tony will be home?" she asked, sitting back and relaxing to the sound of the ocean.

Lisa shook her head. "Tony gave me a quick kiss on the cheek and left with Zach. Said he'd see me later, but didn't say when later was."

Arianna filled her plate with some chicken Caesar salad and began to eat. "Zach had a gun with him last night. Being with him, I felt safe, and for a moment, I almost forgot about the situation I'm in. But sitting here now, a thousand questions are racing through my mind... things I want to ask him, such as why he carries a gun?"

"Good luck getting answers," Lisa said, nibbling on some fruit. "Every time I try to ask Tony something, he changes the subject or gives me some evasive answer."

Arianna moved to the edge of the porch and stood there sipping her wine. "I'm feeling very anxious all of a sudden, and I really want to go home. If Zach would just tell me the truth about what is going on, maybe I could help. After all, as a journalist, I'm used to snooping around and getting to the bottom of a story."

"I'd love to go home, too," Lisa added, "but for now, I think we need to sit tight and let Zach and Tony handle this."

"Yeah, maybe," Arianna said, as they packed things up to go back to the house. "Lisa, do you realize my life has been in upheaval for almost six months now. Ever since I was kidnapped and woke up on this island, one bad thing after the other has happened to me. And now that I have this new relationship with Zach, I don't know..." Her voice trailed off. "I just want this over with. I want my old life back."

ARIANNA SPENT the afternoon working with the lawn crew and then, returned to her room to clean up for dinner. She showered and actually took some time to style her hair and apply a bit of make-up for a change. Looking good was a priority now, but the contents of her closet dismayed her. Whoever had grabbed her clothes from Lisa's house had left all her better things behind. She had nothing nice to wear. Shallow, but this was yet another reason to get back to her normal life.

At about five, she came into the kitchen where she found Pilar preparing dinner. She looked out on the veranda, hoping to see Zach, but the patio was empty.

"I thought Zach might be back by now," she said to Pilar. "Do you know when he's due back?"

Pilar looked up at Arianna and sighed. "I'm afraid he won't be back for a couple of days. Tony, too," she added, seeing Lisa come in behind Arianna. "He had some pressing business to take care of."

"Pressing business? What kind of pressing business?"

"He didn't say. I just know he'll be gone for a few days."

"So, how do you know this?" Arianna had a dubious look on her face. "Did he call?"

"Maybe, but not me," Pilar said as she tossed the dinner salad. "Carlos told me."

"Carlos? So what, Carlos can't tell me? He has to make you the messenger? Zach can't call me himself?" Arianna began to pace back and forth, obviously troubled by this bit of news. She stopped pacing and stared at Pilar who was pulling a pork tenderloin roast out of the oven.

She handed Arianna an electric knife. "Here, would you please carve this for me?"

Arianna took the knife, but hesitated. She wanted to carve something right now, and it wasn't this roast. She felt like she didn't matter. That she was just a pawn in a game whose rules she didn't understand. Did no one trust her? People came and went. Didn't talk to her. Didn't answer questions. Kept her in the dark. She felt her life was totally out of control, and she hated it.

"I don't get it. Lisa, did you hear from Tony?"

Lisa shook her head. "But I'm not as shocked you. Tony told me that sometimes when he works, they go places where there's no internet or cell service."

"Oh, that is so lame! You mean, we're supposed to believe these guys are off in some jungle or third world country somewhere with no way to contact us. He was able to contact Carlos. Why not me? I don't get it. I don't like this." Arianna was becoming more and more agitated as she talked.

Pilar came over and took the knife from her and set it down. She looked her directly in the eye and held both of her arms. "Arianna, listen to me. I know you do not understand this, but do you trust me?"

'Nothing is normal around here, I..."

"Arianna, do you trust me?" Pilar squeezed her arms, as she looked her in the eye. "Calm down, and listen to me."

Arianna was silent and looked at Pilar.

"You need to relax. Zach would not leave unless it was important. He would call if he could. He will explain everything when he returns. If you trust me, then trust him, and be patient until he comes home."

Arianna let out an exasperated sigh. Pilar was right. She needed to relax and stop worrying. Nothing else was normal in her life so why not this.

"Thank you, Pilar. You're right. I need to calm down. My nerves have been shot lately."

ARIANNA SLEPT restlessly and woke the next morning feeling anxious. Just when she thought her life was moving smoothly in a new direction with Zach, things had taken a disappointing turn. Of course, she knew he hadn't disappeared for good, but still, his sudden departure and silence was just another aspect of this saga that was beginning to get to her.

She remembered the first day she arrived here when Pilar had asked her to make Zach's bed and how she had informed Pilar she was not about to lift a finger around here. Time changes everything as they say because now, working and staying busy was the one thing helping her keep her sanity.

Today, her job was to mow the lawn. Jostling along on the riding mower was a menial task that allowed her time to think. In fact, she was so lost in thought, trying to figure out her future she almost missed it. The front gate. It stood wide open with no guards in sight. Surely, this could not be. She circled the mower closer and closer, continuing to watch for any sign of a guard. No one appeared.

Her heart beat faster, and she became more and more excited as she stared at the open gate. She knew leaving was risky, but the prospect of freedom was a huge magnet. She could go where no one could find her. What would be the harm? Zach could continue his pursuit of whoever was supposedly trying to kill her, and when it was safe, they could get back together again. Also, if she had the freedom to move about, she might even be able to help solve this case herself.

On one level it made perfect sense, though a *tiny*, little voice inside her kept saying that somehow Zach wouldn't think her leaving was such a good idea. But really, what was not to like about it? As long as she was safe, why would he care whether she was here or somewhere else? He was gone... he'd left without saying a single word to her. Maybe it was time to step back and take a fresh look at things. Take some of her independence back. Time away from him with time to think, could give her a fresh perspective on things. She was going to go for it.

To get off this island, she needed her passport and picture ID in her room. It had arrived with her purse and clothing brought from Lisa's house. She steered the mower around to the side entrance and rushed down to her room. Scooping up the contents of her purse, she stuffed everything into her pockets and hurried back outside.

Back on the mower, she started riding toward the front gate. A guard was talking to a man by a delivery van up by the front entrance to the house, but the gate was still wide open. She parked the mower behind some tall bushes and shut it down. Sneaking up through the shrubs near the entrance, she turned and slipped out the gate. Once outside, she dashed into the tree line and ran quickly down the side road until she came to the main highway leading back into the city. It didn't take long before she saw a pick-up truck approaching. She waved her hands, and the driver stopped and rolled down his window.

"I work at the casino in town," Arianna said to the young kid driving the truck. "My car wouldn't start. If I miss work one more time, I know they're going to fire me."

"Oh, we can't have that," the kid said. "Hop in."

Thanking him, she jumped into the truck, keeping one hand on the door handle in case this guy turned out to be an ax murderer, and she needed to leap to safety. "Mind if I use your phone?" she asked, seeing his cell phone lying on the seat.

"Sure. Help yourself," he said, smiling broadly, checking her out.

That he found her attractive was both a good and a bad thing, she thought. It could work to her advantage or really cause her problems. She wasn't sure about this hitchhiking thing, but what choice did she have?

"Meet me in front of the *Poseidon* in about fifteen minutes," she told a shocked André when he answered his phone. "I can't talk now, but I'll answer all your questions when I see you."

She needed André's help to get off the island, so she was very thankful to find him waiting for her when she arrived at the club. Thanking the driver, she jumped out of the truck and into André's car.

"Thanks for meeting me," she said, giving him a big hug. "I need your help."

"Arianna, what in the hell are you up to?" André asked. "Does Zach know where you are?"

"No, but look. I had a chance to leave so I took it. I decided to go home."

"Okay. What's going on? I notice you just got out of a pick-up truck. What? Zach's too poor to offer you a ride? And what about that boyfriend who was stalking you? I take it he's out of the picture, now. Otherwise I know you wouldn't be wandering around like this by yourself, right?"

"Oh, André, there's so much I'd like to tell you, but I just can't right now. Please don't ask a lot of questions. Just help me, okay?"

"You know I will, darlin', but I think I liked it better when you were nestled away at Zach's estate."

"Oh, you worry too much. I'll be fine. You see, Zach and I kind of got involved, and I think I fell in love with him. Well, he fell for me too, but he left for a few days, and I have no idea when he's coming back. Anyway, on top of everything else, I think it's just best if I get away and think things through. Everything is happening so fast."

"You and Zach? Man, oh man. Some girls have all the luck," André said.

"You weren't listening to me, André. I said he left and didn't tell me where he was going."

"Well, duh! Maybe he had a good reason. You mean that's why you just decided to take off? Arianna Grant, when are you ever going to learn? Please tell me that's not the only reason you're skipping out of here."

"No, of course not. There are other reasons. I haven't seen my mom in ages and other stuff."

André had a strange look on his face. "Sure. Other stuff. Right, so that's why you arrived in a pick-up truck, with no extra clothes, luggage... nothing, and asking for my help. Yeah, uh huh. All of this would be too much for Zach to help you with, of course. I believe this like you can believe I'm going to screw the town whore tonight."

Arianna giggled.

"Hey, it's not funny," he said. "Is it even safe for you to be traveling around by yourself?"

"As I said, you worry too much. I'll be fine. But right now, I need to get to the airport and get a flight out of here so drive on, please."

CHAPTER

32

H i, sweetie. I was just thinking about you," a surprised Kathryn Garrett said at hearing Arianna's voice on the phone. "Where are you?"

"I'm in Milwaukee, Mom, and I have a lot to tell you, but it will have to wait until I see you."

"Great! I'm just in the process of closing up the office. Are you on your way home?"

"Uh, well, not quite. See, I'm only going to be in town overnight, and I'm staying at a hotel. Can you meet me somewhere for dinner?"

"What? You're staying at a hotel? Why not at home?"

"Well… it's a long story. I'll tell you when I see you. How about meeting me at *Fridays* at Keystone Mall, maybe around seven o'clock? Also, I need you to go home and grab some clothes for me. Nothing too fancy. Some jeans, underwear, and t-shirts will be fine."

There was a long silence on the other end of the phone. Finally, Kathryn asked, "Arianna, why am I bringing you some clothes, and why are you staying in a hotel? What is going on? Are you okay?"

"I know this all sounds weird, Mom, but trust me. I'll explain everything when I see you, and Mom, don't tell anyone I'm in town, okay? It's very important you not tell a soul I'm here."

"Arianna—"

"Really, Mom. Trust me. I can't answer any questions now. I'll fill you in when I see you. Seven o'clock at *Fridays*." She hung up before her mom could ask any more questions.

She knew her mother had to be very confused, but it couldn't be helped. How would she even begin to tell her all she'd been through in the last six months in one short phone call? Leaving the phone booth, she walked across the street to Walmart. She wanted to purchase some toiletries and get a prepaid cell phone. In order to do some investigation on her own, she would need a phone... one nobody could trace. By draining her bank account in Costa Luna, she had been paying cash for everything. She didn't want anyone to be able to trace either her phone calls or to leave a credit card trail.

Next, she went to the Hyatt Regency next to the mall and reserved a room. She knew she couldn't go to her mom's house since Zach said it was being watched. She hoped her mother would spend the night with her. She had missed her, and they had a lot to talk about. She also needed a ride to the airport in the morning. She was catching a flight to New Jersey where she would connect with her old boss, Harold Major. He had contacts who might be able to help her get to the bottom of all this. She was tired of this death threat hanging over her head and instead of sitting idly by as a victim, she was determined to try to do her part to resolve the situation.

After completing her room reservation, she left the hotel, went to *Fridays,* and took a seat at the bar to wait for her mother. As she sipped on a glass of merlot, she felt her body relax for the first time since she had left Zach's house that morning. Not totally relax, however. Doubts began to creep in.

Thinking things through now, it occurred to her how flawed this plan really was. Plan was probably too strong a word actually. This move was more like an impulsive, knee-jerk reaction to seeing an open gate... a gate that spoke of quick freedom and had drawn her through it like someone sucked into a vortex. Sure, she told herself this was the chance to go home, connect with her mother, and have some time to relax. To think her situation through. Once she found a secure place to stay, the plan was to call Zach with her location and everything would be wonderful. After all, he wasn't even home right now himself. It would be hard for him to miss her.

Only problem was, she now realized she didn't even know Zach's phone number…or email address. Nothing. She had no way to contact him. How stupid was that? Not hopeless… she figured André could get a message through to Zach, but this move rated right up there with one of the more impulsive, irrational, stupid things she'd ever done. As the sun faded, a feeling of trepidation crept over her, and she began to question her decision to leave. No going back now, however. She needed to forge ahead, stay out of sight, and be safe.

She saw her mother enter the restaurant, so she threw some money down for the bar tab and then rushed over to meet her. As they embraced, tears began to form in her eyes. She didn't want to break down, but something about finally being with her mother again, caused her to nearly fall to pieces.

Kathryn took a step back and began to wipe Arianna's tears. "Hey, sweetie, what's wrong? I know something's wrong, Arianna. This whole arrangement is crazy. What's going on?"

Arianna snuffed up her tears and did her best to pull herself together. "I have a lot to tell you, Mom, but first, let's get a table. We can talk over dinner."

The hostess led them to a table, and a waitress welcomed them and took their order.

"I've been following you on Facebook," Kathryn said as the waitress left. "The last posting I saw said you were in London working on a story. When did you get back to the States?"

Arianna shook her head. Someone had sure done a good job of fabricating her life to all her Facebook friends. Not even her mother thought she was missing.

"No, Mom. That was all made up."

"What? You just made that up? Why would you do that?"

Ahh! Where to begin? As they sipped their drinks and waited for their food to arrive, Arianna began to share the Cliff note's version of all that had transpired since she'd been in Kervistan. Kathryn's mouth was agape from the moment Arianna first said the word kidnapped until her last words about leaving Costa Luna earlier in the day.

"Wow! This is unbelievable, Arianna. Also quite scary. Thank God for your friend Zach. Seems like he saved your life. I can't wait to meet him."

Arianna's heart caught in her throat. Yes, she indeed owed him her life and yes, she too couldn't wait for her mother to meet him. But it was just too difficult for her to think about him right now.

"From what you've told me though, I don't think he'll be very happy to have you running around all by yourself," she heard her mother say. "Is it even safe for you to be here? You said someone is watching my house."

Arianna sighed. There was a definite risk to her being in the city, but she didn't want to scare her mom by expressing any personal concerns she had.

"As long as no one knows where I am, I'll be safe. I'm flying to New Jersey tomorrow to connect with my old boss. I'm pretty sure he'll hide me out, and I know he has some connections that can help resolve this. In the meantime, I'm hoping you can stay with me tonight so we can spend more time together."

Kathryn yawned and nodded. They had been talking for almost three hours. "I'd love to. It's getting late to drive home anyway. Shall we take some dessert to go? I think there's more to discuss. Let's settle in for the night and continue this discussion over coffee and cheese cake."

They left the restaurant and proceeded to Kathryn's car to retrieve Arianna's clothing. Out of nowhere, a van came skidding to a stop beside them. Two masked men jumped out, grabbed them, threw them into the van, and then, sped off. A cloth with a strange odor covered Arianna's face, and in seconds, she blacked out.

When she came to, she found herself on the floor of an office in what looked like an abandoned warehouse with her mother lying beside her, still passed out. Two men were sitting at a nearby table, guns lying prominently in front of them. Her worst nightmare had just come true. One of the men was Dan Jeffers, the FBI agent. The man Zach said wished to do her great bodily harm.

Arianna reached over to check her mother, gently shaking her, trying to rouse her. God! What had she gotten her into? What had she gotten herself into? Fear such as she'd never known before, gripped her. Leaving Zach's house had been a terrible mistake. She didn't know how these men had found her so fast, but at this point, it didn't matter. They had, and she knew it would take a miracle for her to make it out of this predicament alive.

A hand grabbed her and dragged her up and into a chair. "Ah, Miss Garrett. We meet again," Jeffers, aka Karl Reichter-CIA mole, snarled. "We need to finish our little talk which was so rudely interrupted on the beach."

Arianna just glared at him.

"I have many questions, and I think if you value your mother's life, you'll tell me everything I want to know."

Yes, she'd do anything to protect her mother, but she was smart enough to know once he got the information he wanted from her, he'd kill her and her mother. The only hope for one or both of them getting out of here unharmed was to try to negotiate with him. She'd promise to give them the information he wanted in exchange for her mother's safe return home. Once she knew her mother was safe, she'd give him the information he wanted. She didn't know how she'd get out alive, but at least her mother would live.

One problem. She remembered Zach said they were after information she couldn't give them because she didn't have it. If that was true, she'd have to make up something pretty convincing or there would be no negotiation…only termination for both her and her mom.

She looked around for possibilities of escape. Things didn't look promising. Reichter stood over her, breathing down her neck. There were two other men in the room and possibly someone outside the door. Escape seemed impossible.

Seeing her mother stir, Arianna jumped down from the chair, brushed past Reichter, and went to her side. "Mom, are you okay?" She tried to help her to a sitting position.

"Mmmm!" Kathryn moaned, holding her head. "Where are we? What happened?"

"Mom, I'm afraid we're in some really bad trouble now. This is the guy who has been looking for me," she said, a slight quiver in her voice.

"Arianna, you have to try to be brave," Kathryn said. "Maybe if you tell them the information they came for, they will let us go."

"Sure, Mom," Arianna replied, but she knew it was just the opposite. As soon as she told Reichter what he wanted to know, he would kill both of them. No sense adding to her mother's concern so she said, "Try to relax, Mom. I'll handle this." She looked back at Reichter who was glaring menacingly at her, and repeated, "I'll handle this."

F uck!" Zach snapped his phone back in its case and signaled to Tony and Juan to break off the operation and move out.

Tony was the first to catch up to Zach as he threw his gear into the SUV.

"What the hell? Why are we scrubbing this op?"

"Arianna's been kidnapped."

"What! How? When?"

"I have no idea," Zach fumed, "but someone fucked up. Get in. We need to get to Milwaukee ASAP."

The team had been on a stake out, waiting for the CIA mole, Karl Reichter, to come for a meeting with Kevin Baxter. He was already a half an hour late. Now, they knew why. He had gone to Wisconsin to interrogate Arianna. Zach and his team had to play catch up.

FOR A month, it had been a case of surveillance and counter surveillance. This mole had put local people in place to watch Kathryn Garrett's house and had monitored her home phone hoping Arianna would either show up or call. On the other hand, Zach had his own people who were watching these people to make sure Kathryn was safe in case they decided to snatch her in an effort to bring Arianna out of hiding.

So it was thanks to the men working for Zach, that they were able to pick-up right away on the women's kidnapping. They weren't quick enough to prevent it, but they were able to follow and see where the kidnappers held the two women. In fact, the local agents had been told to stand down and wait until Zach arrived.

"How the hell did Arianna get to Milwaukee anyway?" Juan asked.

"I have no idea," Zach replied as the SUV sped toward the airport. "Someone fucked up back at the house. Trust me. Heads are going to roll when I get home."

"I doubt that, Zach. Whoever was asleep at the switch and let Arianna slip out of there is probably long gone because he knows he's toast as soon as you get your hands on him."

After a two-hour flight, Zach and the team arrived at the warehouse where the women were being held. It was now around two o'clock in the morning. Several men from the Agency met them there. Zach, Tony and Juan had already changed into full camo. No one, not even Arianna would recognize them. There may come a time when he might divulge to her just how he made his living, but not tonight. Veritas had sent some agents to the scene to set up surveillance. All they'd been told was that an elite rescue team would be joining them soon and that this was their op to execute.

"Here's what we have," the lead agent said as he began to brief Zach. "We think there are about seven men inside, identities unknown, weapons unknown. One man arrived alone about an hour before you got here. Don't know if that's significant or not."

Zach wasn't sure either. He could only hope it was the mole. He not only wanted Arianna safely out of there but also wanted to eliminate this spy to remove the death threat hanging over her head.

"All of this information is sketchy," the agent continued, "because we've had to run surveillance from a distance to avoid detection. We've got a helo up with infrared thermal-imaging capability. It picked up the images of five people in this room on the second floor," he said pointing to a rough map of the warehouse. "We think this where they are holding the girl and her mother. We've also got images here, here and here... probably additional guards," he said pointing to a rough map of the warehouse.

"What about audio?" Zach asked. "You have any ears in place?"

"Negative. We were told to stand down and let you handle this so that's what we've done."

"Roger that," Zach said and pulled Tony and Juan aside. "I don't think I have to tell you what's at stake here," he said grimly. "We've got to get to Arianna and her mother before we're detected. If they hear or see us coming, those woman are history."

The men nodded.

"I figure they'll work Arianna over to get the information they think she has. I'm guessing it won't be pretty," Zach continued. "If she doesn't give them the information they want, they'll kill her. They'll kill her one way or the other," he said with a slight catch in his throat. "We've got to get to her fast."

Zach would use the local agents to get the women safely away after they were rescued, but he only trusted himself and his men to execute the rescue. They were trained for this. This is what they did for a living, but never had the stakes been so personally high. He had to forget who was in the room up there and check his emotions at the front door.

The building was pitch black, so they needed night vision goggles in order to pick their way quietly to the second floor. They were mic'd though they would maintain strict radio silence. They had enough firepower to blow the building, but that wasn't even close to being the plan. With luck, it would be a quick bang, bang, bang... bad guys dead. Ladies rescued. Good guys go home.

"Okay. Time to get your sneak on," Zach said as they approached the side door.

Juan slipped the door open while everyone waited, hidden in place. A man came to see who was there. Tony stepped up behind him and snapped his neck, dropping him silently to the ground. Zach tossed a pebble through the doorway and waited for a response.

Seeing and hearing nothing, the three of them moved inside and switched to night vision.

As Zach edged his way through the building, he began to pick up sounds of men yelling and, what seemed like women crying out or screaming, he couldn't tell which. He knew they must be interrogating Arianna, and if they had her in tears, this was not a good sign. She had to be enduring some pretty rough treatment.

Zach was on point, and when he turned a corner heading up the stairs, his night vision picked up the image of a man down the hall. He quickly ducked back and waited. Wanting to draw the guy's attention, he again tossed a pebble across the floor. When the man came to check the noise, Zach grabbed him from behind, swiftly and silently snapping his neck. Pulling the body back into an alcove, the way was now clear to move to the second floor.

The sound of yelling and a woman crying was quite distinct as they got to the top of the stairs, and he saw a light coming from a door just down the hall. The three of them moved to the entrance and waited. Zach threaded a thin fiber-optic camera through the crack in the door and what he saw, caused his blood to boil.

The kidnappers had tied Arianna to a chair with her hands bound behind her and her blouse ripped open. Blood was running down the side of her face. A man Zach did not recognize, but who he hoped was this illusive mole, was leaning over Arianna, barking questions at her as he ran his hands across her chest. Infuriated, Arianna spit in his face causing the guy to rear back and slap her soundly. Kathryn let out a scream and attempted to rush to her aid as Arianna and the chair hit the floor hard.

Damn, as much as he'd admired Arianna's courage in the past, he feared it now. This time it would only get her in more trouble than she could handle. The man righted Arianna's chair and started to interrogate her once more. Zach prayed this time she would just sit there meekly and not piss this guy off again. Probably not going to happen. The Arianna he knew would fight and resist with all her might. As he watched, he struggled to contain himself. Tony's hand on his shoulder helped him recall his SEAL training. Keep your emotions in check and execute the mission.

He'd seen enough. It was time to act. Using only sign language, he signaled the plan to Juan and Tony. Tony would blow the door open, and he and Juan would push through. By the time Zach finished with the signals, each man knew exactly how many hostiles were in the room, their location in the room, what kind of weapons everyone had, where Arianna and her mother were located, and which direction each of them would take upon entry. The last signal reminded them they would go as soon as the door was blown and to go loud.

They'd been through drills like this before and had practiced this situation until they could execute the maneuver with precision. They would hit hard and fast, and one way or the other, it would be over in seconds. The only difference was, never before had the stakes been so personally high.

Zach was waiting for the mole to move away from Arianna for even a second. He seemed intent on hovering over her, copping feels, and spitting questions at her…questions about him he could hear clearly through the door.

"I know you know who the guy from Kervistan is. You are either going to tell me, or I am going to kill your fucking mother," Reichter said and moved toward Kathryn.

This was it. The time was now. "Three, two, one." Zach counted down and signaled, "Go time."

Tony blew the door, and with no hesitation, Zach and Juan rushed through, rolling right, rolling left and back to their feet, weapons blazing. The attack was on.

Zach took Arianna's chair to the floor with a swift but firm kick of his foot, getting her out of the line of fire. Reichter and his men got off a few shots, but missed Zach and his team. One by one, they cut down every hostile in the room. But the fight was not over yet. Two more men came through another door firing. Zach dropped to one knee and took out the first man with a shot to the head, while Tony shot and killed the second assailant.

ARIANNA COULDN'T believe what was happening. Swarming out of nowhere, she saw three commandos, camouflaged from head to toe. One commando had swiftly taken her chair to the floor, putting her safely below the gunfire. She saw her mom lying nearby, pushed behind a desk by another commando. She'd never been so scared in her life. Real bullets, real blood, and real people lying dead all around her.

When the action died down, the first commando came back to her side and sat her chair upright. Untying her, he made a quick inspection of her face, pausing to examine the cut on her lip and a gash above her eye. Blood was pouring down her face, so he grabbed a bandana from around his neck and tied it around her head to stem the bleeding. He made a quick check of her arms and legs for other wounds and then, pulled his t-shirt off and put it on her, covering her shredded blouse.

Arianna was so happy to finally be safe she threw her arms around the commando's neck and sobbed. Whoever this guy was, she owed him her life.

"You saved my life. Thank you so much," she cried as she clung onto him. For an instant, the man returned her embrace, but then, suddenly, he pulled her arms off of him and sat her into a chair and signaled she should stay there. He moved away and began snapping pictures of the dead men while the other commandos removed wallets and cell phones and put them in bags. Finally, her commando savior returned and took her by the wrist, then signaled to the rest of the men to move out. They all headed silently for the exit.

In contrast to the initial tenderness he'd shown, as they made their way out of the building, the commando now had a painful grip on her arm and was dragging her along in such an abrupt manner, her feet hardly touched the ground. *Boy! This guy is rough.* She glanced back over her shoulder and was happy to see her mother was at least being carried gently out of the building by one of the other men in the group. As for herself, her escort seemed angry and in a hurry, dragging her swiftly along behind him.

The women were hustled to a waiting SUV where another man in a suit greeted them. Before Arianna knew what was happening, the commando hoisted her unceremoniously into the backseat. Her rescuer took one long, last look at her and then, slammed the door so hard it shook the vehicle. Arianna shuddered at the force and fury of its impact and looked after him. Something about him really unnerved her. The door opened on the other side of the van, and the other commando carefully placed her mother in the vehicle. He reached across and gently rubbed Arianna's cheek with his knuckle and then, left as the man in the suit joined the women in the van.

Such extremely different responses from two of her rescuers. One tender and affectionate and the other seemingly as mad as hell. She looked out the window at the man who had brought her out of the building. He was standing by the car talking to two men in suits. He looked back in her direction one more time and then, left with the rest of the commando team. The remainder of the men in suits piled into cars, and in a matter of minutes, the parking lot was empty. At some point, the local police would find only seven nameless men, lying dead in a room littered with drugs and drug paraphernalia. The true details of what went down tonight would never be known.

"Ms. Garrett," the man in the suit said, flashing a badge she barely had time to look at. She didn't know if he was MPD, FBI, or CIA. He could have flashed a Boy Scout badge for all she knew.

"I just need to ask you a few questions. Are you feeling well enough to talk for a moment?"

Arianna nodded.

"Very good, then. This won't take long," he said as the SUV pulled out of the parking lot. He took out a notebook and prepared to take notes. "First of all, what can you tell me about the guy who questioned you? Was he the same man you saw on the beach in Costa Luna?"

Arianna nodded again.

"What did you tell him about where you've been? Specifically, did you give him any names or talk about the location where you'd been hiding?"

Arianna dabbed at the cut on her head which was still seeping blood. "Nothing. I told him I would tell him everything he wanted to know as soon as he let my mother go. I figured he was going to kill me. Maybe I could save her."

"You're very brave, Ms. Garrett." He offered her his handkerchief. "Are you sure you didn't give out any more information... names, places, anything we should know about?"

She'd stalled and equivocated. As she said, she was determined to at least secure her mother's freedom.

"Sir, Arianna put her own life and well-being in danger, trying to protect me and not implicate anyone else in this situation," Kathryn interjected. "I almost wish she had told them something. It was painful to sit there and watch the brutal treatment she was enduring. I'm so proud of my daughter."

"Yes, her bravery is commendable. I'll put that in my report and let the appropriate people know." He snapped his notebook shut. "Well, that's all the questions I have for now. I see we've reached the hospital. Let's get those wounds looked at. And, Ms. Garrett, I think you can understand that it's probably best you not discuss the events of this evening if you know what I mean."

Of course, she did, yet didn't completely know what he meant, but she'd be happy to not talk about the hell she'd just been through. Thank God, the rescuers had arrived when they did. No one would ever know how close she'd come to caving. She was in shock at the moment, but was sure when the adrenaline wore off, the realization that she'd looked death in the eye and survived would come crashing down on her. With any luck, someone would be there to catch her when she crashed.

CHAPTER

34

Who was that guy? The man had flashed a badge at her, but Arianna took little notice of it. Still in shock, she had no idea what government entity the man who accompanied her to the hospital professed to work for. And who were all the other men at the scene, she wondered? It was so strange how all of them had packed up their cars and left at the same time. No police tape. No police officers milling around. All that remained was an empty parking lot. And of course, she still had no idea what information she was supposed to have that the mole was trying to beat out of her. She suspected the answer to that question rest with Zach, and thus, well...

"I'm afraid we're going to need a plastic surgeon to close this gash above your eye," she heard the ER doctor say, "otherwise you'll have a nasty scar, my dear. Your lip is cut too, but it should heal okay without stitches. And all this bruising and swelling will go down in time. Put some cold compresses on your face when you get home."

As Arianna waited for the plastic surgeon to arrive, her mother came into the examining room. Other than some minor scrapes and bruises, she was in much better shape than Arianna.

"How are you feeling?" Kathryn asked.

"Probably like I look... which is like hell."

Kathryn grimaced. "I wanted to kill that man with my bare hands, but I felt helpless. I'm so glad help arrived when it did."

Arianna lay back on the examining table, not answering. Not wanting to talk really.

"I called Jim to come take us home," Kathryn said. Jim Evans was her longtime boyfriend. "He said he'd be here in about a half an hour."

Arianna nodded and sat up as the plastic surgeon, along with a nurse, entered the room.

"Just a pinch," the doctor said as he administered the first shot to numb the site. "This is the worst part. Once we get you numbed up, you won't feel a thing."

The surgeon attempted to ask her questions about how she received the injury, but Arianna knew not to tell the real story, a story best left as a classified matter, so she made up a lie about being mugged and pushed down to the sidewalk.

"Sorry to hear that, but we'll get you fixed up good as new. This cut is in the brow line," the doctor said as he sutured the wound. "It will never be noticed once I'm finished. I'm also sending you home with some pain meds. You're going to be sore for several days. Come see me in my office in ten days, and I'll take these stitches out. Now, unless you have any questions, you're free to go."

"Thank you, Doctor," Arianna said, slipping off the examining table. She gathered her things and made her way to the lobby where she stopped by admissions to check out.

"There's no charge," the registrar said. "The bill's been paid."

"What do you mean?" Arianna asked. She knew she didn't have any insurance, and she wasn't covered on her mother's anymore either.

"Just that," the woman behind the desk repeated. "Your bill has been all taken care of."

"By who?"

The clerk shuffled through some papers and checked her computer screen. "Hmmm. This is strange. I can't really tell by the information I have here, but it is paid. All I see is balance due, zero. There's an account override and my supervisor's initials. Hey, don't knock it. Looks like someone's been looking out for you tonight."

"Thank you," Kathryn said to the person behind the desk and took Arianna by the arm. "Come on. I see Jim waiting at the curb. Let's get you home."

The three arrived at Kathryn's house as the sun rose on the horizon, but everyone was too hyped up to sleep. Kathryn put a pot of coffee on and decided to make them some breakfast. As Jim and Kathryn ate and Arianna held an ice pack on her cheek and lip, the women attempted to fill Jim in on Arianna's long ordeal and the events of the kidnapping. They had been talking for over an hour, when Kathryn finally asked the question that had been in the back of Arianna's mind the whole time.

"Shouldn't you call someone?" she asked. "Maybe Zach or Lisa?"

Now, there was a question. It seemed logical, but she knew that somehow Zach already knew what had happened. She also felt he must have been connected to this rescue though she wasn't sure how. Yes, calling him seemed like the logical thing to do that was for sure. They could celebrate the fact that this ordeal was over. But no, not really. Somehow, Arianna also knew that calling him was exactly the *wrong* thing to do.

Finally, at about seven, she succumbed to Kathryn's pressure to take a pain pill. Arianna hated medicine, but her head was starting to throb, so she relented. Tired and needing sleep, she made her way to her bedroom. She could no longer think about the narrow escape today, or how scared she'd been, or how thankful she was to be rescued.

Standing in her bathroom, she looked in the mirror and was horrified at seeing her face. She had several noticeable stitches above her eye, a deep purple bruise covered her cheek, her hair was matted with blood, and her lip was cut and swollen. Slowly her eyes trailed down to the blood stained t-shirt the commando had put on her, and suddenly, a rush of sentiment washed over her. He had been so tender, so caring... so protective of her. But like a chameleon, he had also been extremely rough with her as they left the building. She thought it was odd the two extremes from the same person.

Slipping off the shirt, she held it close and smelled it before laying it down. The scent seemed vaguely familiar. She wasn't sure why. Covered with her blood and his sweat, what would be familiar about that? She stepped into the shower and let the water pour over her as she tried to wash away the remnants of her horrible ordeal.

Exiting the shower, she reached for some pajamas, then stopped, drawn back to the t-shirt. She didn't know why, but instead of donning her pajamas, she slipped back into the shirt. She remembered fondly how gallant that commando had been to cover her near nakedness.

She moved gingerly to her bed, the pain pills making her very drowsy. Physically and emotionally spent, she fell soundly asleep wrapped in the warmth of a stranger's t-shirt.

IT WAS late afternoon when she heard the phone ring. As she fumbled for it, every muscle in her body ached, and her head was throbbing.

"Hi, Arianna. It's me, Lisa," the voice on the other end said.

"Oh, hey Lisa," Arianna mumbled weakly, her lip so swollen she could barely talk.

"I called to see how you're doing. Are you all right?"

"Yeah, I think so. Just a couple of stitches and some bruises..." her voice trailed off.

"You still there, Arianna?" Lisa asked.

There was a moment of silence before Arianna answered. "Yeah, I just hurt all over. No major injuries."

"I heard you had a close call. Why'd you leave here anyway?"

"I don't know, Lisa. Why do I do anything I do? I'm dumb, I guess."

"It *was* dumb, Arianna, but you're all right, and that's what's important. At least this thing is over now."

"Yeah, that's good."

"I don't think that man will ever bother us again."

There was a long silence on the phone.

"Arianna, are you still there?" Lisa asked again.

"Yeah, I'm ...." She paused once more. She was in such pain and misery she could barely talk.

"Well, since you won't ask, Arianna, I'll tell you. I haven't spoken to him directly, but it seems like Zach is not very happy with you. He was furious when he found out you were gone. I heard him screaming and yelling all over the house, and I thought he was going to kill that one guard. He had him by the throat up against the wall. Tony had to pull him off of him."

Arianna began to cry softly. She knew she had blown it. Her taking off had been a slap in the face to Zach and all he had tried to do for her. When would she ever learn? Her impatience and impulsiveness always seemed to get her into trouble.

"Lisa, I gotta go," she said.

"No, wait, Ari. Maybe you could just call Zach..."

"Sure and say what?"

"Well, tell him you're sorry."

"Somehow I don't think sorry will be quite enough."

"Well, maybe Tony could talk to him."

"Lisa, listen. You take care, okay?" Arianna said, not able to talk any longer. There was no way Tony would talk to Zach either.

The tears were streaming down her cheeks as she hung up the phone. She couldn't remember when she'd felt such despair and anguish. To find true love after so many years only to lose it because of her stupidity was almost more than she could bear.

There was a soft knock at her door. "Arianna, are you awake?" Kathryn asked, coming into the room. "Oh, hey. What's wrong, honey?" she asked, seeing Arianna's tears.

Arianna completely broke down and sobbed in her mother's arms, crying bitterly for her loss. A loss she knew surely existed. Zach would not call her, and her pride would not let her call him, a call that would bring no good anyway. She didn't think you jerked Zach Acevedo around like this and then, just called him, expecting to pick up where you left off.

"Oh, Arianna, just give it some time," Kathryn said. "If he loves you as you said he did, I believe he'll be back."

"No, Mom. You don't know Zach. He won't."

"WHAT NOW?" Tony asked as they sat by the pool nursing a couple of beers.

"We go back to work," Zach said, taking a long sip of his drink.

"I meant about Arianna," Tony said.

"Yes, I know. The answer is, nothing for now. We go back to work, and we see what happens when we get home."

They were long overdue to report to their next assignment, a month long mission that would find them training a band of contra rebels in Central America. Unofficially, he and his men would be supplying US weapons and training to the rebel forces who in turn would try to oust the current ruling drug lords in their country. If it worked, it was money well spent by the US, not to mention the fact that it didn't put any US soldiers in harm's way.

The mission called for them to work sterile which meant that all their weapons and equipment would be stripped of any "made in the USA" labels in case they fell into the wrong hands. It was a risky operation, but then, they all were. That's why, once again, the government was paying him a small fortune to do this.

But Arianna. She weighed heavily on his mind. He loved her. He knew he did, despite how mad he was at her right now. He was concerned about how she was doing, but his man had phoned him from the hospital with the doctor's report, and it was pretty much as he'd suspected. Other than the nasty gash and a cut lip, there were no major injuries.

Emotionally was a different story, however. She was really shaken up, but in a way, it served her right. Leaving here in defiance of his specific orders had almost gotten her and her mother killed. She ought to be shaken up. In fact if she were here right now, he'd be tempted to give her something even more to be shaken up about. It was just as well for her that she was a thousand miles away.

So, now what, Tony had asked? With the elimination of Reichter, there was no further need for Zach's protection. Arianna could safely return to her former life. Only one small catch. He wanted her to be a part of his life. To come live with him, eventually anyway.

The problem was, he led no ordinary life. Certainly not one that lent itself to sharing it with anyone on a fulltime basis. But his work had been enough until now. Now, he realized he wanted more. He wanted his work *and* her if he could have both of them.

But this incident had proven just how difficult it would be to bring anyone into his world. He had just rescued the woman he loved but couldn't even reveal himself to her. Could never let her know how he made his living or provide any valid explanations for his long absences from home. How long would she tolerate that in a relationship, or would she? Even this incident now had started because he'd left without telling her his whereabouts.

He didn't know how their relationship would work out in the end, but he did know that she had captured his soul, and he'd be forever restless if he let her go.

So, for now he didn't plan on doing anything but let her reflect on her erroneous choices. He figured he'd see how he felt when he returned from Central America. Time apart might provide more clarity.

"Lisa talked to her you know," Tony said.

"And?"

"And, I guess she feels really bad. I think she knows she screwed up."

Zach just shook his head and drained the rest of his beer. "She should feel bad. She almost got us all killed, and since we'll be gone for a month, she'll have plenty of time to ponder her mistake."

But then he'd also have a whole month alone without her so she wouldn't be the only one feeling bad. He was suffering, too.

CHAPTER

35

I t had been a week, and Arianna languished in bed. The physical aches and pains had subsided, but the ache in her heart raged on. How ironic that she had rationalized leaving Zach's house by saying she needed time and space to sort out her feelings. Separated from him now, there was nothing to sort out. She loved him totally and completely and desperately wanted him back.

As time passed, that seemed less and less likely. He had not contacted her, and her pride would not let her contact him. But it wasn't just the pride thing. She couldn't see it doing any good.

In the beginning, she'd been skittish about a relationship with Zach because of the differences in their economic backgrounds. Now, she could have cared less. However, it was too late. Since she had totally insulted him and screwed up his efforts to keep her safe, she figured she'd made an irreconcilable mess of things. Reluctantly, she realized she'd just have to live with the consequences of her actions and move on, but she was tortured by her tragic blunder.

Lisa had called. She was home in Chicago and wanted Arianna to come visit her.

"The guys have gone on some kind of business trip," Lisa said, "so I came home to visit my parents. I think Tony said they'd be gone for several weeks. It didn't make sense to me, however, something about the way Tony looked at me, told me not to ask questions, so I just dropped the subject."

"That's a long time," Arianna said.

"Yeah, so why don't you come visit me?"

Arianna wanted desperately to see Lisa again, but she knew it would be too painful right now.

"Lisa, I'm trying to put this behind me and seeing you would be a painful reminder of what I've lost."

"Oh, that's silly. I think you're just being overly stubborn, and I also think you should contact Zach when he gets home."

Arianna knew she wouldn't. "I've never called a guy in my life, and I'm not about to start now, especially not Zach. I'd be making a complete fool of myself. My pride just won't let me."

"That's exactly what I mean," Lisa said. "You're being *way* too stubborn for your own good. You were wrong and should apologize."

"Lisa, I think I could apologize, however, my instincts tell me anything that's going to be done will be done within Zach's time frame and on his terms if at all. I think if I called him now, he would more or less tell me thank you but no thank you. I'm not about to set myself up for rejection like that. So you see, there's really nothing I can do."

Lisa thought about it and decided Arianna was probably right. She just prayed Zach would come to his senses and call her when he came home. She really couldn't see him doing that either. He could be just as stubborn as Arianna when he wanted to.

IF IT had been left solely up to Arianna, she would have been content to continue to languish in her room. Her mother had other ideas. There had been another time when she'd seen her daughter like this. It had been Arianna's senior year, and she'd been dumped by Derek Watson. Kathryn vowed to never again let Arianna mope around in despair for weeks on end as she had over Derek. Having tragically lost a husband, Kathryn knew from experience the best thing one could do for themselves was to get busy. Arianna needed to go back to work.

"Mom, I really don't think I'm ready," Arianna protested, when Kathryn brought up the subject. "I need to rest some more."

"No, ma'am, you do not," Kathryn said. "Your eye has healed, and you can barely see where you were hurt. Just a little touch of make-up and you'll look as good as new." She knew there were still wounds... internal wounds of the heart only time could heal.

Arianna had no enthusiasm for this idea but grew tired of her mother's constant nagging. She knew she would not hear the end of it until she found a job and made an attempt to return to a normal life. So, she took the path of least resistance and called André. Singing with his band would give her a bit of income and get her out of the house without having to put any effort into what she was doing. In other words, she could stay lost in an emotionless limbo.

"Well, you're in luck, darlin'," André responded, when Arianna called him. "I have a gig lined up in Miami if you're interested."

Not really but, if she expected to get her mother off her back, she knew she had to take it. So, it was with a heavy heart she found herself on a flight to Miami. She'd go through the motions, hoping that time would eventually ease the constant dull ache she had in the pit of her stomach.

André had booked a gig in one of the trendy nightspots of South Beach. The city teemed with the young, the beautiful, and affluent, and an abundance of phony relationships. The women gave and the men got... and gave, too, usually with their wallets. Money, jewels, and a large assortment of other luxury items. One way or the other, they gave. And the number of lasting relationships ever really formed was likely miniscule.

Arianna detested this environment. She much preferred performing for the college crowds at the spring break locations. She had to start working again somewhere, so this place was as good as any.

Todd Martin had attended every one of her performances for two weeks now, and he'd asked her out every single time. He was handsome enough, and it didn't hurt that he was one of Miami's wealthiest residents, but Arianna felt nothing for him. Besides, her heart was closed. Walled up and sealed off, it was impenetrable at the moment.

Now, Martin wanted to hire André's entire band, including her to perform for his quests at a weekend bash he was hosting at his multi-million dollar, ocean side mansion. In addition to performing, he'd insisted that she and André spend the weekend as his special guests.

"No way," Arianna insisted, when André brought it up. "He's just looking for a chance to hook up with me, and that's not happening," she told André.

"Please," André countered. "He's one of Miami's wealthiest residents. He can open all kinds of doors for me professionally. This is a great business opportunity."

Arianna shot him a look that said, please tell me you're kidding.

"Pretty please," he pleaded, looking at her with big puppy dog eyes.

"Okay," she'd said begrudgingly. She owed André so much. How could she say no? "But if Todd makes one wrong move, I'm out of there."

"Deal! Thank you. Thank you. Thank you," André said, very glad Arianna had agreed.

The plan was for them to arrive on Friday evening with the rest of the guests. They would enjoy a poolside cookout and then, dancing to music provided by a DJ. On Saturday, Arianna and the band would give one short performance in the afternoon and a longer one after dinner.

Todd agreed Arianna would have her own private bedroom, and he encouraged her to make herself at home and enjoy the weekend with the rest of the guests. Arianna's translation of all this was that he considered her his date and thus had high hopes of making it with her before the weekend was over. She'd indulge his misguided fantasy for the sake of keeping things status quo, but in truth, there was no way she was going to become romantically involved with him.

Friday night's cookout actually turned out to be just as dismal as she'd anticipated. Todd seemed to be right at her elbow every time she turned around despite her best attempts to avoid him. Finally, weary of the battle, she feigned a headache and turned in early, leaving André by himself to schmooze the guests in search of future bookings.

She slept in as late as she dared on Saturday, and then asked for some breakfast to be sent to her room where she stayed until noon. Realizing that she had finally run out of excuses for not appearing, she dressed and made her way to the pool where most of the guests had congregated.

Todd was the first to greet her, thrilled she had finally joined them. Normally, the life of the party at any pool gathering, on this day she sat stoically by herself off to the side. Todd continued to smother her with attention to the point she was relieved when three o'clock rolled around, and it was time for her afternoon performance.

It was in the middle of this set that she saw him. Zach strolled into the party followed by Tony, Lisa, Juan and his girlfriend. On Zach's arm was a stunning brunette. Petite and delicate, she had a radiant smile that was captivating. Arianna's heart clinched in her chest and for a moment, she couldn't breathe. It took all the internal fortitude she could muster to stay on the stage and keep singing.

Zach's expression was unreadable, and he never took his eyes off her, though Arianna took great care not to look at him. Seeing Zach alone would have been shock enough. Seeing him with another woman was excruciating.

"Hey, Zach!" Todd said, slapping him on the back. "I was beginning to think you weren't coming, but you came just in time. Isn't she something else?" he asked, motioning toward Arianna singing on the stage.

Zach returned Todd's greeting, never responding to his question about Arianna.

"Yeah," Todd beamed. "She's not just the entertainment, you know. She's my date for the weekend."

Zach instantly saw red. The thought of Todd being with Arianna caused him to do a slow boil. "No, I didn't know," he said, struggling to tamp down his anger.

"Yeah, but hey, who's this lovely young lady?" Todd asked, looking at the girl standing beside Zach.

"This is my sister, Camilla Acevedo," Zach responded. "She's visiting from Puerto Rico."

"Ah, so nice to meet you, Camilla. Now, I see the resemblance. Welcome to Miami. I'm glad you could join us," he said kissing her hand.

Turning to Zach he said, "I thought I heard you were dating one of your servants. Had to consider the source though. Ran into Lydia a couple of weeks ago, and she was ranting on and on about your breakup. Any chance you two will get back together?"

"No, none."

"Well, anyway, grab a drink and make yourself at home. There are actually several single ladies floating around here. Who knows? You just might get lucky. When this set is over, I'll introduce you to Arianna, but just remember she's with me," he said with a wink.

ZACH WAS shocked to see Arianna at the party. His people in Milwaukee were slipping. They were supposed to be keeping tabs on Arianna and her comings and goings while he was away on his latest mission. No one had indicated she had left the city. He'd be making some personnel changes when he got home. You couldn't make these kinds of mistakes and continue to work for his organization.

Zach made sure he stayed far away from Todd. He didn't' want to be anywhere near him when Arianna came off the stage and joined up with him. He hadn't planned on, and thus wasn't ready to talk to her today. A month of guerilla warfare hadn't cooled his ardor for her, not to mention he was dying for the company of a woman. When he next spoke to her however, he wanted it to be in the right place and the right time. This party was neither of those.

But maybe he was too late anyway. To hear Todd tell it, the two of them were an item. Evidently she'd found someone new. If that were the case, he didn't plan on sticking around to watch some other man make off with the woman he loved.

IT WAS fitting that the last song of the set was "Let It Go" from the movie *Frozen*. That's exactly how Arianna felt... frozen in her tracks with a strong need to let it go. Try to let go of the raw emotion, hurt and pain she felt. As soon as the song was finished she rushed into the house, threw her belongings into a bag, and was dashing out the front door when Lisa caught up with her.

"Arianna! Wait up," she yelled, scrambling after her.

Arianna turned and looked back. "Oh, Lisa! Hey. How are you?" she asked, stopping to give her a big hug.

"Good. Missing you. Wishing you'd be back with Zach."

Arianna grimaced. "Sure," she said, shaking her head. "But anyway, I was just leaving so maybe I'll call you sometime." She paused to negotiate with someone's limo driver for a ride back to where she was staying in Miami.

"No wait," Lisa said, running up to her just as she was getting in a car. "Please, Arianna. I'm dying to talk to you. Can't we work something out?"

Arianna stared at her, not speaking. It was Zach she was running away from, not Lisa. She couldn't think of any valid reason for not seeing her. Besides, this would be the last time they would get together. Now that it looked as though Zach had moved on, it would be too painful to spend time with her ever again because of the memories it would conjure up.

"Okay," she said finally. "When?"

"Awesome," Lisa said. "Now listen. It has to be tonight because we're leaving tomorrow. I'll tell Tony I have a headache and leave the party early... maybe around eleven, twelve o'clock. It'll be perfect because the guys have an all-night poker party planned so we won't be interrupted. I'll leave a key at the front desk of our hotel...the Adam's Mark on Key Biscayne Drive. Just come on up when you arrive."

Arianna hesitated. "Are you sure? I do not want to run into Zach."

"I'm very sure. No one will be around but me and you. If that changes, I'll call you."

"Okay," Arianna said, waving the driver on. "I'll see you tonight then."

CHAPTER

36

I t was quite a test of their friendship. Andre took a lot of heat over Arianna's leaving. He told Todd she'd suddenly become ill, but Todd wasn't buying it. Only by agreeing to perform for free was he able to stave off a potential lawsuit for breach of contract.

Arianna spent the rest of the day, debating whether to actually meet Lisa or not. Should she inadvertently run into Zach, she knew it would be a major disaster. On the other hand, she very much wanted to see Lisa, for what in her mind, would be one last time.

Shortly after midnight, she stopped at the front desk of the hotel to retrieve the key Lisa had left. Taking the elevator to the seventh floor, she was constantly on the look out for Zach or any of the other men. She made her way to Lisa's room, slid the key into the door, and entered the darkened suite. Evidently Lisa had turned in early, probably thinking Arianna wasn't going to show.

Tiptoeing softly to the bed, she bent down to gently waken Lisa, when a hand reached out and grabbed her arm. In a blink of an eye, she was slammed to the bed. As the light snapped on, she found herself staring into the barrel of a 9 mm, which Zach had aimed at her head.

"Holy shit! What the hell are you doing here?" he yelled, pulling the gun back. "You almost got yourself killed."

"Uh, uh...." she stammered, more embarrassed and shocked than scared. "Uh... oh, my God! This is all a mistake."

It was a huge mistake. She had no idea how she'd wound up in Zach's room, but she planned to get the hell out of there as fast as she could. The problem was her sandals had flown off when she'd been slammed to the bed and her purse and its contents were scattered all around the room. Quickly scrambling to her feet, she began searching for her possessions.

"Umh, you see, you were supposed to be Lisa," she said looking under a chair. "I mean, Lisa invited me to come see her, but I think there was a big mix up, because uh, uh I have your key, and I don't have any idea why I have your key and not her key. I... I picked up the key she left me."

Zach just stared at her, not speaking.

"I mean, I'd never, or well, ahem, I know that since I screwed up, well uh, I can see that you'd never want to have anything to do with me again" she yammered as she searched around the room for her shoes. "And... and I don't blame you so I'm just going to get my things here and go, but ah.... I can't seem to find..." and her voice trailed off, as she continued to frantically look for her sandals and purse under chairs and behind curtains.

Complete panic was setting in. She found one sandal on top of the armoire and the other under a chair, but her wallet was nowhere to be found. She needed it, at least the money it contained so she could get a cab back to her hotel across town. Without it, she was stranded not to mention her driver's license was in there too. *This is a disaster.*

"I...I understand why you hate me," she continued, glancing quickly at Zach then looking away. "I messed everything up because I'm such a fool sometimes, but I really didn't mean to, it's just that I thought I could, oh.... I don't know what I thought," she said and tears of frustration began to roll down her cheeks as she still struggled to find the contents of her purse.

Her wallet was nowhere to be found, and it didn't help that Zach just kept staring at her without saying a word. She would have felt a lot better if he'd yelled at her or something. She decided she'd have to leave without the wallet and find some other way home because she couldn't take being in his presence any longer.

She walked to the door and had just begun to open it when Zach stepped up behind her and slammed it shut in front of her. Startled, she turned to face him, tears flowing freely now. He stood only inches from her face. Being this physically close to him caused her to quake inside.

"I'm sorry," she whispered, her lip trembling as she looked up at him timidly. "I— I—", then bit her lip, unable to continue.

"Stop talking," Zach snapped.

She stared back at him, tears streaming down her face.

"Forgive me, Arianna if I seem less than sympathetic right now, but you should cry," he said angrily. "You almost got yourself *and* your mother killed. Do you realize what would have happened if help hadn't arrived when it did?"

She slowly nodded her head as the thought of her near death experience brought on a fresh wave of tears. "I was so stupid, but I... I just wanted to go away and think, but it was all wrong—"

"Think? What were you going to *think* about, Arianna?"

She shook her head. "I don't know. You. Us...my situation. I mean, I didn't want to be in love with you Zach, but I was, and it scared me."

"Was?" he asked, grimacing.

Completely frustrated, she turned and tried to open the door again. It was too painful to admit to him that yes, she was still in love with him. She'd totally blown any chance for a relationship. He had a new girlfriend...she'd seen her at the party today. All she wanted to do was leave. No matter how hard she pulled however, he held the door shut.

Slowly she turned to face him again. "Zach, please. Just let me leave. It'll be better for both of us if I just go."

"Oh, really?" he said, pounding his fist into the door, causing her to jump with fear. "And that'd be twice now you've tried to determine what's best for both of us? What makes you think your judgment is any better this time than the last time?"

"I... I just thought—"

Once again he smacked his hand against the door, his temper flaring.

"Well, don't think any more, Arianna. Just listen, damn it!"

Exhaling deeply, he stepped away from the door and raked his hands through his hair. It was the moment of truth, and he wasn't sure he could do this.

He knew what he wanted to say, but it was a first. He'd never really committed himself completely to a relationship before, and he wasn't sure how to begin. Wasn't sure it was wise. Just this latest debacle alone should have been reason enough to warn him off.

This whole situation had proven just how tough it would be to bring anyone into his world. In the beginning she'd thought he was the enemy, and even when he personally rescued her from a certain death, he couldn't reveal himself to her. Could never let her know the true nature of his work. If she lived with him, as he wanted her to, she'd see things. Intuitively know things, and in his world, knowing too much could get you killed.

He wasn't sure what the right thing to do was, but if the last month had shown him anything, it was that he'd never find peace as long as he was without her. So, now there was no doubt in his mind what he would do. He just needed to find the right words to say.

Turning back toward her, he said, "You have a T-Shirt that belongs to me. Black and covered with blood the last time I saw it."

Arianna gasped and her eyes popped wide open. Of course. Hadn't she known it all along? Hadn't she said that in addition to Reichter, Zach and his men were professional *somethings*? Now, she knew what those professional somethings were, at least kind of.

He'd saved her life. Personally saved her life. And it must have been Juan that carried her mother out, and Tony must have been there, too. These guys were trained commandos. Zach was a trained commando! Trained for what though, she wasn't sure.

"Y...you," she stammered. "That warehouse? That was you?"

He nodded ever so slightly.

"B...but—"

He cut her off and moved to but inches from her face. "Arianna, listen to me. Despite that dumbass move you made in leaving that nearly got us *all* killed, I still love you."

Tears flooded down her face. How could he still love her after what she'd done?

"You do?" she asked.

He reached up and attempted to wipe the tears from her eyes.

She grabbed his hand and kissed it. "I'm sorry," she whispered, choking back tears. "I love you Zach, and I'm so sorry for leaving. So sorry for putting everyone's life in danger."

She began to cry even harder.

"Shh," Zach said. "Arianna, it's all right. Don't cry."

"I can't help it, Zach. This, plus all the trouble I caused at your house. You probably thought I was some unappreciative little bitch," she said sobbing.

"It's okay, Arianna," he whispered. "You didn't know. We were all under a lot of stress. I forgive you."

He held her close, soothing her as a father soothes a child. "Look at me," he said, drying her tears once more. "It's over, and we're going to put that all behind us." He leaned down and kissed her softly then held her close, telling her not to cry. When he thought she'd calmed down and regained her composure, he added, "But you're right. You were an unappreciative little bitch."

Arianna pushed away from him and slugged him in the shoulder. "Well, thank you very much, Mr. Nice Guy, but you made me do it. I had to fight back somehow."

He tucked a strand of hair back behind her ear, kissed her lightly on the forehead, then her cheek before finally placing a light kiss on her mouth. There was so much to talk about. So much to still work out between them, but it would have to wait. Slow tender kisses quickly ignited a raging desire between them.

One kiss more ardent than the other, he finally pressed her against the door and devoured her with a long sensuous kiss. His hands flew up and down her body, wanting to touch her everywhere, wanting to ravage her. Totally, and without patience, he pulled her shirt off over her head and reigned kiss after kiss across the swell of her breasts before finally ripping her bra apart and sucking greedily on her naked breasts.

Unfastening her pants he pushed them down off her hips and ran his hands in and out of her panties, the palm of his hand massaging her rhythmically. His fingers combed her moist curls before finding their way back to her breasts where he pinched and teased her senseless.

Arianna was moaning wildly with pleasure…her breath coming in gulps, not able to get enough of him fast enough. His arms, his chest, his buttocks… she was groping him everywhere, wanting every part of him. She reached between his legs and felt his strong erection, and all but impaled herself on it.

Ripping clothes off each other, they fumbled their way to the bed in a frenzy of desire. Stripped naked, Zach straddled her and began to penetrate.

He deftly thrust in an out, taking her higher and higher with each stroke. Within minutes she burst into an orgasm that shook her from head to toe. Zach lost all control as well, collapsing on top of her on the bed, a deep groan escaped his lips.

They lay nestled together, relishing each other's embrace. Zach placed soft kisses on Arianna's cheek and held her fast to him as if he never wanted to let her go. God, he'd missed her.

Sighing heavily, he sat up and leaned against the headboard, pulled Arianna up beside him, and wrapped his arm around her.

Arianna, we need to talk," he said, still holding her tight. "I've thought a lot about us last month. With Karl Reichter out of the way, there is no threat to your life. You can safely go wherever you want." He paused as if searching for the right words. "I want you to come live with me on the island."

"I—" she started to say.

"Wait. Before you say anything, there are some things you need to understand. Things such as what I do for a living." He got up and moved over to the window, staring out into the lights of the city. This was hard. He struggled to find the right words.

"It's complicated," he said, turning back toward Arianna. "You can never ask me about my job. Never discuss what you think it is I do with anyone else, either. You already know too much, and that's not safe for you, or me."

"If you hadn't shown up when you did, I'd be dead right now, Zach. I owe you my life."

"It was a close call, but it's not out of gratitude I'm asking you to live with me." He moved back to the bed and sat down beside her. So much to say. He was in foreign territory for sure. "I'm in love with you Arianna, and I don't want to be without you anymore."

Arianna melted inside and was overwhelmed with emotion. This was quite a declaration coming from Zach. She didn't think he'd said that too many times in his life, maybe never.

"Last month was hell without you, Zach. I never realized how much I loved you until I thought I'd lost you."

"You never lost me, but I have to admit, I was pretty pissed. It was probably good we were thousands of miles apart."

Arianna hung her head. She couldn't blame him. Her carelessness had put a lot of people's lives in danger. "You started to date again, I see."

A puzzled look crossed Zach's face.

"The girl at the party yesterday… I saw her."

"That was my sister, Camilla. She's visiting from Puerto Rico. There's been no dates."

Relief swept over her.

"And you?" Zach asked. "Todd said you were his date for the weekend."

"No. Not true. He was hoping to get lucky, but no way. It was strictly business. I wasn't even remotely interested in him."

It was Zach's turn to breathe a sigh of relief. "Arianna, you have to understand, my work is intense and at times requires my full attention. It also requires me to be gone for long periods of time. And while I'm gone, it would be important that I not worry about where you are or what you're doing. I can't be distracted by any drama back home."

"Ahhh! Well, I'm pretty independent and impatient," she said. "I'm afraid I'd be driving you crazy with my impulsive escapades."

He turned and gave her an ominous look. A look she thought she'd seen before under not so pleasant circumstances. "That's just it, Arianna. No, you won't because I'd put an end to those wild escapades quickly. That's why you need to be very sure you understand what you're committing to."

She knew he was dead serious. Doing anything to distract his attention while he was gone would surely lead to the demise of their relationship.

"But I...."

Zach held up his hand, interrupting whatever she was going to say. "Let me finish. I've got to get this all out before you speak. Even of more concern is that I have enemies. My enemies would be your enemies, and they may try to get to me by hurting you. You'll need a bodyguard wherever you go from now on, meaning I'll know where you are every minute not to mention there would be some places you could never go."

Arianna sat up and scooted closer to Zach. "What about working?"

He shrugged his shoulders. "Possibly..."

"I have a degree in journalism. I'd like to go back to work."

"Maybe, I'm not ruling it out." It was a lie, kind of. He knew he'd fiercely oppose her taking an assignment like she had in Kervistan, for example. This was the point he was trying to make without specifically saying it... afraid it was a deal breaker for the relationship. It would take a lot for him to be okay with high risk assignments.

"You don't have to work, you know?' he said. "I can give you every luxury you ever dreamed of. You could live a lifestyle that would be the envy of everyone you know."

Arianna shook her head. "I can't imagine it. I think I'd feel like a 'kept' woman not to mention, I'm not the 'sit around' type."

"Not a kept woman. Never that." He pulled her close and wrapped his arms around her. "I'm offering you so much more than that. I'm offering you my love. I would never interrupt my former life just to have a 'kept' woman around. But have no illusions, Arianna. Missteps in my life have deadly consequences. I don't want to micro manage your life, but to be honest, you'd be living under a benevolent dictatorship."

Silence enveloped the room. Life with him would indeed be complicated. Maybe that's why he'd never made this commitment before. Maybe that's why she'd never fully committed to a relationship, especially to someone like Zach. This was the tomorrow they'd both been denying for a long time. But the day... the time, had arrived when both of them would need to put their prior lives behind them in pursuit of a new life together.

"I love you, Zach," Arianna finally said. "Whatever it takes, I don't want to be without you."

He kissed her passionately, holding her tight. This was the happy ending he'd been hoping for. "I have an idea," he said, finally pulling himself away from her embrace. "Let's get the hell out of here and go home."

'Yes, good idea." She couldn't wait to get back to the island and begin her new life with him. "Take me away," she said and planted a big kiss on his cheek.

ARIANNA STOOD looking out the window while Zach packed. What a journey it had been as she thought back over the past few months. Her life had changed drastically.

She heard him make a call to Tony, telling him they would be leaving in two hours.

"Zach, I was thinking," she said, scrunching up on the bed watching him pack.

"Yeah? About what?"

"Us. Me. This whole saga. It all started when I was abducted from Kervistan. I have nightmares about the guy who kidnapped me. Do you know who he is?"

Zach's head snapped up. He stared at her, not speaking...

ACKNOWLEDGEMENTS

I would like to acknowledge all my friends of the Wannabe Writer's Group for their valuable guidance and inspiration.

ABOUT THE AUTHOR

Ann is a former English teacher who currently lives in sunny Florida. She spends her time training dogs, writing, and enjoying the company of her own two dogs, Georgia and Duke. She has always had a special affinity for the written word, especially her own. "I have to admit. I love to see what I write in print. It is so much fun to paint a picture or evoke an emotion with words." Her dogs, ever faithful critique partners, have heard every word of *Deny Tomorrow*, and agree, it's a great read. Look for the sequel, *Capture Tomorrow*, to be out soon.

34612122R00157

Made in the USA
Charleston, SC
13 October 2014